The Good Knight

The Gareth and Gwen Medieval Mysteries

The Bard's Daughter
The Good Knight
The Uninvited Guest
The Fourth Horseman
The Fallen Princess
The Unlikely Spy
The Lost Brother

The After Cilmeri Series:

Daughter of Time
Footsteps in Time
Winds of Time
Prince of Time
Crossroads in Time
Children of Time
Exiles in Time
Castaways in Time
Ashes of Time
Warden of Time

The Last Pendragon Saga

The Last Pendragon
The Pendragon's Quest

Other Books by Sarah Woodbury

Cold My Heart: A Novel of King Arthur

A Gareth and Gwen Medieval Mystery

THE GOOD KNIGHT

by

SARAH WOODBURY

The Good Knight: A Medieval Mystery

Copyright © 2011 by Sarah Woodbury

This is a work of fiction.

www.sarahwoodbury.com

Cover image by Christine DeMaio-Rice at Flip City Books
http://flipcitybooks.com

For my Gareth

A Brief Guide to Welsh Pronunciation

c	a hard 'c' sound (Cadfael)
ch	a non-English sound as in Scottish "ch" in "loch" (Fychan)
dd	a buzzy 'th' sound, as in "there" (Ddu; Gwynedd)
f	as in "of" (Cadfael)
ff	as in "off" (Gruffydd)
g	a hard 'g' sound, as in "gas" (Goronwy)
l	as in "lamp" (Llywelyn)
ll	a breathy "th" sound that does not occur in English (Llywelyn)
rh	a breathy mix between 'r' and 'rh' that does not occur in English (Rhys)
th	a softer sound than for 'dd,' as in "thick" (Arthur)
u	a short 'ih' sound (Gruffydd), or a long 'ee' sound (Cymru—pronounced "kumree")
w	as a consonant, it's an English 'w' (Llywelyn); as a vowel, an 'oo' sound (Bwlch)
y	the only letter in which Welsh is not phonetic. It can be an 'ih' sound, as in "Gwyn," is often an "uh" sound (Cymru), and at the end of the word is an "ee" sound (thus, both Cymru—the modern word for Wales—and Cymry—the word for Wales in the Dark Ages—are pronounced "kumree")

Cast of Characters

Owain Gwynedd – King of Gwynedd (North Wales)
Cadwaladr – ruler of Ceredigion, younger brother to Owain
Cadwallon – elder brother to Owain and Cadwaladr, deceased
Rhun – Owain's son
Hywel – Owain's son
Elen – Owain's daughter

Meilyr – court bard to Gruffydd ap Cynan (Owain's father d. 1137)
Gwen –Mcilyr's daughter
Gwalchmai – Meilyr's son
Gareth – Knight

Cristina – Owain's love interest

Anarawd – King of Deheubarth
Cadell – Anarawd's brother

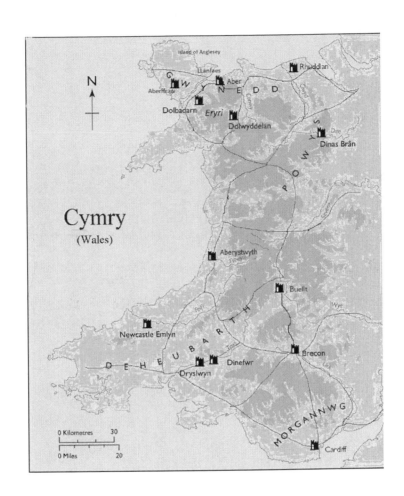

1

August, 1143 AD

Gwynedd (North Wales)

"Look at you, girl."

Gwen's father, Meilyr, tsked under his breath and brought his borrowed horse closer to her side of the path. He'd been out of sorts since early morning when he'd found his horse lame and King Anarawd and his company of soldiers had left the castle without them, refusing to wait for Meilyr to find a replacement mount. Anarawd's men-at-arms would have provided Meilyr with the fine escort he coveted.

"You'll have no cause for complaint once we reach Owain Gwynedd's court." A breeze wafted over Gwen's face and she closed her eyes, letting her pony find his own way for a moment. "I won't embarrass you at the wedding."

"If you cared more for your appearance, you would have been married yourself years ago and given me grandchildren long since."

Gwen opened her eyes, her forehead wrinkling in annoyance. "And whose fault is it that I'm unmarried?" Her fingers flexed about the reins but she forced herself to relax. Her present appearance was her own doing, even if her father found it intolerable. In her bag, she had fine clothes and ribbons to weave through her hair, but saw no point in sullying any of them on the long journey to Aber Castle.

King Owain Gwynedd's daughter was due to marry King Anarawd in three days' time. Owain Gwynedd had invited Gwen, her father, and her almost twelve-year old brother, Gwalchmai, to furnish the entertainment for the event, provided King Owain and her father could bridge the six years of animosity and silence that separated them. Meilyr had sung for King Owain's father, Gruffydd; he'd practically raised King Owain's son, Hywel. But six years was six years. No wonder her father's temper was short.

Even so, she couldn't let her father's comments go. Responsibility for the fact that she had no husband rested firmly on his shoulders. "Who refused the contract?"

"Rhys was a rapscallion and a laze-about," Meilyr said.

And you weren't about to give up your housekeeper, maidservant, cook, and child-minder to just anyone, were you?

But instead of speaking, Gwen bit her tongue and kept her thoughts to herself. She'd said it once and received a slap to her face. Many nights she'd lain quiet beside her younger brother, regretting that she hadn't defied her father and stayed with Rhys. They could have eloped; in seven years, their marriage would have been as legal as any other. But her father was right and Gwen wasn't too proud to admit it: Rhys *had* been a laze-about. She wouldn't have been happy with him. Rhys' father had almost cried when Meilyr had refused Rhys' offer. It wasn't only daughters who were sometimes hard to sell.

"Father!" Gwalchmai brought their cart to a halt. "Come look at this!"

"What now?" Meilyr said. "We'll have to spend the night at Caerhun at present rate. You know how important it is not to keep King Owain waiting."

"But Father!" Gwalchmai leapt from the cart and ran forward.

"He's serious." Gwen urged her pony after him, passing the cart, and then abruptly reined in beside her brother. "*Mary, Mother of God...*"

A slight rise and sudden dip in the path ahead had hidden the carnage until they were upon it. Twenty men and an equal number of horses lay dead in the road, their bodies contorted and their blood soaking the brown earth. Gwalchmai bent forward and retched into the grass beside the road. Gwen's stomach threatened to undo her too, but she fought the bile down and dismounted to wrap her arms around her brother.

Meilyr reined in beside his children. "Stay back."

Gwen glanced at her father and then back to the scene, noticing for the first time a man kneeling among the wreckage, one hand to a dead man's chest and the other resting on the hilt of his sheathed sword. The man straightened and Gwen's breath caught in her throat.

Gareth.

He'd cropped his dark brown hair shorter than when she'd known him, but his blue eyes still reached into the core of her. Her heart beat a little faster as she drank him in. Five years ago, Gareth had been a man-at-arms in the service of Prince Cadwaladr, King Owain Gwynedd's brother. Gareth and Gwen had become friends, and then more than friends, but before he could ask her father for her hand, Gareth had a falling out with Prince Cadwaladr. In the end, Gareth hadn't been able to persuade Meilyr that he could support her despite his lack of station.

Gwen was so focused on Gareth that she wasn't aware of the other men among them—live ones—until they approached her family. A half dozen converged on them at the same time. One caught her upper arm in a tight grip. Another grabbed Meilyr's bridle. "Who are you?" the soldier said.

Meilyr stood in the stirrups and pointed a finger at Gareth. "Tell them who I am!"

Gareth came forward, his eyes flicking from Meilyr to Gwalchmai to Gwen. He was broader in the shoulders, too, than she remembered.

"They are friends," Gareth said. "Release them."

And to Gwen's astonishment, the man-at-arms who held her obeyed Gareth. Could it be that in the years since she'd last seen him, Gareth had regained something of what he'd lost?

Gareth halted by Meilyr's horse. "I was sent from Aber to meet King Anarawd and escort him through Gwynedd. He wasn't even due to arrive at Dolwyddelan Castle until today, but ..." He gestured to the men on the ground. "Clearly, we were too late."

Gwen looked past Gareth to the murdered men in the road.

"Turn away, Gwen," Gareth said.

But Gwen couldn't. The blood—on the dead men, on the ground, on the knees of Gareth's breeches—mesmerized her. The men here had been *slaughtered*. Her skin twitched at the hate in the air. "You mean King Anarawd is—is—is among them?"

"The King is dead," Gareth said.

2

Could this situation be worse? Gareth couldn't imagine how. Facing Gwen over a handful of dead bodies was one thing—not pleasant, but something with which he could cope. It was something else entirely to face Gwen's *father* after not seeing either of them since Meilyr had rejected Gareth's offer for Gwen. Meilyr oozed resentment, as if a better life could have been had than singing for the lords and kings of Wales. At least Gwen's presence indicated that he'd not restrained her more than needful, nor sold her to the highest bidder. That she stood in front of him as beautiful as ever, and as if the intervening years had never happened, took his breath away.

At the sight of her, he wanted to either punch the air in exaltation or pull her into his arms, but did neither. Instead, he said, "Are there more of you? Are you traveling with a company?"

"No." Gwen looked up at him, tears in the corners of her eyes. "We'd hoped to ride alongside King Anarawd, but my father's horse went lame and delayed us at Dolwyddelan. The King and his men left without us."

"Praise God they did," Meilyr said. "If we'd traveled with him, we'd be dead too."

Leave it to him to think about his own skin first, though in this instance, Gareth couldn't blame him. If he'd had Gwen and Gwalchmai to protect, he'd have felt the same way.

"Gwalchmai seems a sturdy lad," Gareth said. "If I give him my horse, can he ride back to Dolwyddelan? We need carts to transport the dead. It's only a few miles—"

"I know how far it is," Meilyr said, reverting to his habitual scorn. "We've just come that distance."

That told Gareth all he needed to know about the state of Meilyr's nerves. It was bad enough for Meilyr to ride into Aber Castle after so many years away and ask King Owain Gwynedd for entrance, even if he'd been invited. It was quite another to do the same with the dead body of the bridegroom thrown over his horse.

"Do you have any idea who did this?" Gwen said.

"Not specifically." Gareth forced his eyes away from her, willing to talk to Gwen but not wanting to relate what he knew in front of Gwalchmai and Meilyr.

"Did you see anyone on the road to the north?" Gwen stepped closer to him and his arm itched to go around her. He stayed his hand. They'd fallen in love shortly after Meilyr's falling out with King Owain, but now hadn't spoken for five years. Their last words, while not thrown at each other in anger, had been full of pain. *Christ. I was more a child than she was, for all I've seven years on her.*

"No. I would have expected more traffic, given the upcoming wedding." Gareth glanced at Anarawd's body and added "—which won't be taking place now."

"Why would anyone want to stop Anarawd from marrying Elen?" Gwalchmai asked this with all the innocence of a twelve-year old. "It's a perfect match."

"I don't know about that," Gareth said, "but it looks as if the men who ambushed Anarawd chose the perfect moment."

"Perfect?" Meilyr's voice was full of outrage.

"I apologize for the poor choice of words," Gareth said, suppressing his irritation at how quickly Meilyr grew angry. "I only meant that they must have planned this very carefully, as well as had fortune on their side."

Her hand to her throat, Gwen stared at the dead men. Their bodies lay as if a giant had tumbled them together. Gareth thought about taking her arm after all, fearing she'd retreated dangerously inside herself and might be going into shock.

But then she spoke. "No company of men could cause so much death and leave nothing of themselves behind. There must be something here we can link to their identity. A token, a fallen surcoat, something…"

"Don't—" Gareth reached a hand to stop her from entering the battlefield but in one step she moved out of his range.

"Let her be," Meilyr said, his voice back to a growl, but not as disapproving as Gareth might have expected, given that his daughter picked her way among the dead. "It's not the first time she's been a part of a scene like this."

"What do you mean?" Gareth said.

"She spies for Owain's son, Hywel." Gwalchmai blurted out the words and then swallowed hard at Gareth's incredulous look.

"You're not serious." Gareth glanced from Meilyr to Gwalchmai, who gave him a weak smile. "You are serious?"

"She didn't ask my permission, if that's what you mean," Meilyr said. "Just told me one day that I might stop her from marrying the man she wanted—that would be you—but she was going to follow her own road in this and I didn't have any say in the matter." Meilyr dismounted, his legs jerking stiffly. "Not a thing I could do to stop her."

Gareth barked a laugh. "If I remember anything about her, I remember that." He turned to Gwalchmai and handed him his own horse's reins. "Here, boy. Don't stop for anything or anyone."

"What about the men who did this?" Gwalchmai's voice trembled as he asked this question but then he firmed his chin.

Gareth placed a hand on the boy's shoulder to reassure him. "They're surely gone by now. And they wouldn't be on the road to Dolwyddelan, regardless."

"You'll be fine. Ride straight back the way we came," Meilyr said.

"Yes, sir." With a last look at his father and a nod to Gareth, Gwalchmai spurred away. Galloping hard, he disappeared around a bend in the road, the echo of the horse's hooves fading into the distance.

Gareth canted his head at Meilyr. "I could have sent one of the men-at-arms, but thought it would be better if Gwalchmai had something to do besides look at dead men."

"Thank you."

Gareth restrained his disbelief that Meilyr would thank him for anything and just nodded, not knowing what else to say.

Gwen had come to rest beside the fallen Anarawd and looked up at Gareth as he approached. "I can't believe I spoke to King Anarawd only this morning. I can't decide which feels more like a dream, then or now."

Gareth had no words to comfort her. "I wish we were dreaming." He studied the body of the downed king. Anarawd sported a few gray hairs, but even at forty years old, had the physique of a much younger man, with shoulders used to wearing armor and no sign of a softened belly.

"Tell me what you wouldn't speak about in front of the others," Gwen said.

Trust her to read me that well, even after all these years apart. Gareth thought for a moment, reliving the scene, and then indicated the rise in the road a hundred yards north of their position. "I'd just crested the ridge there when the two sides met in force below me. I could do nothing to help Anarawd, being only one man, so I rode to find the scouting party from Caerhun, led by my friend Madog, whom I'd encountered by the river earlier." Gareth shrugged. "The battle here was over by the time I returned with Madog and the other soldiers."

They both glanced at the host of men he'd brought. All wore the red and yellow crest of Gwynedd on their surcoats, as did Gareth himself. They'd begun to shift the dead men, laying them out side by side on the road. Gareth knelt beside Gwen, drawing her attention back to him. "Tell me what you see."

Before Gwen's family had come upon him, Gareth had stripped the armor from Anarawd's body and pulled open his shirt, exposing the fatal wound, a slender cut between two ribs where his attacker had thrust a blade into Anarawd's heart.

"It looks..." Gwen hesitated, and then tried again. "The wound is different from all the others, isn't it?" She traced the cut with one finger. "Narrower."

"Yes," Gareth said. "A sword couldn't have caused it."

"A knife, then?"

"One with a notch in the blade."

Gwen looked more closely. "That's why it didn't cut cleanly?"

"Yes."

"What do you suppose this means?"

Gareth tugged down Anarawd's shirt to cover his ruined torso and straightened. The wind blew through the trees and he listened for unnatural sounds above or beneath it. Rain had fallen in the night and now that the sun had risen high in the sky, light filtered through the leafy trees and the damp earth gave off an oppressive heat. "I couldn't say. Not yet anyway." He studied the ground around Anarawd. "What I can tell you is that Anarawd didn't die where he lies."

Gwen got to her feet too, though her head was still bent and her eyes on Anarawd. "How do you know?"

"By the lack of blood underneath the body and by the dirt and scuff marks on his toes," Gareth said. "Someone dragged Anarawd face down from the place where he was killed."

"Why would he drag him face down?"

"So he didn't have to look at Anarawd's expression and dwell on what he'd done?" Gareth said.

Gwen thought about that. "It would have been easier to drag him by the feet, surely. Much less awkward."

"But then the skin on Anarawd's face or the back of his head, were he face up, would have become marred," Gareth said. "Anyone who found him would have asked questions."

"As it is, the killer didn't reckon on you."

Gareth glanced at her, his expression deliberately unreadable, but it didn't matter since her face remained downturned. She'd complimented him. He tried not to wonder if he still meant something to her. Then he gestured towards Anarawd's chest. "From the stains on his shirt, he was standing up when he was stabbed and didn't bleed out lying on his back."

"Can you find where he fell?" Gwen said.

"Perhaps." Gareth traced the perimeter of the battle with his eyes. "Anarawd knew his killer. He must have, to have allowed him to get so close."

"All of a sudden, the quiet feels menacing, doesn't it?" Gwen said.

One of the other men approached Gareth. "The attackers might still be out there, my lord. They might even return."

"I know that, Madog. But Anarawd wasn't just ambushed. He was murdered. I'll need to examine his body more closely once we reach Aber. Right now, however, I must survey the area and discover whatever I can before the men trample all the evidence."

"I'll come with you," Gwen said.

Gareth met Madog's gaze. His friend gave him a quick nod before moving away, out of earshot. "I'm not sure that's a good idea..." Gareth's words trailed off as Gwen moved closer to him.

"Hywel trusts me," she said. "I can help you."

Gareth glanced to where Gwen's father stood, his hands on his hips and his mouth in a thin line, staring at them. Gareth saw disapproval in his face, but whether he objected to Gwen's close proximity to him or to the situation they were in, Gareth didn't know. "And maybe with the two of us working together, we can get this over with more quickly so that you can get to Aber Castle sooner rather than later?"

Gwen nodded her head sharply.

"You're worried about your father."

"We're all worried about this meeting with Owain Gwynedd," she said. "King Owain may have invited my father to sing at the wedding, but it was my father who swallowed his pride first and asked for King Owain's patronage. Now, with Anarawd's death, King Owain will be very angry. How much harder is that going to make his meeting with my father?"

"As I recall, it was a mere spat that shouldn't have solidified into enmity so easily."

"You're right," she said.

"Remind me what happened." The words came out an order, and he thought to backtrack since it wasn't his place to order her about, but Gwen only shrugged and told him.

"It was nothing. After King Gruffydd died, Owain Gwynedd didn't immediately choose my father to continue in his service as court bard. My father was offended."

Gareth smirked. "That is an image I have no trouble picturing."

Gwen made a rueful face. "So we left. We've returned now only because my brother needs a patron and my father would do anything to find a settled place for him. We lived among the royal court during all my growing up years. The king held his hand over us, and that was worth almost any kind of sacrifice, though it could hardly have been called that. That is something my father would like to establish for Gwalchmai before he dies."

"Before he—" Gareth couldn't finish the sentence. "Your father looks well."

"He is well. He's just feeling morbid." Gwen gestured to the bodies. "Which this will do nothing to help."

"So Meilyr doesn't actually want the position of chief bard for himself?" Gareth tried to keep the incredulity out of his voice but didn't think he was entirely successful.

Gwen shot him a brief smile. "No."

"That's a tricky position to be in—for everyone—but particularly Gwalchmai, upon whom all your father's hopes rest."

"You can see why it would be better to have some idea of who did this when we bring Anarawd's body to King Owain," Gwen said. "Anarawd was the king's friend and the man who would have been his son-in-law."

Gareth looked towards Gwen's father again. Meilyr had stopped studying them and was rummaging through a satchel in the back of their cart. "Let's see what we can find. And it would be better if we hurried."

"Do you think whoever did this will come back, like Madog said?"

Gareth read real fear in Gwen's face. He didn't like seeing it. "I assured your brother that they wouldn't, but—" Gareth tensed his shoulders and then relaxed them. Nothing about this day had gone right. The longer they stood here, the more worried he became. "This might not be over. Not by a long shot."

3

How can it be that he's here? Gareth of all people? As she followed Gareth through the woods, Gwen cursed herself for her muddy hem and unkempt hair—and the fact that instead of greeting him and throwing herself into his arms as she wanted to, she was examining a murder scene for Hywel. That was so like her and her luck. How many nights had she lain awake, imagining herself in her best dress, her hair perfectly coifed, singing without mistake for a company of noble lords in a hall. Halfway through the evening, Gareth would appear and fall in love with her all over again.

It had never happened, of course, and she'd long since given up hope of ever seeing him again. She'd half-convinced herself that he'd died in some far away land, fighting someone else's battle.

"What's this about you spying for Hywel?" Gareth said, as they picked their way among the trees.

"Who told you that?" Gwen said.

"Gwalchmai," Gareth said.

Gwen sighed at her brother's too-free tongue. "Hywel's position in his father's household has always been precarious. It was bad when we left and has gotten worse since then. Not long after I last saw..." she stopped, swallowed, and rushed on, " ... I last saw you, Hywel visited the home of his cousin in Powys and it happened that we played there that winter. He spoke to me then about keeping an eye out for trouble and I said I'd see what I could do."

"And have you?" Gareth said. "Seen what you could do, I mean."

"I can't say what value I've been to him. My reports are mostly on the comings and goings of his people, both high and low," Gwen said. "Who conspires with whom; who has sued whom over what land; whose marriage bed is colder than it should be."

"Your father said you've been among the dead before."

"I never thought to involve myself in anything dangerous," Gwen said. "But we served in many households, and ... things kept happening. My father was even accused of murder once and it was up to me to find the truth because nobody else would."

"If I'm ever accused of murder, I would be delighted if you would extend me the same courtesy," Gareth said.

Gwen smiled, as she was sure he meant her to, but then sobered, looking over her shoulder at the men strewn along the road. "Nearly two dozen men, all dead, all put to the sword either in battle or once they lay stunned on the ground. All except Anarawd, who was killed with a knife."

Gareth crouched low to the ground. "Here." He brushed away a few fallen leaves to reveal a man's footprints, clearly embedded in the soft earth. Further on were more footprints, and then more again.

"How many men in the party, do you think?" Gwen said, glad they could talk about something else, even if it was murder.

"More than enough to surprise Anarawd's troop," Gareth said. "Anarawd and his men stood little chance, taken unawares as it appears they were." He eyed the road and the woods beyond. "The attackers waited here—probably here and in the trees opposite—for Anarawd's company to ride past. King Anarawd and his men would have been unconcerned and unsuspecting of danger. They were well within the confines of King Owain's territory and only an hour out of Dolwyddelan. They'd gone—what?— four miles at most?"

"Something like that." Gwen and her family had ridden that distance at a walk, which was all the horse who drew the cart could manage most days. They'd left two hours after Anarawd and his men. That meant the ambush had occurred at least two hours before this moment and more likely three, which made sense since the bodies were still warm, but stiff. Unmolested, the company would have nearly reached Aber by now. Gwen pursed her lips as she studied the footprints. "You knew what to look for," she said. "You've seen this type of thing before?"

"Ambushes are the easiest way to eliminate a rival," Gareth said. "And like yours, my tenure with Hywel has been—" Gareth paused to glance up at Gwen, an actual smile hovering around his lips as he sought for the proper word, "—irregular."

"My father told me that you'd hired yourself out to the highest bidder," Gwen said. At the renewal of Gareth's uncanny stillness, she kicked herself for not keeping that question to herself, but she *had* to know. "You fought as a mercenary."

Gareth took in a breath that was almost a curse. Throughout their conversation, Gwen had found it difficult to look into his face because she was afraid of what she might see there, but now it was impossible. She scuffled at the fallen leaves and dirt that made up the floor of the forest. No glint of metal or other indication of men appeared, other than their trampling footprints.

"That's true as far as it goes," he said. "When I left Prince Cadwaladr's service, I had nowhere to go. I was skilled with a sword and such men are always needed in Wales, with the Vikings, the Irish, and the ever-present English hemming us in on every side."

"I wasn't criticizing you." Gwen's voice went soft. "Just asking. How long have you worked for Hywel?"

"Almost four years," he said. "Despite what your father might think, I'm good at what I do and those for whom I fought recognized it. Hywel was one of several lords who offered me a permanent place in their *teulu*."

"You wear a fine ring," Gwen said.

"A gift." Gareth fisted the hand that wore it. "It was given to me along with my horse when I joined Hywel's band. Prince

Hywel's brother, Rhun, knighted me six months ago after a skirmish with the Normans near Chester."

Six months. He's been a knight for six months, and yet ... Gwen shook herself and held her tongue. Five years was a long time to carry the memory of someone in your heart—someone you'd not seen and had no reason to think still loved you. It wasn't surprising that he'd not bothered to find her.

The sharp twang of an untuned note carried through the heavy air. With his legs swinging nearly to the ground, Meilyr sat in the bed of the cart, holding a lyre. He could always find comfort with an instrument in his hands.

"I would have brought more bowmen than the attackers did." Gareth turned back to their task. "I find it odd they had so few. It seems shortsighted to me. It makes the success of an ambush less certain."

"Maybe none of the men our murderer trusted were archers," Gwen said.

"Yet he found enough men to do his dirty work," Gareth said. "That sounds like a man with noble blood—with power and reach."

"It doesn't sound very noble to me," Gwen said.

"You and I both know that many ignoble men inspire fierce loyalty in those who serve them," Gareth said.

"Or fear."

"Or the lord who ordered this made promises his men thought he could keep. Damn it." Gareth spun on one heel to look back to the road. "We need answers *now*. Owain Gwynedd won't want to wait until some lord's men are curiously richer or rewarded more than their due. We will be bringing King Anarawd's body to him at Aber *today*."

Gwen's heart turned cold at the memory of King Owain's temper, and then even colder still as another thought struck her. "What if the man who ordered King Anarawd's death *is* Owain Gwynedd?"

4

They were still arguing about it two hours later as they led their horses down the road towards Caerhun. Every man walked, while his horse had a dead man flung over it, even Meilyr's borrowed horse, Gwen's pony, and Gareth's Braith. As Gareth had hoped, Gwalchmai had convinced the castellan at Dolwyddelan to help and had returned at the head of a half dozen carts, one of which now held Anarawd, lying in state. Gareth held his horse's reins in his right hand and was sorely tempted to clasp Gwen's hand in his left, but refrained, even though it would have assuaged some of the ache in his heart.

Too soon.

"Why would he have contracted with Anarawd for his own daughter if he was going to kill him before the wedding?" Gareth said, exasperated that Gwen was suspicious of the one person he was certain couldn't have ordered the ambush. "His daughter doesn't even inherit King Anarawd's domains now."

Gwen wrinkled her nose, clearly not wanting to admit he was right, but nodded her grudging acceptance. "All right. I can't argue with that, though I submit he could have changed his mind.

My question then is, if not King Owain, who? Who knew King Anarawd's travel plans? Who benefits from Anarawd's death, commands enough power to order it, *and* is secure enough in his own dominions to withstand King Owain's displeasure when he eventually finds out? Because he will. You know he will."

"Our culprit might not know King Owain as well as we do," Gareth said. "He might not realize the extent of his determination and reach. Arrogance is not in short supply among our nobles."

"I guess I have to grant you that too," Gwen said, with a laugh.

"The first item, however, isn't too hard to figure," Gareth said. "Anarawd's list of enemies was long. He's fended off the English barons in Deheubarth for years, and in addition, while his Welsh rivals aren't too many to count, they're numerous. He controls rich farmland in the south, not to mention herds, mines, and trade routes."

"It's the other two characteristics that will narrow the possibilities," Gwen said. "Who has the power and the reach? That's why I suggested it could be King Owain."

"For now, we must look beyond him." Gareth glanced at Gwen. "And you mustn't even hint of your suspicions to Prince Hywel."

"Why ever not?" Gwen said. "He's used to the machinations at court. If I don't bring it up, he will. Given his position, and for his own survival, he has to suspect everyone, even his own father."

"That may be true," Gareth said. "It is certainly why he recruited you and who knows how many others to spy for him. But let him come to this on his own, if that's what he's going to think. It serves you not at all to impugn his father's name."

"I still don't agree," Gwen said. "He needs those of us he trusts to see the arrow flying towards him before it hits. If I tell him what I suspect, he'll trust me later when it counts for more."

Hywel was many things: reckless, brave, impractical, creative, imaginative, and intelligent. But also could be dreadfully irresponsible about other people's thoughts and feelings. Except when it came to serving his father. To him fell the lot of the younger son, always passed over in favor of his elder brother Rhun—for attention, for honors—always trying to live up to the pre-set standard. And admittedly, Hywel didn't often fail.

But he didn't tug his father's heartstrings like Rhun did and Hywel knew it. He'd always known it. Gareth didn't know if it was because Hywel's mother, whom King Owain had apparently loved, had died at his birth, or because he and his father were far too much alike. Both of Gareth's parents had died from a wasting sickness when he was five years old, so what he knew about families he'd learned from watching others.

In addition, Hywel was Owain Gwynedd's bastard second son. While the Welsh accounted a man legitimate if his father acknowledged him, the lords of Wales had a growing sense that the Welsh royal family must bow more and more to the dictates of the English Church. An illegitimate son might become king if no legitimate son was available, but King Owain had legitimate sons, with more, undoubtedly, in the works.

"He already has younger brothers, as you know," Gareth said. "But have you heard that they'll be more still? King Owain woos again."

Gwen nodded. "It's no secret."

"There are barriers to the match, however," Gareth said.

"Because King Owain and Cristina are cousins?" Gwen said.

"Because she's a witch."

Gwen laughed and choked at the same time. "Don't say that within King Owain's hearing. He'd have your head."

"All I know is that he has eyes only for her and he trails after her like a lost puppy."

"Does she share his bed?" Gwen said.

If Gareth had underestimated the work Gwen had done for Hywel, that question put to rest to any uncertainties in that regard. Gwen was no longer the sixteen-year-old innocent he'd known and sought to marry. "Not yet—not until the contracts are signed is my guess, no matter how persuasive he can be."

"Then all is not yet lost," Gwen said. "He might change his mind."

Gareth was opening his mouth to express his skepticism when Braith stopped in the middle of the road. The rest of Owain Gwynedd's men filed around them, some of them smirking at Gareth's stubborn horse as they passed. Gareth tugged on Braith's reins, but the beast refused to budge. Rather than hanging her head as Gareth might have expected, given her unhappiness with her present burden, Braith lifted it and pricked her ears forward.

Gwen, who had walked a few paces on, came back to Gareth. "What is it?"

"I don't know," he said.

They'd not yet left the mountains, though they'd descended some distance from the highest point on the path, which was a mile beyond the ambush site. The road led down from this point to the Conwy River valley. When the road had run through the old slate mines some distance back, it had been a good fifteen feet wide. A quarter of a mile ahead of them, however, it narrowed to accommodate the gorge through which the road ran, and was just wide enough for the carts to pass in single file, with a man walking beside.

Gareth moved his gaze to the hills on either side of the road. Braith wasn't as temperamental a horse as some. Gareth had learned to listen to her. By now, he and Gwen had fallen twenty paces to the rear of the company. Those in front were nearing the narrow point in the road. From his journey south in the early hours of the morning, Gareth remembered that the path curved in on itself just ahead, following the creek on their right that flowed towards a fall.

"Madog!" Gareth shouted above the rush of the water and the sound of feet and horses' hooves.

At the front of the line, just about to enter the narrow gap, Madog put up a hand and turned on a heel to look back at Gareth and Gwen. Owain Gwynedd's forces, well acquainted with the chain of command, stopped immediately. Silence descended, with each man listening as hard as he could for anything amiss. The forest around them quieted too, which gave Gareth no comfort. It meant the animals and birds were on alert. Other than the occasional whicker of a horse in the middle of the company, the pounding in his own ears was all Gareth could hear.

"Gareth! Watch out!"

Gareth spun around, recognizing the voice but stunned that its owner could be here. Then, an eerie scream split the air, trailing off at the end as the crier caught his breath.

Madog shot out a hand. "Move!"

The entire company obeyed: every man pulled out his sword, crouched into a defensive posture, and turned to face outward, shields up.

They'd reacted just in time.

Arrows flew from the peaks on either side of the road, hurtling into the company. The rain of arrows didn't last long but as soon as it stopped, men followed, flying into Owain Gwynedd's men as if they themselves were shot from hidden bows. The trees on both sides of the road erupted and in a heartbeat, more enemy soldiers appeared between Gareth and his friends. With Gwen to protect, Gareth didn't try to rejoin his company.

Thrusting out his arm, Gareth shoved the body off Braith, launched himself onto her back, and pulled Gwen up after him. From his vantage point, Gareth quickly surveyed the field and saw that, unlike Anarawd's company, he and his companions outnumbered their attackers.

Sword in hand, Gareth hesitated, looking towards Meilyr, who twisted in his seat on the cart and waved his arm in a shooing motion, his face contorted. "Ride! Get her out of here!" Without waiting to see if Gareth obeyed, Meilyr launched himself from his seat into Gwalchmai who'd been walking beside the cart, and rolled with him into the ditch beside the road.

Gareth turned Braith's head, but his initial hesitation cost him his opportunity. Two men appeared around the turn in the road behind them, galloping towards the battle from the south, swords raised high. Forward or back, Gareth had no choice but to fight. He urged Braith into the seething mass of men. Using the advantage being mounted gave him, he swung his sword at the first enemy soldier he came upon. As it sliced through the man's shoulder, Gareth tried to remain contained, breathing steadily to control the rush of energy that poured through him. It worked about as well as it usually did, which was to say, hardly at all. Instead, he felt as if he were flinging his sword about uncontrollably.

A second man attempted to waylay them and Gareth killed him with a sharp thrust to the throat. Gwen, meanwhile, clung to him, her arm clenched around his waist, while she slashed with her belt knife at any man who came at them from Braith's other side. Again Gareth thrust his sword, this time at a man who was trying to catch Braith's reins. Gareth killed two more men before he reached Madog, who, though heavily beset, was holding his own.

Gareth swung at an assailant's head and then launched himself from Braith's back, taking down a second attacker. Without pausing for breath, he pushed to one knee and shoved his sword through the man's midsection. And with that, the flow of battle moved away from him and his senses began to work again.

He turned, looking for Gwen. She'd managed to gather Braith's reins and stay on the horse's back. Gwen's breath came in gasps and her eyes were wide with fear, but like Braith, her head was up and she wasn't screaming. Beyond, men and horses pushed back and forth at each other, some in such close combat that their swords weren't doing the fighters any good. Despite the ferociousness of the attack, Owain Gwynedd's men had been able to withstand the initial assault. Even the two horsemen who'd ridden into the fray from behind had gone down.

"They overestimated their ability to surprise us," Gareth said. "And we had the greater numbers."

Madog grunted and moved towards the thick of the fight, calling to the men, "Keep one alive!"

"If they can't hear you, we've got one here." With his boot, Gareth toed the side of one of the men he'd downed.

Madog turned back and crouched beside the wounded man. A gash in his side bled heavily, but he was still conscious.

"Who sent you?" Madog said.

The man grinned, revealing blood-stained teeth, and answered in Welsh, but with a thick accent. "Why should I tell you?"

Madog glanced up at Gareth, who nodded. Just by speaking, the man had told them plenty. Now, they were looking not only for a rich, powerful lord, but one with the wherewithal to buy mercenaries from Ireland. Either that, or someone from

Ireland wanted Anarawd dead and had put great effort into ensuring it.

"You should tell me who it was, because no matter how much he paid you, you won't collect the money now. Why not bring him down with you?" Madog said. "No use dying here for nothing."

The man grinned again and seemed about to speak, but then choked as blood from his lungs bubbled into his mouth. He coughed, tried to lift his head, and then fell back, his mouth slack.

"*Cachiad*," Madog said. "We'll have to find another."

Gareth turned, prepared to search among the other fallen men for one who was still alive. Then Gwen, who still sat astride Braith, gave a cry. "Father!" She spurred Braith back the way they'd come.

5

"Thanks be to God, you're all right." Gwen fell to her knees beside her father and Gwalchmai. The latter sat up, rubbing the side of his head.

Meilyr patted Gwalchmai all over. "You're not hurt? Your chest, your fingers..." Meilyr clasped both of Gwalchmai's hands in his.

"We've routed them." Gwen put a hand to her chest, feeling her heart slow.

"I'm fine, Father." Gwalchmai pulled away. "And so is Gwen."

"I can see that." Meilyr glanced at his daughter once before turning his attention back to Gwalchmai.

Gwen smiled inwardly at the usual pattern: her father ignored her and Gwalchmai remembered. It was always he who reminded their father that he had another child. When Gwen was ten and her mother died at Gwalchmai's birth, she'd taken over Gwalchmai's care—and her father's too, truth be told—the best way she knew how, lavishing all the love she had on her little brother. Her father had been undone by grief and had never thanked her, never mentioned her mother or their mutual loss that whole first year. They'd barely spoken to each other beyond brief discussions of court politics, about which Gwen hadn't cared in the slightest.

By the time she reached womanhood, Gwen and her father had come to a grudging accommodation, which had been instantly undone by Meilyr's rejection of Gareth. Gwen had said things to her father then—things she couldn't take back or amend because they were the truth—but which she later regretted. At the time, she paid for them and maybe that had made her father feel better and allowed him not to face his own neglect. That he was the adult and she the child had mattered little in the end.

Gwalchmai's value, however, was undeniable. When Meilyr thought of him, he was thinking also of his own livelihood, which would come to depend more and more on Gwalchmai in the coming years. Meilyr was growing old, and while he taught as well as he sang, few households but those of high lords and kings could afford him. Gwalchmai's voice, a voice which came along perhaps once in a generation, could support them all.

"Whose men were they?" Meilyr got to his feet and brushed grass and leaves from his cloak and vest.

"We don't know," Gwen said. "At least one of them was from Ireland. It's possible they all were. Gareth will find out."

Her eyes went automatically to Gareth, who was working side-by-side with Madog. They'd taken on the gruesome task of sorting through their own men: who was alive, who was going to die, and whom they could save. Gwen's throat constricted at the horrors she'd seen today. It was all *too much*. Tears pricked her eyes again. She swallowed them back, gritting her teeth and telling herself that she would shed them later, when nobody was watching.

"Is that so?" Meilyr's eyes turned thoughtful as he looked at her. "This move is not what I would expect from the Irish—or those Dublin Danes for that matter—not when attacking King Anarawd's band and ours means inciting the wrath of King Owain Gwynedd."

"They were over-confident," Gwalchmai said. "Do you remember that time I sang in King Padern's hall? I'd sung that particular song so many times I could do it in my sleep. But because of that, I didn't prepare as you taught me and when I opened my mouth, no sound came out."

Battling over-confidence was something Gwalchmai would have to deal with his whole life, but Gwen could appreciate his point. "They attacked us because they thought they could ensure that nobody lived to tell the tale," she said. "They must have been paid a great deal to be willing to sacrifice their lives in Wales for such an ignoble cause."

"No Welshman would have done this," Meilyr said. "We are ignoble often, but not as willing to die so far from home. We're far more practical."

"How much time have you spent with Irishmen to know them so well?" Gareth came to stand beside Gwen. His hand hovered for a moment at the small of her back and then dropped to his side. The pounding of her heart, which had eased once she knew her family was safe, sped up again.

"We've sung along the west coast of Wales for many years. Gwalchmai is right, as far as it goes." Gwen gestured to the carnage before them. "It would be interesting to know how much of this their master ordered, and how much they took upon themselves."

"That's the Irish for you," Gareth said. "A lord might bring them here, but then not be able to control them."

"And how do you know that?" Gwen said.

"I've spent time in the Emerald Isle," Gareth said. "Hywel's mother was Irish and we traveled there together to renew his family ties."

"He'll need them if he ever has to fight his younger brothers for the throne of Wales." Meilyr surveyed the battle scene and what was left of their goods. "Them or his Danish cousins."

The horse who'd drawn their cart had panicked, upending their possessions on the way to pulling the cart off the road. He'd come to rest between two trees but had been unable either to force his way between them or free himself from his traces. He stood now, head hanging, exhausted from his own fight.

Gwen noted her satchel, squashed but unopened beneath a box containing musical instruments. Her best dress, when it came time to wear it, should be undamaged. Gwalchmai noticed the box at the same time she did, and with a cry, ran towards the cart.

"Those two are much alike," Gwen said, as she watched Meilyr and her brother set the box upright, open it, and begin to examine the contents. Gwalchmai held up an injured drum, showing his father the hole punched through the skin stretched across the frame. "And Hywel for a third. Always thinking of music."

Gwen felt Gareth looking at her, his eyes questioning. She didn't want to meet them. She kept seeing the rise and fall of his sword as he fought. But Gareth was thinking along entirely different lines. "Are you more to Prince Hywel than just his spy?"

"What?" Gwen turned to Gareth. "What do you mean?"

Gareth studied her. "Are the two of you lovers?"

"Of course not."

The notion was ridiculous and Gareth should have known it if he'd thought about it for longer than a heartbeat. If anything, Hywel thought of her as a sister. Admittedly, Gwen had loved him as long as she'd known him, but understood almost as quickly what a lost cause that was, and how bad for her Hywel would be if she ever shared his bed. He was a Prince of Gwynedd and she a bard's daughter. His father would never allow him to marry her and she wasn't going to settle for anything less, not even from him.

For Hywel's part, he'd never shown any interest in her, not in all the years that he'd wooed and loved the dozens of women he'd taken to his bed. By now, she was grateful for that, because it made them friends, or at worst, employer and employee, without the complications of romance.

"If you say so." Gareth squeezed her hand once. "Come. We've more downed men than before—some of whom are still alive—and it's a long way home to Aber."

"Surely you don't intend to attempt the journey today? After all this?" Gwen glanced upwards. Although most of the day had passed and the sun had fallen halfway down the sky, as it was early August, they had at least five more hours of daylight. That would give them just enough time to get the exhausted soldiers, the dead, and the wounded, to safety before dark.

Gareth shrugged. "Once we get the wounded to Caerhun, I must ride. Hywel and Owain Gwynedd need to hear what has transpired as soon as possible and I should be the one to tell it."

"Then I will come with you," Gwen said.

"Your pony can't keep up with my horse, and Braith can't carry two that far with any kind of speed," he said.

"I'll borrow my father's horse," Gwen said. "He fears King Owain more than he values his own dignity. He will loan it to me." The horse in question cropped the grass beside the road, still with a dead body on his back, but seemingly unconcerned about either it or the activity around him.

Gareth caught Gwen's chin and looked into her face. It had been a long time since they'd gazed at each other like this. She wasn't sure she could read him anymore and for a moment didn't know if he would agree—and what she would do about it if he didn't. But then he nodded.

"You'll tell me next that Hywel would want me to let you come."

"He would. You know he would," Gwen said.

Gareth narrowed his eyes at her, but Gwen shrugged him off and walked toward the fallen cart as if the matter was already decided. It would be a bad start to their renewed friendship if she had to force his hand, or follow him from Caerhun without him knowing. A quick look through the jumble of belongings on the ground produced the bag of medicines and bandages that her father had kicked to one side in his anxiety to determine the state of his instruments. She'd tied the top tightly when she packed it to protect what was inside and now crouched to open it. Then Gareth was beside her again.

"Do you know what these all are for?" He pawed through the collection of vials and herb boxes, picking up one and then another to study the labels. She almost laughed. It shouldn't have surprised her that in the five years since she'd last seen him, he'd learned to read. It was just like him.

"As well as anyone who spent half her life in the company of an active younger brother, I suppose," Gwen said. "My father worked very hard to control Gwalchmai, and perhaps that's why when he was allowed out, he ran wild—and inevitably injured himself or his friends." She paused. "And you?" She wished she could read Gareth as well as the letters on the vial, as he shot her yet another look she couldn't interpret.

"I've spent far too much time in the company of wounded men. I know less about healing than I would like, but certainly enough to help you doctor these men until we can get them to someone more knowledgeable."

"Then come," Gwen said. "We've work to do."

But this time, Gareth didn't reply. He stood frozen to the spot, a few steps from the cart, and then walked quickly to a body that had fallen underneath two others. He shoved at them and Gwen trotted up to help.

"What is it?" she said.

"I pray—" Gareth stopped speaking and swallowed hard instead. He'd revealed the face of a man who was still alive, but hadn't long to live.

"Bran!" Gareth knelt to cradle the man's head. "Talk to me!"

Bran opened his eyes and brought a hand up to Gareth's cheek, before dropping it. "Glad you're alive."

"What? Why? Why are you with these Irishmen?"

"Not Irish. Danes. We had to come back. Didn't know you'd be here. I tried to warn you." Bran moaned and would have closed his eyes again but Gareth shook him to keep him awake.

"*Why* did you have to come back?"

"Had to get Anarawd's seal. Prove the king was dead."

"Prove to whom, Bran! Who bought you—"

Silence.

Gwen reached over and closed Bran's eyes while Gareth settled Bran onto the road. He put a hand to his forehead, with his elbow resting on his knee. He held that position, his throat working, though he didn't make a sound. Gwen put a hand on his shoulder and Gareth reached back with his other hand to grasp it.

"Who was he?" she said.

"He was my milk brother. Though why—" Gareth swiveled to survey the men around his fallen brother.

"Why would he ride among Danes?" she said.

"I don't know," Gareth said. "The last news I had from him was that he rode in Anarawd's *teulu*. I looked for him among the fallen earlier, thinking he might have died defending Anarawd, and was relieved to find him absent. But now..."

Gwen didn't know what to say other than, "I'm sorry."

Gareth got to his feet, his shoulders stiff and frozen. He stared at his brother's body as if he would stand there forever. Then he gave a deep sigh and ran a hand through his hair. "Come. We've work to do."

"Why would Bran have been with a Danish company if he rode with—"

"I don't know, Gwen." The words came out sharp and she knew instantly that it would be better not to ask what he didn't want to answer. Not with the grief so near. And betrayal.

In silence, they labored among the dead and wounded. With the help of Madog's surviving soldiers, they stripped the foreigners to their loincloths. Their own soldiers could use the armor and weapons and it gave Gwen and Gareth an opportunity to look for any indication of who had paid the mercenaries, if that was indeed what they were. Perhaps the King of Dublin himself wanted Anarawd dead, though Gwen couldn't imagine why.

They found nothing useful, no seal or ring that a lord might give to an underling to provide him safe passage through Wales. A pair of boots appeared beside Gwen's knee.

"It's time to put the lyre on the roof." Meilyr dropped her satchel of clothing beside the body of the man she'd searched most recently. "Here. It's time to go."

"I hate giving up," Gwen said. "Owain Gwynedd will not be pleased."

"Then he can come himself and search," Meilyr said, uncharacteristically dismissing his lord's concern. "It's time we were going if we are to arrive at Caerhun before darkness falls."

Gwen got to her feet and hefted the two satchels—one of clothing and the other of the much-depleted medicines. Madog needed their repaired cart to carry the dead and a soldier had calmed their horse enough to haul it. For the rest, they piled the weapons, bodies, and goods in the already heavily laden carts, and traveled the last miles to the Conwy River. Meilyr and Gwalchmai carried the box of precious instruments between them.

Madog spent the journey grilling Gareth and Gwen about King Anarawd's death and everything they'd culled from the Danish soldiers. Unfortunately, there wasn't much. Most of the loot would be divided among Madog's company, with a tithe set aside for Owain Gwynedd. Gareth had acquired a short knife, which now rested at his waist.

"Take these." He handed three coins to Gwen.

"I—I can't," she said, rejecting them out of hand, even though her eyes widened at the sight of them. Coins were rare in Wales and she'd never had any of her own.

"What do you mean, you can't?" Gareth said.

Gwen shook her head. "A man who is dead last held those coins. Perhaps the lord who ordered Anarawd's death gave them to him. How can I take them for myself?"

Gareth tsked at her through his teeth but didn't push them on her, and instead slipped them into his own scrip. "I'll hold them for you until you need them."

Gwen hadn't banished the sick feeling in her stomach at the events of the day. "I can't believe someone has plotted to murder a king."

Gareth laughed under his breath. "What you can't believe is that you witnessed it. Murdering one's king is a well-established tradition in Wales and you know it."

Of course Gareth was right. And if Gwen were smarter, she wouldn't be the one to tell Owain Gwynedd about this particular murder. Unfortunately, leaving the task for Gareth alone was the coward's way and that was a path Gwen refused to take.

It was another long walk before the fort of Caerhun rose before them, half-finished—or rather, half-falling down and patched here and there with wattle and daub or foraged stone. King Owain understood the importance of the old Roman fort. It guarded a centuries-old east-west road across Gwynedd. The Romans had built the fort and improved the road, but the Welsh themselves had passed this way for as long as they'd peopled these lands.

The English had sought to force the Conwy River many times over the years. While today King Owain's domains were at peace and stretched all the way to the city of Chester on the border between England and Wales, that hadn't always been the case. King Owain, and his father Gruffydd before him, had chosen to defend what amounted to the only useable ford on the Conwy River.

Gwen checked the sky as they turned into the entrance. The long summer dusk was upon them, giving them perhaps another two hours of light. They'd traveled all of ten miles the whole day— a few hours' walk when things were going well. A pity they hadn't. Particularly for Anarawd.

"How long before we must ride?" she asked Gareth.

"Give me an hour, two at most," Gareth said. "Both Braith and your father's horse need food, rest, and the comfort of a stall for a short time at least."

Gwen nodded and turned towards the dining hall with some of the other men, looking forward to the opportunity to sit down. She bent at the waist, stretching her back. Her hair had come loose and she pushed it out of her face, and then looked up to find Gwalchmai planted in front of her.

"Father says you're going on without us."

"Yes," Gwen said. A wave of soldiers swept around and past them and she wrinkled her nose at the press of humanity. Maybe she wasn't hungry after all if she had to eat with all of them.

"I'm sorry about Father," he said. "You know he doesn't mean anything by what he says. Or doesn't say."

Gwen smiled at her brother. He was only an inch or two shorter than she was. By next year he'd top her and the year after that he'd be a man, according to Welsh law. "Thank you for trying to protect me, but there's no need and you'll only make Father angry."

"It's time someone stood up to him," Gwalchmai said.

"Isn't that what I've been trying to do?" Gwen shook her head. "Leave that to me too. You have a great future ahead of you, from the moment you sing your first note in King Owain's hall. And it's Father who's taught you everything he knows, who's poured all of his love of music into you. There's nothing there to feel sorry about or regret."

A man brushed past her and Gwen started when she realized it was Gareth. He glanced back at her and winked before entering the hall.

"Are you sure?" Gwalchmai said.

Gwen's heart swelled with love for her brother. If nothing had gone the way she'd wanted in her own life, at least she'd done the right thing by him. "I'm sure. As I told Father years ago, I'm ready to follow my own road."

6

Gareth and Gwen had ridden through the dark and now reached the highest point on the road that led across the high, windswept moors of Gwynedd from Caerhun to Aber. The standing stones of Bwlch y Ddeufaen stood stark in the moonlight, looming over them eight feet high on either side of the road that wended among the hills. Those stones had guarded the pass from all comers since before the Romans came. At least the fine weather continued, and they weren't forced to ride these ten miles in the rain.

"What did my father say about me traveling with you?" Gwen said.

"This and that," Gareth said, having no intention of sharing anything about that conversation.

At first, all Gareth had done when he'd encountered Meilyr standing with his hands on his hips, blocking Gareth's retreat from the dining hall, was hand him the few coins Madog had set aside for Gwen. Gareth hoped she'd accept them later, even if they made her uncomfortable now. Although he didn't like Meilyr, the man was neither a wastrel nor a miser. He would save them for Gwen.

"Fine time for you to appear," Meilyr had said. "You mind telling me what you've been up to all these years before I allow my daughter to go off with you?"

Gareth could read nothing in Meilyr's face but his usual suspicion, so he ventured to reply. "You heard I was a mercenary?" Gareth asked the question even though he already knew the answer from his earlier conversation with Gwen.

Meilyr gave him a short nod.

"Those days are past," Gareth said.

"Landed on your feet, then?" Meilyr's voice remained casual, denying the intensity of his expression.

Gareth warred with himself as to whether or not to tell Meilyr the truth. If Meilyr was going to give his approval, Gareth preferred he gave it to him because he trusted him, instead of being blinded by an obsession with rank. Still, if he was to have any chance with Gwen, it was better if Meilyr heard it from him.

"I am a knight."

Meilyr grunted. "Are you now?"

"I understood it to be the requirement," Gareth said.

"Left it a bit late."

"Is she betrothed?" Gareth's gut roiled. Gwen hadn't said as much to him but she might not, given how awkward that conversation could become.

Meilyr laughed, but the sound came out more sour than humorous. "Could have been. Just last month I had someone asking for her. Wasn't thinking of you, of course, but I couldn't let her go to just anyone, especially not a spoiled child-man like him."

Gareth's heart settled a bit. He still had time. "With your permission, I'd like to speak of this further. For now, I'm afraid I've work to do." He gestured towards the stables where Braith waited. "Aber isn't getting any closer and King Owain won't like to have been kept waiting."

"Owain Gwynedd doesn't like anything that he doesn't control or foresee," Meilyr said. "How did you end up under his wing?"

"I'm not under his, but Hywel's," Gareth said.

Meilyr grunted again, acknowledging the difference.

"Though it was King Owain's eldest son, Rhun, who knighted me, and that raised my standing in the King's eyes," Gareth said.

"King Owain knows of your troubled history with his brother, Cadwaladr?"

"He knows," Gareth said.

For the second time that day, he'd had a civil conversation with Meilyr. With that, Gareth hadn't wanted to tempt his luck any further, not after the traumatic events of the day, and retreated to the stables.

"What did your father say to you?" Gareth said. "When you demanded to come with *me*, that is." He smiled because he had no doubt that's exactly what Gwen had done.

Gwen didn't rise to the bait. "He accepted it, and since the kitchens at Caerhun would be there to prepare his breakfast in the morning, he could dispense with me. He didn't want to give me his horse, necessarily, but in the end he gave way. What payment did you promise Madog to get him to loan my father a better one?"

"Gwen—"

"Don't try to deny it. I know how these things work." Gwen matched him smile for smile, as if to indicate that she was comfortable with these kinds of machinations and her own perceived value. He wasn't fooled.

"Your father loves you," he said.

"Does he?" Gwen said. "Fathers are supposed to love their daughters, but ... Would he miss me if he awoke one morning and I was gone forever?"

"He loves you enough not to give you to just anyone," Gareth said, and then bit his tongue because of what that statement gave away.

Gwen glared at him. "He told you about Rhys?"

"Not his name," Gareth said. "But the circumstances."

"I've had enough of my father's opinions," she said. "Don't make me dislike yours as well."

"I know it's been hard—"

Gwen cut him off. "I've not wasted all these years mourning your absence," she said. "I'd hoped we'd have three children by now, and be living on a bit of land somewhere by the sea." She shrugged. "It wasn't meant to be. I can accept that we can't always live the life we imagined."

"I've paid for my choices, Gwen," Gareth said. "I'd prefer not to have to keep paying."

Gareth felt Gwen's eyes on him, but didn't know if he should say anything more as she didn't. Cadwaladr had dismissed him the same day he'd intended to ask Meilyr for Gwen's hand. She'd been only sixteen, he twenty-three and far more sure of himself than he should have been. Cadwaladr had been right to dismiss him, if outright disobedience was grounds for dismissal. But then, Cadwaladr's insistence that Gareth cut off the hand of an eight year old boy who'd stolen a piglet had been one order too many for Gareth. Still, looking at Gwen now, it was hard not to have regrets.

The lights of Aber shone in the distance and they slowed. "It's been a long time for you, hasn't it?" he said.

"Six years. I cried when we left." Gwen paused, and then to Gareth's surprise, added, "I was pleased to work for Hywel again because of those memories. But you can't go back, not really, even if you follow the same road."

Gareth swallowed. Was that comment meant for him? Was she telling him to walk away from her? "I do think Hywel missed you," he said, instead of asking either of those questions. And then kicked himself again. What compelled him to mention Hywel's name every third sentence?

"Did he?" she said. "He didn't even seek me out to say goodbye." Before Gareth could formulate a reply, they reached the walls and Gwen's mouth fell open at what confronted them. "What are they doing to the castle?"

King Owain didn't have the wherewithal to improve the defenses of all his holdings, but Aber was an important seat, his stronghold on the north coast of Gwynedd. He'd ordered the building of a stone wall around the fort, turning what had been little more than a large manor house nearly into a fortress. Many of the English bastions along the border between England and Wales were going up entirely in stone. It was dangerous not to keep up with the times, but the cost was exorbitant.

"The English are coming," Gareth said. "Perhaps not this year, but eventually. Hopefully by the time they get their affairs in order, King Owain will be ready."

"I'm not so much worried about the English today," Gwen said. "This ambush of Anarawd indicates that King Owain has a very angry, very dangerous enemy."

Gareth took in a breath. "Perhaps it's time he knew of it."

They urged their horses the last yards to the gatehouse. Gareth's face gained them admission and in the shelter of the courtyard, they faced off in the darkness. At this hour—nearly midnight by Gareth's reckoning—most of the torches had been allowed to die, leaving two by the front door to the hall and two by the gate. The bulk of the garrison slept in the barracks, while the peasants and craft workers had settled into their huts and stalls. Dawn came early in August and they and their animals would be up before it.

"Should we speak to Hywel first?" Gwen said.

Gareth glanced towards the great hall, some thirty paces away. The King kept odd hours, but midnight was as late as Gareth had ever seen him leave the hall. If he held true to form, Gareth would have to wake him, which thrilled him not at all. Better to take the cowardly route. He grasped Gwen's arm and tugged her towards a side entrance to the main building, for which the hall formed the central room, with offices, storerooms, and sleeping quarters leading from it.

"Hywel's rooms are along here." Gareth opened the exterior door and entered a long passageway. Still tugging Gwen with him, he halted in front of a half-closed door and knocked.

"Come."

Gareth pushed through the door, with Gwen at his heels. For once, Hywel was alone, though that wasn't to say a woman wasn't lounging on his bed in the room adjacent, waiting for him to return. Hywel's charm and appearance—black hair, deep blue eyes with long lashes (ridiculously long if Gareth's female observers could be trusted), and muscular physique—had drawn women to him from before he'd even become a man.

One of the most treacherous battles Gareth had ever been in was when he'd ended up defending Hywel from a horde of angry farmers, roused by a cuckolded husband. They'd been outnumbered twelve to one, and yet managed to escape by luck and the timely appearance of a priest who told the farmers off. Had he known the reason for their anger, he might have felt differently, but at the time, all he'd seen was peasants confronting a prince.

As they entered, Hywel looked up from the household accounts on his desk in front of him. A grin split his face. "This is a surprise." Hywel's eyes tracked from Gwen to Gareth.

Gareth gritted his teeth. His lord had a tendency to perception and just now, his relationship with Gwen was not something Gareth wanted acknowledged, or worse, discussed. "My lord." Gareth put his feet together and gave Hywel a stiff bow. Gwen curtseyed beside him.

"I hoped to have seen Gwen earlier today—and you not until tomorrow, Gareth," Hywel said. "How is it that you arrive together, and so late?"

Gareth and Gwen exchanged a look. Her expression told him that she'd prefer him to speak. Choosing nobility, he plunged on: "We've ridden through the night to tell you—and your father—of a terrible event that has transpired. King Anarawd was ambushed by Danes on the road just north of Dolwyddelan. He is dead."

"What!" Hywel was on his feet. "By the Saints, say it's not true!"

"I'm sorry, my lord," Gwen said. "It is true."

"Who, what—tell me more!"

Gareth and Gwen relayed the story, including their search and the second ambush, taking turns with the parts they knew best. By the end, Hywel had settled into his chair again, a horrified expression on his face. Made worse by his news for them: "You should know that I and some of my men tracked these Danes across Gwynedd today, nearly to the road from Dolwyddelan where you tell me Anarawd died."

Gareth took a step forward. "But, then—"

Hywel shook his head, in what Gareth interpreted to be stunned disbelief. "You know those hills are full of paths. We thought we had them—we followed them for some distance—but lost them when they backtracked west. Or, rather, we thought they went west. By the time we reached the Roman fort, we found no sign of them. Instead, they must have taken a different route north to ambush you."

"You heard nothing?"

"There is a river there, running through a series of falls. The path runs beside it. It would have drowned out any noise of battle. And since the Danes didn't ever reach the road, or so we thought..."

"But they did," Gwen said.

Hywel sighed. "Why was Anarawd even there? He shouldn't have been. He wasn't due until tomorrow."

"He was in a hurry to reach his bride, apparently," Gareth said.

"Was there any sign, any token, of who could have ordered this?" Hywel said.

"No," Gareth said. "Not that we've found so far. I'd like to return to the initial site without the feet of fifty other men treading on it."

"You'll have that chance," Hywel said, "if I have any say in it."

"Whoever paid for this crime has incredible power and reach, my lord," Gwen said. "The Irish connection is critical."

Hywel got up and began to pace in front of the open window by his desk. They both knew better than to interrupt his thoughts, but then he halted in front of them. "This news cannot wait. We must wake my father. It will be worse for everyone if even one more hour goes by without him hearing of it."

7

Owain Gwynedd, however, was not asleep, though he was less than pleased to see Hywel stride into the room, interrupting his late night meal with Cristina. They sat together at the high table in the great hall, alone but not private, an odd paring at first glance, his middle-aged bulk a contrast to her petite youthfulness.

Gareth bent his head to Gwen's. "As far as I've seen, she refuses to dally for more than a few moments alone with the King. She has her eye on the main chance."

"He's obviously smitten."

"It seems to me since everyone's here for Anarawd's wedding," Gareth said, "they might as well go ahead and marry themselves instead."

"Don't say that!" Gwen said.

"We're all waiting for it."

"Even if we're dreading it," Gwen said.

Their feet echoed in the hall, thudding hollowly on the wood of the floor as they made their way among the mostly empty tables. Hywel came to a halt in front of his father, with Gwen and

Gareth a pace behind him to his left and right. "Sir. I bring bad news," Hywel said.

King Owain studied his son, a smile twitching at the corner of his mouth, despite his earlier annoyance. "Let's hear it, then."

Gwen had the sense that they were playing out an oft-repeated scene—as if Hywel had often brought King Owain bad news, and this was the least painful way to relay it.

Hywel took a deep breath and let it out, still hesitating. His father leaned forward, perhaps realizing that this news was going to be worse than usual. "Anarawd and his men were ambushed on the road from Dolwyddelan by a company of Danes," Hywel said. "King Anarawd is dead."

King Owain surged to his feet, knocking back his chair, even Cristina forgotten. "How do you know this?"

"My man found him." Hywel gestured to Gareth who stepped forward and bowed.

"Tell me," King Owain said.

Gareth bowed again, and then related how he'd observed the start of the battle and returned with reinforcements to find King Anarawd and his men dead. He touched on the presence of Gwen and her family but didn't emphasize it, and then described the second ambush. "The wounded are being cared for at Caerhun, my lord."

King Owain gazed at Gareth, then looked past him to the few other knights and men-at-arms who'd gathered to hear the tale. "Arrest him." He pointed at Gareth with his chin.

"What?" Gwen stepped forward. "You can't—" She cut herself off as Hywel grabbed her arm.

"Hush," he said, and then turned to the King. "Father, this is—" and then he broke off himself as three men surrounded Gareth and pinioned his arms behind his back.

"What are you doing?" Gareth cast a pleading glance at Hywel, looking for help. "I had nothing to do with this! I found them."

"Did you not leave King Anarawd to die?" King Owain said, his face suffused with red and his voice thundering. "Are you not experienced in the use of a sword?"

"Yes, but—"

"I've tolerated your presence up until now because my sons trust you, but I heard about you from my brother," King Owain said. "The truth will out more easily from a cell." He waved a hand. "Take him."

Gareth's jaw bulged. Gwen thought he was going to dig in his heels when his shoulders tensed, but then his eyes met Hywel's. Gareth must have read something there that convinced him to back down, because he allowed the guards to turn him, his legs moving stiffly, and lead him away. He didn't look again at Gwen.

"Father." Hywel faced King Owain, his voice back to reasonable. "Gareth had nothing to do with this. He hasn't the money to pay—"

But King Owain was still on fire. "I never said he paid for it! But he could have been bought and paid for! That I will believe!"

"Father—" Hywel tried again.

"You have something to say?" His voice thundered throughout the hall. "You question my orders?"

Hywel took a step back. "No, Father." He ducked his head. "But I will discover the truth. Gareth has served both you and me well. He is not at fault here."

King Owain wasn't listening. He turned and kicked the fallen chair out of his way. It skittered across the floor. Owain Gwynedd paced towards the fireplace and then back. "Who bought him? Who seeks to strike me in the heart, in my own lands?"

By now, Gwen had slipped away, fading into the background as much as she could, with her back against the wall out of reach of the firelight. It was clear that calling any kind of attention to herself would be a major mistake. King Owain, however, had not forgotten her and after haranguing Hywel a while longer, he spun towards her. "You tell me your father comes too! Was he injured in this fight?"

"No, sir," she said. "Both he and my brother are safe at Caerhun."

"I am besieged on every side." King Owain returned to his pacing.

"Whoever killed Anarawd has enough money and power to buy a troop of men—from Ireland no less—and point them in whatever direction he chose," Hywel said. "Either that, or this is an attack from Ireland itself."

"Don't tell me what I already know!" King Owain said, the storm returning. "Where's Rhun?"

"At Aberffraw, my lord," Hywel said. "He was to escort Elen here tomorrow."

"*Coc oen!*" King Owain said. "This is just what I need."

At his flagrant profanity, Cristina rose to her feet, risking his wrath far more than Gwen could have imagined she might, and put a hand to his arm. "There is nothing more to be done tonight. Madog will come from Caerhun tomorrow with Anarawd's body. Until then, strategy is best conceived with a cool head."

King Owain turned on her at the implied criticism of his temper but she stood steady before him, gazing unblinking into his eyes—and raising her standing considerably in Gwen's estimation. He glared at her for another count of ten, and then his shoulders relaxed and he even laughed. "I bow to your wishes, my dear. We will retire."

Hywel took a step forward. "About Gareth, my lord—"

"He will stay where he is," King Owain said. "He has not told me as much as he will." He strode from the room, Cristina on his arm.

It was as though the fire had gone out of the hall. It was colder, darker, and far, far calmer without King Owain's presence. Gwen moved to Hywel's side. "Is there something Gareth knows that he's not telling the king?"

Hywel gave her a cryptic look. "Many things, but since you confirm his story, I don't see what more he can tell us about Anarawd's death."

"Does Gareth really have to stay in a cell tonight?"

"You're asking me to defy my father? You've spent all of a half of an hour in his company in the last six years but already you should know better," Hywel said.

"But, my lord—"

"You've felt only a taste of my father's wrath. I cannot release Gareth on my own accord—not yet—not until pressed to absolute need. Besides, it sounds worse than it is for him. We don't actually have any cells here. This isn't the Tower of London."

"Yes, my lord." Gwen cast her eyes down so she wouldn't have to look at him—or embarrass herself with begging.

She could feel Hywel's eyes on her. "We will speak in the morning," Hywel said. "I'll have my father's steward find you a place to sleep."

8

Jesus! In his wildest imagination, it hadn't occurred to Gareth that the result of being the one to tell Owain Gwynedd that King Anarawd was dead was that he'd end up here. *What if King Owain leaves me here? I'll rot while Gwen is left to wander the castle alone.* The thought of her on her own amongst the garrison was enough to have him punching his fist into the wall again. That it was wooden and not stone was the only thing that saved him from a broken hand. Of course, it also showed him how easily he could kick his way out of his rickety prison if he had to. He could take some comfort in that.

His cell sat at the back of the stables. It was ten feet on a side with knot holes and slits in the wood that allowed him to see through the slats to the curtain wall. This section had already been replaced with stone, indicating that freedom, were he to pursue it on his own, wouldn't be as immediate as he might hope. The pungent smells of horse and excrement were making him lightheaded in the confined space and he paced around his cell, trying to stay awake until someone came. Hywel? Gwen? A guard to beat the truth out of him? At the very least, he was looking for someone to talk to him, to come and tell him this was all a mistake.

Fortunately, the guards hadn't yet roughed him up. Hell— they weren't even guards, but friends. Evan had brought him a flask, a crust of bread, and dried meat, with an unspoken apology in his eyes. None of his friends had been happy with their appointed task, but they did it. They did it because their lord ordered it and it wasn't their place to question Owain Gwynedd's orders. If Gareth had learned that lesson sooner, he might have married Gwen. They might have had those three children she'd mentioned.

After he'd spent an hour alone, a light appeared on the other side of the door. Gareth braced himself—whether for fight or flight he hadn't yet decided—but it was Hywel who appeared. To his credit, he didn't bother to apologize for Gareth's predicament, but stood with his hands on his hips in the doorway with the door open wide behind him.

"You won't run, I assume," he said.

Gareth eyed the space behind his prince. He could knock Hywel over; maybe even make it out of the stables and through the postern gate before anyone was the wiser. But he didn't. Instead, Gareth took Hywel's words as a vote of confidence and as indication that at least Hywel didn't believe in his guilt.

"It would set your father further against me, wouldn't it?" Gareth said.

"Likely," Hywel said.

"Except I don't even know what I'm supposed to have done." Gareth felt like punching the wall again. "Is he accusing me of betraying you? Of being in the pay of another master? Does he think I helped kill King Anarawd and two dozen of his guardsmen?"

"I expect he isn't accusing you of anything but being in the wrong place at the wrong time," Hywel said. "But he'll hang you for it anyway if we can't find the true culprit."

"*Christ*!" Gareth swung around to kick at a bucket in the corner. It had an inch of stale water in it which he wouldn't have drunk anyway. God knew what they kept in this room when they weren't using it as a prison cell. He hoped few men had the pleasure of it before him, though his friends had known without discussion where to take him when they'd hauled him away from King Owain.

"At least we're not at Dolbadarn—they've dungeons there," Hywel said.

"I should thank him for that small favor, should I?"

Hywel smiled. "I'm sure my father will see to addressing that lack when he rebuilds the hall in stone. In the meantime, you're safe enough here."

"I'm a pig in a pen, waiting for slaughter," Gareth said.

Hywel canted his head as he studied Gareth. "Use your anger and frustration to concentrate your mind on what might really have happened. Though they were all abed when you arrived, the barons have gathered at Aber. They came for the wedding, which won't happen now, but they'll meet in council anyway as my father intended. If any one of them is guilty of this treachery, they'll think themselves safer for your confinement. We might catch someone off guard."

"Tell that to your father," Gareth said.

"I won't need to," Hywel said. "By morning he'll think of it himself, even if he won't admit it. We can, however, take advantage of his hasty action."

"By leaving me in this cage?" Gareth said, not any happier with this idea, even if it was a good one. "I would be more useful on the outside!"

"We'll see." Hywel smirked at Gareth's outraged expression, and then added, "You're a bit easier to control in here." He held up an iron key. "I will lock the door because my father expects it, not because I don't trust you."

Gareth managed to tamp down his temper enough to tip his head at Hywel who, still smirking, closed the door behind him. Personally, Gareth thought Hywel was putting a bit too much faith in his father's good sense, which Gareth couldn't quite discern from where he stood. He thought it much more likely that King Owain would hang him, if only to make himself feel better and put some kind of conclusion on this affair—especially if he never found out who'd really ordered King Anarawd's death.

Gareth hadn't managed more than a few more paces around the cell, stewing in his anger and resentment, when a new knock came and then the sound of a key turning in the lock. He strode towards the door, furious that Hywel had come back to mock him some more, but then came to an abrupt halt a foot from the door as it opened. Gwen stood before him with a platter of steaming broth and a jug of mead.

"I bribed the cook with my recipe for spiced scones," she said.

Gareth warred with himself, as she was the last person he wanted to see him so powerless, but the smell of the soup made his stomach growl and he chose not to fight her—or to sulk. "Come in." He bowed low, one arm out like a courtier welcoming her to his home instead of a room lined with dirty straw.

"Hywel made me promise not to free you."

"I gave him my word that I'd stay." Gareth said. "He has some idea that if I'm confined, it will embolden the real villain. Give him confidence that nobody suspects him, which of course we don't since we have no idea who did this." The thought made Gareth want to kick something again, but he didn't. He took in a deep breath and let it out, getting hold of his temper.

Gwen handed him the tray of food. As he reached for it, he was surprised to see her eyes tearing. "I was that worried. King Owain was so angry."

"He's known for his astute strategizing," Gareth said, "but it's not uncommon for him to act first and think later. Look at what happened with your father. They have an argument about something that should have been resolved within half a day—and which King Owain probably doesn't even remember now—and they don't speak for six years. Hywel says that King Owain could still hang me for this, were we to fail to uncover the real culprit."

"That's what I fear. I spoke with several of your friends among the garrison. They don't think you're good for this, even if you've done some things in the past of which you are less than proud." She paused. "You don't have to tell me about those things."

"We've all done things we regret," Gareth said. "After Cadwaladr dismissed me, I learned that even what he'd asked me to do were minor offenses compared to what was possible." He shrugged. "A lord feels much more loyalty to his regular men-at-arms and knights, whose families may have served his family for generations, than to the mercenaries he hires. That's why a lord always assigns a mercenary the dirtiest work."

"Much like Hywel," Gwen said.

Gareth looked up from his soup bowl. "What makes you say that?"

"Wouldn't you agree?" Gwen said. "Rhun is the heir; Owain Gwynedd has things that need doing that he might not mind doing himself—if he had the time—but is loathe to have them sully Rhun's hands. But Hywel..."

"Yes," Gareth said. "I would say that you're right."

"It's always been that way," Gwen said. "I remember the first time. Hywel was only fourteen. One of King Owain's knights had neglected his duties to the king; he'd refused service and tithes in a strange act of defiance. It was Hywel that King Owain sent to see to him."

"And what did Hywel do?"

"Burned the man's house and barn to the ground, along with everything in them. The knight escaped with only the clothes on his back." Gwen glanced at Gareth, her gaze inscrutable. "None died, if you're wondering."

Gareth nodded. Such was the way of kings. "It could be worse. Hywel could have been born in the time of Gruffydd ap Llywelyn. If the stories of his reign are true, Gruffydd had half the men in his family killed to prevent any chance of them usurping his throne. Someone had to do it; someone had that blood on his hands, even if he was only doing as Gruffydd told him."

"King Owain has his hands full enough with his brother." Gwen poured the mead she'd brought into a cup and handed it to Gareth. He took it but didn't answer. He should have known she couldn't be silenced so easily. After another look, she said, "I gather, then, that we aren't going to talk about Cadwaladr either?"

"What's there to say?" Gareth said. "Even after all this time, he spreads lies about me. What I can't understand is why I'm even in his thoughts. I was a tiny speck on his cloak that he flicked off with one finger all those years ago."

Gareth had come to Cadwaladr after the death of his Uncle Goronwy, who'd served King Owain's elder brother, Cadwallon. Goronwy fell in battle with Cadwallon in 1132, in a war against a king of Powys over something Gareth couldn't remember now. Land or power, it was all one to Gareth. He'd been a soldier for two years already, though in truth still a boy and fighting on the fringes of the battle. He'd been posted among the archers since they'd been short of men with bows and his shot was better than average.

Upon Goronwy's death, Gareth, now orphaned for the second time, had transferred his allegiance to Cadwaladr at King Gruffydd's request. It was unfortunate for Gareth that this youngest prince hadn't even half the courage of the eldest.

"Apparently you weren't a negligible speck to him," Gwen said. "Now that you're among Hywel's company, Cadwaladr has been reminded of what happened and how you stood up to him. Perhaps you are one of the few men who ever defied him openly."

"The only one, I think," Gareth said. "Or rather, the only one who lived to speak of it. He's learned since his dealings with me that it's not enough to dismiss someone. Better to kill him."

Gwen shook her head. "I really don't want to know that. We've sung in his castle at Aberystwyth many times." She leaned against the wall, her hands behind her back, studying Gareth. "I actually didn't mean to talk about what happened between you and Cadwaladr, though we can. What I meant to point out is that Prince Cadwaladr is one of the few men in Wales who exactly fills the description of someone who'd want to murder Anarawd."

"Why is that?"

"Because he rules in Ceredigion, on lands adjacent to Anarawd's. Perhaps he didn't want King Owain to control them through his daughter, possibly at Cadwaladr's expense."

Gareth scrubbed at his face with both hands. "It's true he has Irish connections. As do all the royal families in Deheubarth and Gwynedd."

"More than that, he lived there as a child," Gwen said. "Hywel tells me that he only returned to Gwynedd upon the death of Cadwallon because his father felt that the remaining brothers must stand together to defend Gwynedd."

"We must keep speculation to a minimum," Gareth said. "You might as well accuse Hywel, for he shares a similar pedigree—his mother was Irish!"

"I'm not accusing anyone of anything," Gwen said. "But speculation is how mysteries are solved. We ask good questions, and we see if any of the answers we find fit our questions."

Gareth ran his hand through his hair. "Good questions, you say? I've got one for you—when do I get out of here?"

9

Gwen lay still and silent on her pallet, thinking of Gareth and hoping he wasn't too uncomfortable in his cell. When she'd returned to Hywel, he'd laughed off her concerns about Gareth's well-being, but she didn't think he was quite as complacent as he conveyed. Hywel had to know that even though King Owain had lost his temper and acted rashly, the king might not want to admit he was wrong about Gareth, even if they never found proof of his guilt.

In addition, King Owain should have known by now that his brother, Cadwaladr, didn't always relate the most accurate version of events. As she gazed up at the ceiling, she had a vision of that day five years ago when she'd lain in a room very like this one, but in Ceredigion, sobbing her eyes out over the loss of Gareth. Prince Cadwaladr had summarily dismissed him and Gareth had ridden away with only his sword and his horse. Cadwaladr hadn't even allowed him a moment to return to his quarters to gather the rest of his things.

It was Gwen who'd done that. Though Gareth didn't know it, she still had one of his spare shirts, stuffed into the bottom of her satchel, and wore his mother's cross around her neck. She should have given it to him first thing, but had forgotten about it until this moment. She pulled it out and clenched it in her fist.

To be fair, she had to acknowledge that Prince Cadwaladr had been beset at the time and much like his brother, may have allowed his temper to run away with him. Not long before, the Normans had beheaded Gwenllian, a younger sister to Owain and Cadwaladr, for leading a rebellion against them. Gwenllian's husband—who just happened to be Anarawd's father—had been in Gwynedd at the time, seeking an alliance against the Normans. As a result, Cadwaladr and Owain Gwynedd had gone south to avenge her death. Their losses had been compounded by the death of Gruffydd, their father, not long after in 1137.

These past realities made Anarawd's murder all the worse. Not only was he a strong ally and the King of Deheubarth, but he was a nephew-by-marriage to both Owain and Cadwaladr since Gwenllian had been Anarawd's step-mother. These family ties were powerful and compelling, not just for King Owain and Cadwaladr, but for any Welshmen. While the victory over the Normans had allowed King Owain to annex Ceredigion, it could not replace what they'd lost. It was Cadwaladr, now, who ruled those lands. And if Cadwaladr had something to do with Anarawd's death...

Thinking of the possibility made Gwen's stomach ache.

The next morning, after a restless night in which she feared she'd repeatedly woken many of the other women, Gwen forced herself from her pallet and back downstairs. Chaos confronted her in the hall. Men, huddled in groups small and large, talked and gesticulated to other men who nodded sagely back. The news of Anarawd's death was not easy for any of them to encompass.

"Will our tribulations never cease!"

That was Cadwaladr, holding court near the fire with three other barons. Taran, Owain Gwynedd's steward, stood a few feet away, speaking grimly with several other men. Hywel was alone by the door. Gwen headed towards him.

"What's going on here?" a woman's voice said.

Gwen looked past Hywel to see Elen, the bride, at the entrance to the great hall. At only sixteen, her marriage would have been a May-December match, but Gwen hadn't heard that she'd complained about it to her father. Her golden hair glinted in the sunlight, forming a halo around her head. As a bride, she had the right to wear it loose and it cascaded down her back in a bright mass.

Hywel caught her arm. "Come with me, Elen. I've something to tell you."

He tugged her in Gwen's direction and Gwen hurried to greet them. Their ages were too different to have allowed them to be actual friends growing up, but Gwen had cared for Elen many times in the years she lived at Aber. Too often, Elen's elders had alternately spoiled and ignored her. Gwen had tried to make up for that, just a little.

"Gwen!" Elen embraced her. "I'm so glad you've come."

Gwen eased back, still with her arm around Elen's waist, and filled with regret at what she was going to have to say next. "We have some bad news."

Elen's face paled. "Father—"

Hywel moved closer, a finger to her lips. "Not Father. Anarawd. He's dead."

"He's—"

"Damn it," Hywel said as Elen's eyes rolled up in their sockets and she collapsed unceremoniously into Gwen's arms. Gwen staggered under her burden, which Hywel eased by catching his sister around the shoulders before Gwen dropped her. Between the two of them, they carried Elen to a bench set against the wall behind them. Hywel laid her on her back and Gwen pulled up her knees.

"It's all right, *cariad*," she said, her lips on Elen's forehead. "You're going to be all right." Elen had never been good with sudden shocks—whether the event was a finger prick from a sewing needle or her grandfather's death. Gwen had nursed her through both in her time.

Cadwaladr had noted his niece's arrival and strode toward them, his gaze fixed on Elen's supine form. The expression on his face was stern but sympathetic and Gwen catalogued in her head the number of times she'd seen him come up with exactly the right outward manifestation, regardless of his inward feelings. Then again, the whole royal family was good at hiding what they thought—even King Owain had a devious mind when he chose to use it. He was the King of Gwynedd after all. By necessity, he'd learned deception in the cradle.

Hywel glanced up and allowed exasperation to cross his face for a heartbeat before schooling his expression. Gwen wondered how many people in the room would have preferred to be anywhere but where they were right now. Then King Owain blew in from his upstairs chamber.

"What's all this noise?" He surveyed his domain with sharp eyes.

At his interjection, Cadwaladr changed course, heading towards his brother. Elen opened her eyes. "Oh, Father!"

As if she'd never been ill, she spun off the bench and ran towards King Owain, who clasped her to him. He gazed over her head to Hywel, meeting his eyes, and then jerked his head in the direction from which he'd just come. That must have meant something to Hywel because he grasped Gwen's arm and dragged her with him to a doorway a few paces away leading to a side passage.

"What are you doing?" Gwen tried to pull away from him but his grip was too firm. They entered the hallway and Hywel swung her around so her back pressed against the wall of the hall.

"Cadwaladr shouldn't see you with me." Hywel moved his hand to her shoulder, holding her still, and peered around the door frame. "Another moment and he would have."

"Why does it matter if Cadwaladr sees me with you?" Gwen said. "He knows we grew up together."

Hywel tsked at her under his breath. She found it annoying that so many of the men in her life had a tendency to do that, not to mention drag her wherever they wished like a half-trained sheep at a village fair.

"You found King Anarawd's body, remember? And you did it with Gareth." Hywel ran his hand through his hair and turned to pace in front of her, even if hampered by the confined space. "Cadwaladr is very sensitive to his dignity and views Gareth as a mortal enemy."

"I still don't—"

Hywel hissed into her face. "Cadwaladr doesn't know you work for me and I'd rather he didn't learn of it today. I'm thankful my father thought of it in time."

Gwen subsided. "I think you're being foolish. I sang in his hall three months ago. I'll sing here tonight. He knows who I am."

"My father obviously shares my concern."

That gave Gwen pause. "Fine. But is Gareth safe from Cadwaladr? His cell is designed to keep him in, not others out."

Hywel stared at her. "Bloody hell! I hadn't thought of that either." But then he nodded. "I'll double guard him so no soldier has to deal with any visitors alone."

Gwen relaxed against the wall, studying her employer, who continued to pace as he thought. "Did she love him?" Gwen said.

"Who? Elen?" Hywel said. "She'd only met him once. But she loved the idea of getting married, for all that he was many years her elder. She would have been a princess of Gwynedd and queen of Deheubarth."

Gareth's friend Evan poked his head around the corner, just as a keening wail rose up from Elen. Hywel rolled his eyes at Gwen before acknowledging Evan. "What is it now?"

"Madog has come with the body."

If Hywel hadn't sworn again, Gwen might have. Then he canted his head to Gwen. "Come."

Gwen trotted after Hywel, towards the far door through which she and Gareth had entered the building last night, with Evan at her heels.

Madog and ten men from his garrison milled about a cart with Anarawd's wrapped body in the bed. His face expressionless, King Owain, Cadwaladr beside him, gazed down at the body. A portion of the crowd from the great hall had followed him out the door and now clustered behind him, unsure of what to do. News of King Anarawd's death had been an opportunity for speculation and gossip, but its reality was something else entirely.

"Enough!" King Owain said. "This is not a market stall. Be about your business."

Mumbling among themselves, the people in the crowd dispersed. Cadwaladr clapped a hand on King Owain's shoulder in apparent sympathy and turned away, leaving King Owain and Madog alone by the cart. King Owain lifted his head and looked around the courtyard until he spied Hywel, still standing by the side door with Gwen. With a wave of his hand, he gestured them over.

"You know what to do," he said when Hywel reached him.

"Yes, Father."

King Owain turned away.

"Where shall we put him, my lord?" Madog said. "The weather has been so warm he stinks already."

"Unfortunate but unavoidable," Hywel said. "We'll try to make this quick. Bring him to the barracks."

More curious than she wanted to admit, Gwen went with Hywel and the men-at-arms carrying Anarawd's body. The long, low building sat by the gatehouse. It contained a large, open sleeping space, but also dozens of small rooms. Just as they reached it, Hywel's elder brother, Rhun, stepped from the main doorway. Hywel pulled up short.

He held out his hand to Rhun, who took it, and the two men embraced. "I'm sorry this isn't going to end in a wedding," Hywel said. "You can imagine how upset Elen is with this news."

"Where is she?" Rhun said.

"In the hall," Hywel said. "I saw her greet Uncle Cadwaladr after Father dismissed him."

Rhun choked on a laugh. "I'll rescue her in a moment." He surveyed Anarawd's body and then turned to Gwen who stood quietly to one side. "Are you sure you want to be present when my brother examines him?"

"I've already seen the body," she said. "Sir Gareth and I were the ones who found him."

She didn't say anything of what she and Gareth had discovered about his murder, however. If Hywel was secretive to a fault, Rhun was too open and might reveal what he knew to the wrong person. Everyone might hear about the knife wound soon enough, but she'd wait to tell anyone else until she'd spoken to Hywel about it.

"Then I leave him in good hands." Rhun clapped Hywel on the shoulder and walked away.

Once inside the tiny chamber, Hywel lit the lamps and dismissed the guards. Together, he and Gwen stripped Anarawd of his fine clothes and armor, revealing a well-muscled but oft-wounded body. "This must have hurt." Gwen traced a thick scar under the man's right rib.

"That came from the 1136 war when we defeated the Normans in Deheubarth," Hywel said. "I was fighting alongside him, although I was only sixteen at the time."

"How old is—was—Anarawd?" Gwen circled the table to survey the body from every angle. The man seemed smaller now, more fragile. So he'd proved to be in the end. As they all were.

"Seven years ago he was in his early thirties. He's forty now, maybe," Hywel said. "His father was nearly this age when he married my aunt, who was only fifteen at the time. They eloped." He grinned. "I would have liked to have been there to see my grandfather's face when he found out."

"Your grandfather didn't approve of the union?" Gwen had begun sorting through Anarawd's clothes, emptying the contents of his pockets and now looked up.

"Well..." Hywel said. "You know fathers."

Gwen laughed. "I do."

A moment of silence. And then Hywel added, "Your father was a good teacher."

"He was and is, but being his daughter hasn't been easy." Gwen shot Hywel an irritated look. "And you haven't helped matters."

"You don't have to work for me," Hywel said.

"Oh, I don't regret that," she said. "But he loved you like a son and yet you've not spoken to him more than a handful of times since we left Aber. It hurts him."

"I know," Hywel said. "But he is not my father and Owain Gwynedd is. My need to please the king is greater." He paused, and then added, "I am looking forward to seeing Meilyr back at Aber where he belongs."

"Father was at Caerhun. Since he didn't travel with Madog, I'm sure he'll be along soon. Still, he is wary of this meeting with the King."

"My father invited him, didn't he?" Hywel said. "For all that he has a temper, he's not one to hold a grudge."

"It's my father who's held it all these years," Gwen said, "not yours."

Hywel nodded. "Pride has undone many a lesser man."

Gwen refocused on the body in front of her. "You see the slit between his ribs? That was the killing blow."

Hywel bent to examine Anarawd's skin. "Are you sure? It's very small—too small to be from a sword blade."

"Yes," Gwen said. "That's exactly my point. Or rather, Gareth's, since he was the one who showed it to me."

"But that means—" Hywel broke off. He lifted his head to study Gwen's face.

"That he was ambushed *and* murdered," Gwen said.

Hywel returned his gaze to the body. He stood with one arm supporting his right elbow, his hand rubbing his chin. "Let's walk through what we know: Anarawd leaves Dolwyddelan with twenty-some men. Strangers from Ireland set upon them, slaughtering them all. Anarawd, however, does not die by the sword, but by a secret knife, slipped between his ribs." Hywel looked up.

"Which means that he knew his killer," Gwen said.

"Why do you say that?"

"Look at his clothes." Gwen lifted Anarawd's shirt, which they'd discarded. "Here's the wound"—she wiggled her fingers through the hole in the shirt—"but see how the blood flowed down the front of the shirt? He was standing when the killer stabbed him, not lying on the ground."

Hywel nodded his agreement. "If he'd been lying down, the blood from his wound would have soaked his side."

"Gareth says the killer murdered him in the woods and then dragged him back to the road."

Hywel stared at Gwen. "How does he know that?"

"The blood again, and the dirt and scuff marks on the tops of Anarawd's boots."

"Did he find the location where it happened?" Hywel said.

Gwen shook her head. "We ran out of time. Too many men and horses had churned it up."

Hywel turned back to the body. "So... do we have two villains here, or just one?"

"Someone paid for the ambush, that we know," Gwen said. "But do we have a second man who murdered him? Why not simply let the Danes do it?"

"Perhaps the first paid the second especially to ensure the deed was done," Hywel said.

"But whose man was he?" Gwen said. "Obviously, Gareth's milk-brother betrayed Anarawd, or so it seems right now, but was there another traitor in Anarawd's party?"

"That would be a diabolical plan," Hywel said.

Gwen glanced at him, disturbed that he sounded, if anything, admiring.

"Let's not get carried away," she said. "Perhaps Anarawd was attempting to plead for his life."

"Or flee, even," Hywel said.

"He wasn't stabbed in the back." Then Hywel's words sank in. "Was Anarawd the type of man to flee from battle?"

Hywel shrugged. "Any man might choose that route if his companions were dead and dying. It isn't always ignoble."

"Hmm," Gwen said, not sure what kind of explanation Hywel was giving her.

"Is there anything in his clothing or on his person that can help us?" Hywel said.

"Only a ring." Gwen held it up. "By the way, there's something else you should note on the body: the left edge of the wound is a bit uneven. The knife caught at the skin instead of sliding neatly through."

Hywel gazed down at the body. "You're saying ..."

"The blade isn't smooth. It has a notch along one edge," she said. "Either it was poorly made or very old. Either way, the metal has been worn down—enough to sustain damage."

Hywel narrowed his eyes at her. "You've seen too many murdered men, I think."

Gwen laughed. "It was Gareth who pointed it out, but I'd learned it already from killing a few too many chickens."

"Lord Ednyfed of Powys told me you solved the murder of Llywelyn ap Rhys."

Gwen sighed, remembering. "And that poor boy Rhodri hanged for it. I almost wish I hadn't."

"Rhodri killed a man."

"I know," Gwen said.

Rhodri had been poaching on his lord's land—not a terrible offense, or at least not a hanging one—but he'd shot another man thinking him a deer. It was his bad luck that the river near which he'd buried the body had flooded three days later and exposed his crime.

"—and worse, tried to cover it up," Hywel said.

"And it's for that they hanged him. Men kill other men for every reason under the sun, but when it's an accident—"

"My lord!"

Gwen and Hywel turned to see Evan poke his nose between the door and the frame.

"What is it, Evan," Hywel said. "I asked not to be disturbed."

"Prince Cadell—" Evan stopped, cleared his throat, and continued, "King Cadell of Deheubarth, Anarawd's brother, has arrived."

Hywel met Gwen's eyes. "Has he?" Hywel surveyed the body. "Come, Gwen. We'll leave Anarawd for now. You can meet your latest suspect."

Gwen couldn't tell if he was serious, or only teasing her. "He inherits Deheubarth?"

"He does," Hywel said.

"Why wasn't he riding in Anarawd's company?"

"That, I couldn't tell you," Hywel said.

"Cadell is another with strong Irish connections," Gwen said. "His father fled to Ireland when the Normans took Deheubarth forty years ago."

"As did my own grandfather." Hywel glanced at her, a wry smile on his lips. "I'm sure you haven't forgotten that my entire family is descended from the Dublin Danes and Brian Boru, the High King of Ireland."

Gwen bit her lip. This put how many names on her list of potential traitors? She followed Hywel out the door and back to the courtyard, where the as-yet-uncrowned King Cadell was dismounting from his horse, accompanied by his own company of men, at least a dozen by her count.

"Welcome to Aber." Hywel walked up to Cadell, who looked a bit like Hywel himself, but shorter and slighter. Here was another second son who found himself possessed of a kingdom on no notice at all.

"Thank you, Prince Hywel." Cadell bowed. "It is my great pleasure to see you again. Bards still sing of your exploits in Deheubarth in the last war."

Hywel blinked. "Thank you."

"Has my brother arrived?" Cadell peered past Hywel to the keep. It looked like he expected Anarawd to appear on the steps at any moment.

Hywel cleared his throat. "In a manner of speaking." He glanced once at Gwen as he took Cadell's elbow. "I would have you speak to my father." Everyone in the courtyard bit their tongues as Hywel steered Cadell towards the side entrance rather than into the great hall.

Evan came to a halt beside Gwen. "Who did kill King Anarawd?"

Gwen shook her head. "I wish I knew."

10

Gareth woke with his head in a bucket, heaving up his insides. "I'm fine! I'm fine!" he said, lying boldly. He couldn't remember how he'd gotten here. He'd eaten his noon meal, and then ...

He pushed at the hand that held his head, forcing down a final heave that belied his words.

"You're not fine," Hywel said. "But you're alive, which is the important thing."

Gareth shivered and his hands shook as he wrapped his arms around his middle, trying to stem the contractions roiling his stomach.

Hywel had been the one holding his head and now bent to look into his face. "Are you ready to lie down?"

Gareth nodded and allowed Hywel to ease him to the ground. Gareth pillowed his head with one arm. "I feel so terrible."

"You ate something you shouldn't have," Gwen said. "We had to get the poison out of you."

"By nearly killing me?"

Gwen raised her eyebrows and a smile hovered around her lips. "Now I know you're going to live since you're so ungrateful." And then she softened. "I gave you mandrake. I agree that it's altogether vile."

"You're not jesting about the poison, are you?" Gareth said. Another shudder rippled through him.

"Gwen saved your life." Hywel eased back onto his heels to give Gareth space. And probably to avoid any contents of Gareth's stomach that remained inside him, but might not stay there.

Gareth moaned. "I ate what I was given." He pressed his face into the cool floor. Absent were the scatterings of refuse and straw. It seemed they hadn't survived his illness. "You're telling me that someone sickened me deliberately?"

"Not sickened, poisoned," Hywel said. "The guard brought food and drink at noon and when I came to find you afterwards, you were unconscious."

"You came very close to dying," Gwen said.

Gareth opened his eyes enough to see into her face. The waver in her voice as she spoke gave him just enough pause to spare a thought for her instead of how horrible he felt. "I'm sorry. Why would anyone try to poison me?"

"Clearly, because of your charming personality," Hywel said, a smile twitching at the corner of his mouth. "Your meal was bread and cheese. Even if it was foul, it wouldn't have put you so close to death. It had to have been the mead."

"It didn't taste right when I drank it," Gareth said. "I left most of it in the jug."

"We know," Gwen said. "We didn't dare try it on anyone else, but from the smell, the poisoner used an infusion of belladonna."

Christ!

"Someone *really* wants you dead," Hywel said.

Gareth glanced up at him, noting his dry tone and his familiar amusement at the catastrophes of the world. "What does your father say?"

"He doesn't," Hywel said.

"We haven't told him," Gwen said. "We haven't told anyone yet."

"Why—" Gareth cut off his question. He knew why not; they wanted to catch a killer, not put him on his guard. As long as Gareth remained in this cell, as long as everyone assumed he was the chief suspect in Anarawd's death, the real killer would think himself safe. "You're thinking to keep this a secret."

"I'd like to," Hywel said. "I may not be able to."

"I don't think it's going to be possible, my lord," Gwen said, "especially since you need to convince your father to let Gareth out of this cell. He's far too vulnerable in here."

"And outside?" Hywel said. "Are you prepared to spend every waking moment guarding him—even if he'd let you?"

Gwen blinked. Curious despite his misery as to how she'd answer, Gareth waited, expectant.

"Better that than having him stabbed through the heart like Anarawd or pushed off the battlements," Gwen said, disappointing

Gareth by not blushing. He should have known that she'd take it as matter-of-factly as Hywel had asked the question.

Hywel pursed his lips, thinking. "Stay here. I'll be back."

Hywel left and Gareth rested his cheek on the floor. Gwen scooted nearer and before he knew it, she'd pillowed his head in her lap. "We must be closer to the answer than we think. But to me, the list of potential culprits is only getting longer."

"No, no," Gareth said. "It's shorter. We know that whoever is responsible for Anarawd's murder is *here*, at Aber. Otherwise, he couldn't have reacted on such short notice." He paused. "Admittedly, that does leave us half of Gwynedd and more."

"Yesterday afternoon, I met Cadell, Anarawd's brother, in the courtyard," Gwen said. "He's come for the wedding too."

"And it is he who inherits." Gareth chewed on his lower lip. "Could Bran—" He stopped.

"Could your milk-brother have been working for Cadell?" Gwen finished for him. Her fingers worried at a worn spot on his shirt. If she didn't stop, it would soon turn into a hole.

"Perhaps Cadell objected to the match," Gareth said, "though probably not for the same reasons Hywel did."

Gwen looked down at him. "Why wouldn't Hywel want Elen to marry Anarawd?"

Gareth lifted a shoulder. "He had been known to mistreat his women."

"Oh."

Gareth managed to turn his head to look at her without throwing up. She looked a little ill herself. "Regardless, this moves

Cadell to the top of our list," he said. "He stands to gain the most from Anarawd's death."

"And he's smarmy," Gwen said. "The way he spoke to Hywel…"

Footsteps sounded in the passage outside Gareth's cell, and the man himself reappeared. "Well, isn't this cozy," Hywel said, his eyes alight as he took in the sight of Gwen cradling Gareth.

"Did you speak with King Owain?" Gareth pushed up from Gwen's lap. He struggled into a sitting position and came to rest with his back against the wall beside her.

"I did. He grants that you are unlikely to have poisoned yourself. With reluctance, he is setting you free for the time being within the confines of the castle."

Gareth leaned his head back against the wall and closed his eyes. "I'm delighted to hear it," he said, but didn't move. He opened his eyes far enough to catch the glance Gwen and Hywel shared.

"It's a start," Gwen said. "Was anyone else there when you spoke to your father?"

"Taran and Cristina," Hywel said.

Gwen wrinkled her nose in distaste. "Now everybody will know."

"They would have anyway, the moment Gareth appeared in the hall." Hywel braced his shoulder against the frame of the door. "While we wait for this dashing fellow to recover, why don't you give me news of your travels, Gwen. It's been months since I've seen you."

"Someone tried to marry her, you know," Gareth said before Gwen could say anything.

Gwen stuttered and shoved Gareth's shoulder. "Not that kind of news."

"You turned him down?" Hywel said.

"My father did," Gwen said.

Hywel smirked. "Families are complicated, aren't they?"

Gareth looked away and found Gwen watching him, amusement and the words *they certainly are* in her eyes.

11

"Get up! Get up!" The words hissed in Gwen's ear.

She sat up with a start, thinking that her unsettled dreams had become reality. This most recent one had been full of fighting men, their swords swinging wildly in her direction. Gwen calmed as Gareth settled on the edge of her pallet and put a hand to her arm to hush her so she wouldn't wake the woman next to them. A dozen ladies, many of whom had come for the cancelled wedding and would go home disappointed, slept around her on the floor. Cristina, King Owain's assumed intended, occupied the only bed.

"Anarawd's body has disappeared."

Gwen swallowed hard as she gazed at Gareth, finding it difficult to marshal a reasonable reply. "Will it never end? This gets more complicated by the hour."

Gwen pushed at Gareth to move him out of her way so she could gather her things and get out of the room. With her dress under her arm and her boots in her other hand, she followed him into the corridor. Looking left and right for stray observers, she relaxed against the wall and tipped her head back to gaze at the ceiling.

"Come on," Gareth said when she didn't instantly spring into action.

"This is just too much." Gwen slipped the dress over her head, covering her undyed shift. "It ties in the back." She turned to face the wall. "Can you fix it for me?"

To his credit, Gareth didn't hesitate; far more expertly than Gwen would have thought him capable, he laced her dress up the back. "I never got a chance to examine the body, you see," Gareth said.

After Gareth had felt well enough to stand, the three of them had gone to the great hall and found a spot in the corner for him to rest. Over the course of the evening, Gareth had recovered more fully, until he'd been able to consume a piece of fresh bread and a hunk of cheese. He'd refused the mead, however, for which Gwen couldn't blame him. But still, much to his disgust, she'd insisted on tasting everything he'd been offered to eat or drink before she'd let him have it.

Gwen turned to face him. "You don't think the job Hywel and I did was adequate? We did what we could." That last bit came out defensive and Gwen wished she could take it back.

Gareth shook his head, seeming to understand. "It's not that I don't trust you or respect your abilities, it's just ..." He paused as he thought. "Hywel spoke to me of the ragged edge in Anarawd's wound. You showed it to him?"

"Yes," Gwen said.

Gareth nodded. "Do you remember when you came upon me at that first ambush site?"

"Of course," Gwen said, "how could I forget?"

"Your arrival distracted me, but I was studying how his body was laid on the road. Remember how I said that the murderer had dragged it?"

"From the scuff marks on his toes," Gwen said.

"That and because there wasn't enough blood on the ground beneath his body," Gareth said. "If he'd bled out like his companions, it would have soaked the ground. It hadn't rained the night before and although the earth in the road was damp, it wasn't damp enough to indicate he'd died there."

"But there's more," she said. "You think there's something else?"

"Yes," Gareth said. "Did you notice that his nails were full of dirt?"

Gwen gazed at him. "No. I didn't."

"Anarawd scrabbled in the dirt. Maybe he tried to crawl away from his killer before he died."

Gwen shivered at how cold the killer's heart must be. "You never mentioned this before."

"I thought there was plenty of time to make certain," he said. "I should have inspected the body straight away, but with the singing in the hall, and the dark, I assumed this morning would be soon enough."

Gwen gave him a half-smile. "Do you know the first thing that Hywel told me after he asked me to spy for him?"

"What?"

"Never assume."

Gareth snorted laughter—more in disgust than amusement Gwen thought—and led the way down the stairs to Hywel's rooms. Just like the night they arrived, Hywel appeared to have slept alone. He stood before the fire, his hands clasped behind his back. He looked up as they entered.

"You were still abed?" he said, taking in Gwen's night braid. Although she'd pulled on her boots, she hadn't yet attended to her hair. "It's nearly dawn."

"One of us got to bed later than she liked," Gwen said. "And that would be your fault." Even though she'd gone to bed earlier than Gareth and the men that Hywel had set to protect him, she'd stayed in the hall with him far too late, listening to Hywel sing. His tenor had filled the air with song after achingly beautiful song. Gwen's father, had he been there, would have been pleased with the progress his student had made, even if Hywel had taken what Meilyr had taught him and made the art his own. Most of his songs—the ones he'd written himself—had an unusual meter and rhyme.

"I assume Gareth has told you that Anarawd's body is missing, along with all his possessions."

"Yes," Gwen said.

"Like an idiot, I didn't leave a guard on the room," Hywel said.

Gareth shook his head. "You couldn't have foreseen this, my lord, any more than an attempt to poison me. We've seriously underestimated our opponent. I believe it's time we took all this to the king."

"We must do a complete search of the castle, not only for the body and Anarawd's possessions, but belladonna as well," Gwen said. "We'll need his permission to do that."

Hywel turned back to the fire, hesitated, and then nodded. "I urged something like this on my father after we discovered you'd been poisoned. Now we have to act."

"We should start now, before the nobles and their lackeys are awake," Gwen said. "We might get more assistance from the kitchen and the craft halls when there's nobody watching."

"You two begin the interviews; I'll organize men from the garrison to do a search for the body," Hywel said. "It may be that the culprit was forced to stash it in an out-of-the-way spot inside the castle."

"Yes, my lord," Gareth and Gwen said together and left the room, heading for the kitchens. They'd find breakfast there, warmth, and the loquacious cook, Dai.

"I can't believe I have to do this again," Gwen said. "And at Aber, no less."

"Tell me about the murder Meilyr was charged with," Gareth said.

Gwen shook her head, mentally going over the disaster that week had been, remembering her fear and her struggle to help her father. "I never believed he did it," she said, "though perhaps it was marginally more likely than you murdering Anarawd."

"What happened?"

"During one of our visits to the south of Wales—all the way to Carreg Cennan—a man was found dead, garroted with one of my father's iron harp strings."

"A few twists and one of those could cut through most anything," Gareth said.

"Including the culprit's fingers," Gwen said. "My father always wears gloves when he strings his harp because without them he cuts his hands every time. The murderer didn't know that. Given that my father was in a cell, it was to the murderer's advantage to hold off seeking aid, which he did for three days until his fingers festered and became impossible to hide."

"And you noticed?"

"The fool came to the herbalist for treatment, a friend of mine. By then, we were looking for an injured man and knew he was guilty from the moment we saw his hands." She shrugged. "After few well-placed questions in front of the castellan, Lord Cadfael, the man confessed."

Gareth shook his head over that, but when Gwen glanced at him, he was smiling.

When they entered the kitchen, just as Gwen had hoped, Dai plopped a plate of biscuits, newly churned butter, jam, and a watery porridge in front of them.

"You look serious, Gwen. And you," Dai said to Gareth, looking him up and down, "are a very ill young man."

"Someone poisoned him yesterday with an infusion of belladonna," Gwen said, her mouth full of biscuit.

"Never say so!" Dai took a step back. "Not in my food!"

"The culprit put it in the mead," Gwen said. "Since Gareth had to stay locked in his cell, he doesn't have any idea who did it."

"What was the name of the boy who brought the food?" Gareth said.

"Llelo," Dai said and then without pausing for breath, raised his voice to carry through the kitchen to the pantry. "Llywelyn ap Rhys! Get in here!" A boy of twelve tumbled through the curtain that separated the pantry from the kitchen proper, wiping his hands on his apron, his eyes wide. Dai gestured towards the boy. "Here he is."

"Come here, boy." Gareth waved him closer.

Llelo glanced at Dai, who nodded, and came to a halt in front of Gareth. He eyed the biscuits, licking his lips; Gwen picked one up and handed it to him. He accepted it, still wary and nervous, but not as noticeably stiff-legged. "My lord," Llelo said.

"You brought me my noon meal yesterday," Gareth said. "Tell me about it."

Llelo blinked twice. Clearly this was not what he'd expected to have Gareth ask. It made Gwen wonder what else he'd been up to, though it was probably getting into mischief with the other boys his age—something that he thought might be more serious than it was. "Cook laid your food out for me on the side table and I took it to you straight away, once I came in from chopping firewood."

"And the mead?" Gwen said. "You brought that too?"

Llelo glanced at Dai, who nodded again. Llelo licked his lips.

"Tell them," Dai said.

"Yes," Llelo said. "It was hard to juggle the cup, jar, and platter all at the same time, but I managed without spilling any."

"Good for you," Gwen said. "So between the time you collected the food and drink and when you delivered it to Sir Gareth, nobody waylaid you? Nobody spoke to you?"

"No, Ma'am," Llelo said.

Gareth nodded and Dai jerked his head at Llelo, who departed, much relieved.

"Do you believe him?" Gwen asked Dai.

"I have no reason not to," Dai said. "I saw him leave by the kitchen door. I even told him to take two trips, but of course he pretended he hadn't heard me."

"It was you who set out the food?" Gwen said. "And the mead as well?"

"I tapped it myself," Dai said. "It was the least I could do for his lordship, here." Dai paused and leaned in. "I never thought you killed that foreign king."

Gwen just managed not to laugh at Dai's provincial attitude. *That foreign king.* She and her family had traveled the length and breadth of Wales in the last six years. While a few traditions differed, the language, the customs, and the blood were all the same.

"So then the question is, how long did my meal sit on the table unattended, waiting for Llelo to bring it to me?" Gareth leaned forward to match Dai, his tone earnest.

Dai pursed his lips. "Let's see now—I had the boy at the bucket for water to wash his hands and face. His hands were sticky from wood pitch. He can't seem to chop a single log without getting it all over him. Then back here, so ... a quarter of an hour perhaps? I've four other regular helpers in and out all day, but they were mostly in the hall. We don't usually serve a meal that time of day, but we've been kept hopping with all the comings and goings. I've had to hire another half dozen just to keep up with the roastings and the soups."

Gwen and Gareth looked at each other, inwardly sighing. "We'll have to speak to them all," she said. "Maybe one of them saw something that will help us."

Two hours later, they'd worked their way through all but one of the servants. Of the ten they interviewed, six had remained in the hall throughout the meal, while the other four had run back and forth between the kitchen and the serving tables, keeping the diners well stocked with food and drink.

Owain Gwynedd was known for laying on a fine table, and even in a state of mourning, yesterday had been no exception. None could say anything about who had or had not been in the kitchens. Unsurprisingly, none would confess to being the poisoner. Nor had any of them noticed someone hauling a body out of the barracks in the middle of the night and hiding it.

"It isn't any of them," Gwen said, finally, after the last servant had turned away. "It's got to be this last person we can't find.

"I agree." Gareth stood, stretched, and then guided Gwen out the rear of the kitchen and into the garden beyond. The herbs were in the flush of late summer growth, with green vines winding up the trellises and flowers of every color decorating the beds. "Is any belladonna growing here?"

"No," Gwen said. "I did look."

"You're sure?" Gareth said. "It would be easier if it was."

"I know, but belladonna gives off a strong odor—even a nauseating one as you can attest—when it's crushed or bruised. The culprit would have had to abuse it to contaminate your mead."

"I haven't smelled anything like that," Gareth said.

"Nor I," Gwen said. "And none of the other servants' hands or sleeves smelled of it either. I made certain."

"Someone else could have given them a prepared vial," Gareth said. "He wouldn't have had to touch it at all."

"Of course," Gwen said, "and then the traces would be on him, not a servant."

"We're going in circles," Gareth said.

"Even if we found the servant who did the deed, we'd need to force them to reveal who paid them."

"I'm sure Hywel and I could find a way," Gareth said.

Gwen glanced at him. She was sure he could too. "We need to take a look at your peers."

Gareth's lips twitched. "None of them—whether knight, man-at-arms, or simple soldier—will take well to being questioned by a woman."

"I'll hang back; we'll be nosy but not too much so and perhaps something will come to us. The murderer has been one step ahead of us for two days. We have to catch up; we have to think like him."

"I hope that's harder for you than you're making it sound," Gareth said.

"I'd never killed anyone until two days ago," she said.

Gareth pulled up, tugging Gwen to a halt on the pathway. "What did you say?"

Gwen hadn't meant to tell him, but she couldn't keep it in any longer. "When I was riding with you, when the Danes ambushed us, I stabbed a man with my knife. I even meant to do it, but somehow when the blade went in all the way to the hilt, I couldn't quite believe it."

Gareth clasped both her hands in his and brought them to his lips. "I'm sorry."

"I'm not sorry," Gwen said, "not in the sense that I regret what I did. But I keep seeing him die, seeing him fall." Gwen's throat closed at the memory and she forced back the tears that pricked her eyes. It wasn't that she didn't want to weep in front of Gareth. She felt that if she were to start crying, she wouldn't be able to stop.

"If it's the only man you ever kill, you'll remember it for the rest of your life," Gareth said. "Better that than to be overwhelmed by the sheer numbers of lives you've taken."

Telling him had eased Gwen's heart, just a little, but ... "I don't like thinking of you in that position. Here I cry about one death by my hand, as if you didn't kill men yesterday yourself. And that's only one of a hundred days you've done the same."

"Two hundred," Gareth said. "I serve my lord the only way I know how."

"Owain!"

The scream split the air and after a shared glance, Gwen and Gareth set off at a run for the stables from which the sound had come. Just as they reached the open door, Cristina, King Owain's intended, staggered out, her hand to her head.

Gwen grabbed her arms. "What is it?"

Cristina shook Gwen off, flinging out a hand to point behind her. "There's—there's—" She couldn't speak.

King Owain burst from the hall and hustled over. He wrapped his arms around Cristina's waist and glared hard at Gareth, who took a step back. "What did you do?"

"Nothing, my lord," Gareth said. "Whatever frightened her is in the stables."

"Don't just stand there, then," King Owain said. "Go look!"

"Yes, my lord," Gareth said.

Gwen and Gareth hurried into the airy building that took up nearly the whole of the south side of Aber's courtyard. To Gwen's eyes, the stables appeared as they always had, but then Gareth gave a *tsk* of exasperation. "Another one."

Gwen looked to where he pointed. An arm poked out of the pile of straw which the stable boys used for making fresh beds for the horses. "It wasn't very well hidden. It's almost as if he wanted us to find it."

"I don't know about that." Gareth crouched beside the body, most of which remained under the straw. "And which 'he' and which 'it' we're looking for is the question of the hour."

"What do you mean?" Gwen said. "Isn't this Anarawd's body?"

"No." Gareth pointed with one finger along the length of the arm. "This is not a hand that has ever held a sword." He glanced up at her. "It's a woman."

12

"**G**wenllian ferch Meilyr!"

Gwen swung around to see her father and brother riding through the front gate of the castle. Her father rode a fine horse—finer than the one Gwen had ridden to Aber and equal in breeding to the lame stallion that he'd left at Dolwyddelan. Gwalchmai drove their cart, filled once again with their belongings rather than dead men, with her little pony on a leading rein behind. Gwen had expected her father and brother to arrive hours earlier, if not the day before. Though Gwen admitted to herself that she had felt as if every hour without her father's presence was a reprieve of sorts.

"Welcome to Aber, Father," she said, changing direction.

As Gareth had suspected, the body in the stable had been that of the missing servant. Gwen had detected the scent of belladonna on a spot on her dress, indicating that she'd been the culprit, but who had paid her to poison Gareth—and precisely why—was as unknown as it had been before they started looking. That he'd had the wherewithal to act so quickly was disconcerting.

With the fading of the afternoon, Hywel had told them to put aside their questioning of the inhabitants of Aber for now. Gwen had left Gareth asleep in the barracks with his friend Evan watching over him. Gareth hadn't recovered from his brush with death; although he'd protested that he could help, he would have been underfoot. She wanted to search the kitchen, garden, and surrounding grounds more thoroughly for belladonna without him—because whatever her feelings for him, and however much she wanted to be with him, there was no denying that he pressed on her, distracted her even, and it was time for some clear thinking.

"I trust your investigation is progressing?" Meilyr brought his horse to a halt in front of her.

Gwen canted her head and peered up at her father. That was an unusual—if not unheard of—question for him. Normally, he never inquired about her work. "Not so much that you'd notice. Though the day has been eventful in that we've lost one body and discovered another."

Meilyr grunted. "And the King?"

Gwen smiled. Now she understood the roundabout way her father was speaking and the reason for his delay in coming to Aber. "King Owain has absorbed the news of Anarawd's death. He supports our efforts to find his killer and has not hanged anyone for it yet, though he thought about it. Over the last two days, his temper has cooled."

Meilyr dismounted in the courtyard and straightened his robes while a stable boy ran to take the horse's reins. "Have you spoken to him of me?" He kept his eyes on his own attire instead of on her.

"No," Gwen said. "Only to Hywel. You are expected, however, and a room prepared. Lord Taran, King Owain's steward, asked me to direct you to him when you arrived."

Her father took in a breath and let it out with a sharp laugh. "I'm ready." He turned to Gwalchmai. "Come here, boy."

They both wore worn but unpatched traveling clothes. They'd replace these with finery by evening when Gwalchmai would make his debut in the hall. Gwalchmai seemed to feel none of his father's nervousness. Instead, his eyes glinted with what Gwen read as excitement. She turned to him, smiling. "Are you ready?"

Gwalchmai went up on his toes and back down. "I am."

13

"My lord." Meilyr bowed before King Owain's seat that evening.

"Meilyr, my friend," King Owain said. "I trust you are well?"

"Yes, my lord," Meilyr said. "You remember my son, Gwalchmai?"

"Of course." King Owain nodded his head in a brief acknowledgement of their obeisance.

Meilyr and Gwalchmai bowed once more before stepping back from the table and turning away. Gareth watched Meilyr scan the crowd for available seats at a lower table: above the salt as was their due, but not among the nobles, of which Aber still housed many.

Gareth was amused at how undramatic this much-worried-over meeting had been, a counterpoint to all the events that had led to it. Perhaps that was why it had gone so well—it seemed ridiculous to bear a grudge over a six-year old argument when

Anarawd was dead and the reason for their reconciliation—the wedding—would not come to pass.

"That went better than I expected," Gwen said, in an undertone.

"You mean 'feared'," Gareth said.

Gwen turned to smile at him, but then King Owain spoke, loud enough for all to hear, stopping Gwalchmai and Meilyr in their tracks. "I was hoping for a song."

Meilyr turned back to the King. "Of course, my lord. It would be our pleasure. We have several prepared." Though he'd been looking for seats away from her, Meilyr's eyes immediately went to Gwen. He jerked his head to indicate that she should join them.

Gwen rose from her seat, and then startled Gareth by placing a hand on his shoulder, squeezing once, and leaning in to whisper to him: "Now everyone will see what all the fuss was about."

It felt so normal to have her touch him, as if they were once again as good friends as they'd been five years ago, before his disgrace and subsequent banishment. Looking back, she'd touched him often over the last few days—just a brush of his arm or a bump with her shoulder: affectionate but undemanding. He didn't know whether to be pleased and hopeful, or curse himself for noticing, because now that he had, he'd be on the lookout for it and undoubtedly drive himself mad interpreting every move she made.

As Gareth stewed about that, Gwen made her way to the dais, a portion of which had been cleared of chairs to make room for the three musicians. And, of course, Gwen was right about the song. Three notes after opening his mouth, Gwalchmai had made a place for his family at Aber. He sang a piece from Aneirin's *Y Goddodin*:

> *Three hundred horses galloped into battle*
> *Garlands round their necks*
> *Three hundred men rode them*
> *Swords raised high*
> *Three kings led them*
> *The pride of the Cymry*
> *Alas! None returned.*

Although Gareth focused his attention on Gwen, he acknowledged that it was Gwalchmai's soprano that soared above the others. The song had brought tears to listeners' eyes for five hundred years. Under normal circumstances, grown men cried at the ending. But in Gwalchmai's hands, none could withstand the beauty of it, including King Owain himself, who wept openly. Noblemen on either side of him sobbed, their faces in their arms that they'd folded on the table.

Gareth waited until the last verse, tears tracking down his cheeks despite his best efforts to contain them, before slipping down the side passage to the hall and outside to the castle courtyard. A quick turn around the perimeter of the keep showed him what he'd feared: not a soul—not a guard, servant, noble, or peasant—was in evidence. Gareth had made it his business to know who was on duty tonight, and when each of the men in turn had entered the hall to listen to the singing, Gareth had felt a prickling at the back of his neck he couldn't ignore.

Under these circumstances, a thief or a spy would have ample opportunity to do whatever he liked. Steal a body, maybe? Or murder a servant? Gareth stilled, not sure what he was listening for, but disliking the lack of discipline among King Owain's men, even if many of them were his friends. Aber might be one of the most secure of King Owain's dominions, but to leave the hall unguarded? The front gate unattended? It made no sense.

And then Gareth sighed to see Cristina, the King's beloved, crossing the courtyard at a run. She entered the main building through a side door. He followed and a moment later found his seat still available and Gwen, flushed from the heat and the singing, returned to him. The appreciation of the diners in the hall was palpable.

"Where have you been?" Gwen said as he sat down.

"Outside," he said. "I listened to your family sing until nearly the end, and then thought I'd follow a hunch."

"And that was...?"

"That Aber was, for a time, unguarded. I've never seen anything like it."

"Gwalchmai's voice *is* beautiful," she said.

"As is yours."

Gwen shook her head, though he could tell she was pleased at his compliment. She continued, "You can't blame the guards for wanting to listen to it. They must have thought nobody would notice if they were gone for a short while."

"Of course," he said. "But all of them at the same time?"

"I suppose—" Gwen had been gazing towards the high table as she spoke and now her brow furrowed. "Where is—?" She cut off the words just as Cristina appeared, a coquettish smile on her lips, and sat down a few seats from King Owain.

Gareth leaned close to whisper into Gwen's ear. "She returns. A moment ago I saw her leaving the barracks."

"No!" Gwen hunched her shoulders at how loud that had come out and modulated her tone. "All by herself?"

"So it seems," Gareth said.

"But King Owain has been here the whole time," Gwen said.

"That he has."

Gwen bit her lip. "Why was she in the barracks? Whom did she meet?" Gwen rested her elbows on the table and put her chin in her hands, still studying Cristina. "I don't like this."

"There's no doubt she's conniving," Gareth said. "Though I suspect King Owain softened his stance against me because of her defense. I can't dislike her for that."

"Could she have been with another man?" Gwen said. "It's so unlik—"

King Owain's baritone interrupted their conversation. He rose to his feet, his cup raised and his voice booming to all corners of the hall. "We have feasted today in memory of Anarawd, the

King of Deheubarth, the man who was to be my son. He was a brave man, a good king, and would have made a noble husband."

The hall fell completely silent at his words. Even Elen, who'd begun to sob again at the mention of Anarawd's name, quieted herself. Cristina, seated next to her and three seats down from King Owain, wrapped her arm around the girl's shoulders.

"Anarawd was murdered by a band of Danes from Ireland," King Owain said. "Although I do not yet know why, I will know, and then the perpetrators will be punished! I swear this!" He raised a clenched fist and then his cup.

"To Anarawd!" the King said.

"To Anarawd!"

Everyone drank and then King Owain gestured to Gwalchmai and Meilyr, who prepared to sing again.

"The killer has seriously underestimated this king," Gareth said.

"You know him better than I," Gwen said. "Will he ask someone else to pursue this mystery since we've discovered nothing of use today? Is there anyone else to ask?"

"He always turns to Hywel," Gareth said. "And Hywel turns to me. We still have time. The Council will meet tomorrow morning and the meeting should take all day. You know how these things go."

"I'm sure they will talk about Anarawd," Gwen said. "Will you have to attend Hywel?"

"God forbid!" Gareth said. "Hywel knows I'm no good in council. He has other men for that. He doesn't want me within eye or ear shot of his father either. Hywel may have to face him all day tomorrow, but I have no intention of putting myself in the path of King Owain's wrath again."

"I'm glad," Gwen said. "That's definitely not a good place for you to be."

14

As it turned out, however, that's exactly where Gareth did find himself the next morning, corralled on one side by Hywel and on the other by Rhun. It was an uncomfortable feeling, to say the least.

"You're expected." Hywel grasped Gareth by the elbow.

"Me?" Gareth said, tempted to pull away. "Why?"

"The Council has already heard a version of the story from Meilyr, and now it's your turn," Rhun said.

"Did Meilyr mention me? Did he accuse me of anything?"

Rhun gave Gareth a puzzled look and Gareth forced himself to clear his expression. Rhun was one of those men who went through life loved by everyone. He couldn't understand why other men didn't have the same experience. It wasn't that he wasn't intelligent, because he was, but he was completely guileless.

"All is well, Gareth," Rhun said. "Neither Meilyr nor my father bear a grudge against you. The Council just needs to hear your perspective."

Gareth glanced at Hywel. As usual, a smile hovered around his lips and Gareth thought he could read skepticism in his face, but then Hywel nodded encouragingly. "My brother speaks the truth. Just tell them what you told me."

So, for the third time, Gareth relayed the story of witnessing the battle, returning with Madog and his men, having Gwen and her family come upon them shortly thereafter, and the details of the second ambush. Madog, too, was among the audience and he nodded his agreement at the point where he came in.

"He tells it as it was, my lord," Madog said. "I also might add, that when the mercenaries ambushed my men, Gareth saved my life."

"And now Anarawd's body has been stolen," Cadwaladr said from his seat beside King Owain.

"Yes." That was from Hywel, who stepped into the center of the ring of men. His face filled with an earnestness and sincerity that might have fooled those who didn't know him well, but which, if a man looked more closely, never reached his eyes. Gareth was just grateful to have the council's attention off him. "It happened sometime in the night after Madog brought him here. I regret that I didn't place a guard on the door, not thinking it necessary. I was wrong."

At this bold acceptance of fault, the men around the table eased back in their seats, lowering the tension in the room. Hywel was well-thought of among the nobility, generally well-liked, and in some quarters, pitied. He, of the two brothers, had served as their father's primary emissary to their kingdoms. These lords were comfortable with Hywel and knew him well—or thought they did.

Over the years, Gareth had learned to watch Hywel's other face—the one that showed only in the eyes. When Rhun had knighted him, Gareth had felt Hywel's eyes boring into his brother. Gareth still hadn't decided if it was hatred he saw in them or resentment that Rhun had, as usual, usurped Hywel's prerogative. It was hard to resent Rhun for long, however, and Gareth had never noted that particular look on Hywel's face again. Hywel had accepted Gareth's advancement and even accorded him a small manor house within his own domains on Anglesey.

Although Hywel was telling the Council the truth (as far as Gareth knew it, anyway), his eyes said he wasn't telling all of it. That wouldn't normally have been a cause for concern, since Hywel was Gareth's lord and had protected Gareth as best he could up until now, but this venture was unique in Gareth's experience. Maybe he should see to finding out what secrets his lord was keeping.

For now, Hywel had convinced the Council of his sincerity and Rhun took it further. "I must assure you that Gareth had nothing to do with Anarawd's death. Some of you may have thought it, especially given the presence of his milk-brother, Bran, in the Danish company."

Gareth was disconcerted to see some nods around the table. These men, too, had questioned Gareth's role. It was Cadell, newly crowned by King Owain's hand, who spoke for them. "I understand that King Owain accused him of the deed, yet this man's present freedom indicates you have rejected that notion?"

Rhun plowed on. "While he was locked in the stables, someone put poison in Sir Gareth's mead, nearly killing him. We released him for his own protection. Anarawd's body was stolen that same night, but at that point, Gareth was still recovering and under the guard of several of my brother's men. Unless this conspiracy is far vaster than we presently understand—or are prepared for—he must be absolved of that crime, and thus of the murder as well."

A few different heads nodded and Gareth allowed himself to relax, if just a little. Even Prince Cadwaladr, seated beside his brother, shrugged his grudging admission. Perhaps King Owain had done Gareth a favor by imprisoning him after all. Then Hywel spoke again, stepping into the fray with his wicked smile and a laugh that disarmed everyone with whom he came in contact. "Gareth is a fine swordsman, but even under my tutelage, he'd be hard pressed to coordinate a plot against Anarawd and keep it secret, especially from me!"

Laughter accompanied the comment. *They're going to let me go.* Gareth eased towards the wall, into the shadows. King Owain noticed Gareth's movement, and to Gareth's astonishment, raised his goblet in salute. Gareth bowed. As he straightened, he caught sight of Cadwaladr's face. He was directing a glare of such malevolent loathing—for once not at Gareth but at the King—that Gareth feared it would skewer King Owain then and there.

Having finished speaking to the Council, Hywel had come to stand nearby. Gareth turned to him to tell him what he'd seen, but the young prince put a hand on his arm to stop him speaking—and perhaps to restrain him from leaping between the two brothers to protect King Owain.

"I see it," he said.

15

"I've something you need to see," Cristina said.

Gwen turned, surprised to find anyone—much less the woman who would soon be wife to the King of Gwynedd—in the bath room with her. She was so stunned, in fact, that she didn't answer, just stared at Cristina stupidly.

Cristina didn't appear to notice. "It's lovely isn't it?" Walking down one side of the bath, Cristina trailed her fingers along the patchwork of mosaics on the wall. "When my lord Owain hired masons to rebuild the curtain wall in stone, I asked him to let me borrow them for a time to repair the walls in here too. The decorations aren't complete and I don't know that we'll ever be able to finish them properly, but I'd like to try."

"I've never seen anything like this room." Gwen decided that standing before her future mistress in nothing but her shift didn't bother her as much as she might have thought.

Cristina wore a dress of deep burgundy, fitted in the bodice and with white lace at the wrists and neck. It would have been a dreadful color on Gwen but it offset Cristina's honey-colored hair perfectly. A gold necklace adorned her throat.

Without haste, Gwen began pulling on her stockings. "How does the bath work? The water was very warm and retained its heat far longer than I expected."

"There's a tunnel below this room that leads to a fire," Cristina said. "Owain only lets me light it to heat the water once a week, but when he does, sometimes I stay in here all day."

Now Gwen was worried. "I'm sorry, I didn't know. I should have spoken to you before I used it."

"Oh no." Cristina waved a hand as if it was no matter. "I had my bath this morning."

"Lord Hywel urged me to come in here." Gwen allowed herself a slight laugh. "The road was long and we've been involved in some unsavory things."

"I understand." Cristina shivered. "Dead bodies! It would be selfish of me to keep all this splendor to myself. Besides, this way I can speak to you without interruption."

Gwen straightened, unsure of Cristina's meaning. Cristina continued to trail her hand along the walls. When she'd circled the bath completely, she came to stand in front of Gwen. Then she reached into the scrip at her waist, her eyes never leaving Gwen's face, and pulled out a small box. Opening it, she held it out to Gwen. Inside lay a small, gold seal.

Gwen took the box from her. Warily, she traced the design carved into the metal: a lion rampant. "This is a royal seal. Why are you showing it to me?"

"I found it in King Cadell's rooms," Cristina said, "but it isn't his."

"Whose is it?" Gwen's stomach clenched, since she knew the answer before Cristina spoke.

"Anarawd's," Cristina said. "I recognized it from the paperwork that confirmed his marriage to Elen. It's his personal seal. It was nestled next to the traditional crest of the royal House of Dinefwr, which was also in Cadell's possession."

Gwen closed the box with a snap. "Will you come with me?" Gwen hadn't liked Cadell from the first. She was glad to finally have a proper culprit, even if she had no idea how the seal had gotten from the road near Dolwyddelan to Aber. "Lord Hywel must learn of this."

Cristina stepped back. She held up both hands, palms out, and shook her head. "No. I will not speak of this to Hywel. That's why I brought it to you—and you may take it to him only under the condition that you leave me out of it."

Gwen's eyes narrowed. She found she was no longer intimidated by this beautiful woman, just suspicious. "What do you mean?"

"Just as I said," Cristina said. "Owain must not know that I found it."

Gwen gaped at her. "How am I to explain to Lord Hywel how I acquired it, then?"

"That's your problem," Cristina said. "Owain would be most upset if he knew that I'd been in Cadell's rooms."

That was certainly true.

"Especially after finding the dead body yesterday," Cristina said. "I can have no part in your investigation."

Gwen bit her lip and studied the other woman. "And what were you doing in his rooms?" At this point, Gwen didn't see that she had anything to lose by asking. Her impertinence was slight in comparison to what Cristina had done.

Gwen thought she might have the upper hand for a moment, but Cristina laughed and waved a hand, brushing off her indiscretion as if it was nothing. "I don't know why I'm telling you this at all. It would be far easier to keep this to myself ... but the truth is, I was snooping."

"Snooping?"

"Snooping," she said. "You're not the only one who finds pleasure in the art. First you and that young knight, Gareth, and then later Hywel, hunted all over Aber for information about Anarawd's death. Everyone saw you. But I doubted any of you had the wherewithal to venture into Cadell's rooms."

"With all the barons and nobles here for the wedding, most of Aber was closed to Gareth and me," Gwen said. "Many turned their noses up at Hywel's request for entry as well, for all that King Owain encouraged the barons to cooperate."

"That's what I thought," Cristina said, "so I decided to look for you. I found the seal the other night, during Anarawd's funeral feast. Since Gwalchmai's singing entertained everyone so well, I knew all the barons would be in attendance and for once I wouldn't be missed. The barracks and sleeping quarters were open to me."

"And was it you who sent the guards away?" Gwen said.

Cristina gazed at Gwen blankly. "Guards?"

Gwen bit her lip. "Never mind."

"Cadell styles himself a warrior," Cristina said. "It suits him to sleep in one of the few private rooms on the third floor of the barracks."

Gwen nodded and tightened her grip on the box. Remarkably, Cristina appeared to have done them a favor. "Did you have a reason to look in his rooms particularly?"

Cristina's faced flushed. At first Gwen thought it was in embarrassment, but Cristina's next words told her differently. "He is a close confidant of Prince Cadwaladr, who objects to my relationship with Owain. Both of them have spoken to the King of their *concern* that he might grow too attached to me."

Nothing more needed to be said, did there? Woe to the man who got on the wrong side of Cristina. "You must realize that there's a problem with what you've done," Gwen said.

"And what is that?"

"The real villain might not be Cadell. The killer could have put the seal in Cadell's rooms to implicate him, knowing that if we found it there, we'd accuse Cadell of wrong-doing."

Now it was Cristina's turn to gape at Gwen. "I hadn't thought of that. It does complicate matters."

Gwen glanced down at the box. "At least we know what happened to it. It wasn't on Anarawd's body or among his possessions when we found him, and if Gareth's milk-brother was telling the truth, the Danes set the second ambush specifically to look for it again themselves."

"That's why I brought it to you." Cristina gave Gwen a self-satisfied smile.

"But ... if all the Danish mercenaries are dead, then how did the seal get here?" Gwen said. "Someone must have brought it to Aber—someone who took part in the first ambush but not the second."

"There's someone else we need fear?" Cristina said. "This is all so much more complicated than I initially thought."

Their conversation had felt natural up until then, but these last words from Cristina brought Gwen up short. In a flash, Cristina had reverted to the girlish consort Owain Gwynedd courted, not the competent, somewhat hard-edged woman Gwen thought her to be—and with whom Gwen had been speaking just now. Something here wasn't right.

Still, Gwen didn't say anything more, merely turned to the bench on which she'd left her clothes and slipped the seal into her scrip. She was glad to have it, even if the rest of Cristina's story didn't make as much sense as Gwen would like.

"I'll keep it safe; I promise," Gwen said.

"Thank you," Cristina said. "I'm glad I could help. I'll send a maid to assist you in dressing."

Cristina slipped out the door and Gwen stared after her until her footsteps faded along the passage, thinking hard about what she would tell Hywel. When the maid arrived, Gwen had to bite her tongue not to hurry her along as she fumbled with the ties on Gwen's dress. Finally done, Gwen trotted through the castle to

Hywel's office. She poked her head around the doorframe. The room was empty. She ducked back into the hallway. *Humph.*

She leaned back against the wall and was wondering where in the castle Hywel might be and how long she'd have to wait for his return, when a woman giggled nearby. Gwen peered into the room again. Hywel had left the bedroom door two fingers' width ajar. More giggles emanated from the room, along with a sharp bark of laughter that could only have been Hywel's voice.

Gwen lifted her eyes to the ceiling, hoping Hywel wasn't bedding the daughter of a visiting king. He *usually* had more sense than that. Gwen drew the door to the corridor closed, cursing her employers intemperate ways under her breath, and was about to turn away when Gareth came through the exterior door.

"He's busy," she said.

Gareth halted in mid-stride. "Why am I not surprised?" He studied her. "Why do you want to see him?"

Gwen checked both ends of the corridor to make sure they were alone, pulled out the seal, and gave Gareth the gist of her conversation with Cristina. While Cristina had asked to be left out of it, Gwen had no intention of obeying such a request. The stakes were far too high to muddy the waters with falsehoods.

"I don't like this," Gareth said.

"Don't like what?" The door beside them opened to reveal Hywel, just tucking in his shirt. "Come in. You didn't have to wait outside."

Warily, Gwen stepped into the room while Gareth masked his discomfort with a cough. This time, Hywel had closed the door to his bedroom all the way. Hywel walked around his desk while Gwen and Gareth stopped in front of it. Gwen set the box containing Anarawd's seal before Hywel and opened it.

Hywel took in a long breath. As Gwen had, he fingered the fine workmanship, before saying, "This is Anarawd's."

"It is," Gwen said. "Cristina found it in Cadell's room. She asked that I not tell you that it was she who found it."

Hywel looked up, his eyes lit from that inner well of amusement that he could never quite suppress. "Did she now? And what was she doing there?"

"Helping us," Gwen said. "Or so she said."

"That sounds remarkably unlikely," Hywel said. "And while it's nice to have recovered the seal, it proves nothing. Someone could have left it among Cadell's things to implicate him."

"That's what I told her," Gwen said.

"In fact," Gareth said. "While I did see her hurrying from the barracks last night as she claims, she could be lying about where she found the seal to misdirect us."

"There is one thing I do know," Hywel said. "My father will not take kindly to any insinuations against King Cadell unless the proof of his participation in these events is more substantial."

"If this is Cadell's doing," Gwen said, "and I'm not saying it is, he shouldn't have kept it at all."

Hywel shrugged. "I can see why he did. It was valuable. He couldn't throw it away."

"It's too bad the killer didn't simply keep the seal on his person," Gareth said. "We could have caught him with it and then he could have led us to his master."

"It seems to me, that instead of implicating Cadell, it widens the circle of suspects," Gwen said. "When do we start looking at King Owain's brother, Cadwaladr?"

Hywel's mouth turned down. "Just because he mistreated Gareth, doesn't mean he killed King Anarawd. Why would he?"

"It's no secret that Cadwaladr thinks his lands inadequate," Gwen said, warming to the idea. "Maybe he and Cadell made a deal. Maybe in payment for murdering Anarawd so that Cadell could take his throne, Cadell promised to expand Cadwaladr's holdings in Ceredigion."

"Cadwaladr *has* been very friendly with Cadell of late." Hywel tapped his chin with one finger. "But is it likely? And what about Cristina? What if Cadwaladr is working with her to implicate Cadell? Isn't that equally likely? He could have all of Deheubarth were that the case."

For Gwen's part, she wouldn't put anything past Cristina. If anyone were to threaten Cristina in some way, or betray her, she would take revenge. But her animosity towards Cadwaladr seemed genuine, and Gwen believed her when she said she found the seal in Cadell's rooms. The real issue was who had put it there. Gwen was beginning to admire Cristina more than she wanted to admit.

"She, at least, didn't kill Anarawd," Gareth said.

Hywel threw back his head and laughed. "God help us if she did."

16

This time, Gareth wasn't going to make the mistake of taking the long way to Dolwyddelan. When he'd gone to meet Anarawd before the ambush, he'd followed the well-traveled road from Aber to Caerhun, and then south to Dolwyddelan: the same road he and Gwen had ridden along together in the opposite direction.

He'd had another choice, which he hadn't taken then. He still cursed himself for choosing the longer route. Who knows what could have happened? He could have fallen in with Hywel after seeing the mercenaries. Perhaps he'd have followed their path and warned Anarawd they were waiting for him. Admittedly, he could have also come upon them by mistake and been murdered himself.

A lifetime ago (though really only five days), the attraction of breaking his journey with the mead at Caerhun had been too good to pass up. Since dawn today, however, Gareth had followed a track that ran from Aber straight into the mountains, skirting the peaks of Snowdonia that loomed above him, almost close enough to touch. It was by far the shorter route in terms of distance—as well as in time for one man and horse alone. If it hadn't been so impossible to widen properly, the Romans might have improved this road instead of the one that passed between the standing stones. As it was, they'd given it up as a lost cause. The native Welsh had not, and had continued to use it hundreds of years after the Romans had departed.

He'd said goodbye to Gwen with some reluctance. A warm rain had been falling as he'd left Aber and they'd stood in the middle of it, arguing.

"You could take me with you," she'd said. "Two pairs of eyes are better than one."

"You may be one of Hywel's spies, but that doesn't give you license to do anything you want," Gareth said.

Gwen opened her mouth to protest, but Gareth overrode her. "As it is, Hywel gave me permission to leave Aber—and against his better judgment. Only a few days ago, I was under orders not to leave the castle at all. He's concerned about how this looks."

"The Council dismissed the charges that you were involved in Anarawd's death and King Owain agreed," Gwen said. "It will show all Gwynedd that Hywel trusts you."

"Just as long as nothing else goes wrong," Gareth said.

"That's why you need to bring me with you," Gwen said. "I was never under suspicion at all and I can confirm to the King anything we find."

"Be that as it may, you cannot come," Gareth said. "Your father would have my head. I'll be back by tomorrow morning; it's hardly any time at all." He leaned in closer. "Besides, I need you to keep an eye on things here."

Gwen narrowed her eyes at him. "What aren't you telling me?"

Gareth shook his head. "I don't even know enough to articulate what worries me. Suffice to say I don't trust anyone but you."

That was a significant admission on his part and seemed to satisfy Gwen. It helped that it was true. Gareth did miss her company as the towers of Aber fell away and the mountains hid him from a watcher's view. The higher he ascended into the hills, the more alone he became, but the more his heart eased. He shed the tensions of the last days. Early on in the journey, he encountered a few shepherds, watching their flocks in the higher meadows, but they too disappeared the higher he climbed.

He crossed the barren uplands on which only grasses and scraggly bushes grew, and passed the initial peaks, bare of snow this late in the summer. As he traveled over a ridge and trekked down into one of the high valleys in which a highland lake nestled, the rain lessened and finally stopped, although the wind whipped his hood from his head.

Over the next few miles, the landscape changed further, becoming more treed, with streams and waterfalls racing back the way he'd come. Ultimately, he came out of a long stretch of difficult terrain and reached the abandoned Roman fort that stood near the intersection of several paths. This was where Hywel had lost the Danes. The main road lay further on.

Most of the stones had disappeared into the ground or had been appropriated for other buildings. The fort lay in a valley, surrounded by tree-covered hills and covering nearly four acres. The River Llugwy split the western half from the eastern, larger half, in which Gareth found himself.

The ruins loomed over Gareth, disturbing old wounds that every Welshman felt in his blood. Many of his people refused to approach any Roman structure, claiming that ghosts—whether Roman, Welsh, or both—haunted them. Today, Gareth would have believed it, since a real corpse slumped on the ground against the far wall of the fort.

The man, not well-armored but with an axe at his belt, lay propped against a pillar, his legs splayed. A spear skewered him through his gut and a knife had been driven to the hilt into his chest. Even if his injuries had been less apparent, Gareth would have known the man was dead by the flies that gathered around his head. With more reluctance than haste, Gareth dismounted and headed towards the body, clambering over fallen stones and through ruined rooms to reach it.

Unlike Anarawd, this man had died where he lay, the remains of the pool of blood still evident on the ground around him. The rain that had fallen on the coast that morning had never reached here and the warmer summer air had accelerated the decaying process such that maggots had gotten inside the wounds. Gareth guessed the man had been dead for several days.

Sometimes Gareth hated his job.

He crouched before the man, not wanting to touch him yet—and not just because of the insects that crept and crawled all over and inside him. The man had no weapon in or near his hand, leading Gareth to believe that—like Anarawd—he'd known his killer and been unprepared for the attack.

Although Gareth couldn't tell the man's ancestry from his face, the dead man wore armor and clothing like the other men they'd encountered—and killed—on the road from Dolwyddelan. In addition, the bushiness of the man's beard and the length and color of his hair had Gareth thinking the man was a Dane. Besides, the crest of the King of Dublin was embossed into the leather of the man's vest.

Damping down a squeamishness he couldn't help, Gareth pulled out the spear and set it to one side. He then grasped the rough and unadorned hilt of the knife. The blade slid out easily. The lack of catch told him even before he wiped away the blood so he could inspect the knife that this wasn't the same one that had killed Anarawd. This blade, though newly sharpened, was thicker than the other. It was one a peasant might use for eating or whittling—although the odds of a peasant having killed this man were slim.

Whoever he was, whoever had done this deed, had been more prepared for the act than when he'd killed Anarawd—if indeed the two were murdered by the same person—which now that Gareth thought about it a bit more, he doubted. More likely, this man killed Anarawd and then another person killed him to silence him. Or this soldier had a falling out with his paymaster.

When Gareth had jerked out the spear, the dead man had fallen onto his side, so now Gareth pulled on his legs to flatten him out. He shifted the man's armor and clothing, first of all searching for the knife that killed Anarawd (which would have been quite a find), and secondly for anything that might tell him the identity of this man or the one who killed him. It was rough work. Gareth continued to wear his riding gloves, knowing that, regardless of the waste and the cost of new ones, he'd have to discard them when he was done.

He sat back on his heels to study the body. *What else do you have to tell me?* Holding his breath against the putrid smell and the crawling insects, Gareth stripped off the man's clothing so he could inspect his wounds more fully. It was the spear through the gut that bothered him the most. The knife wound had bled freely, indicating that it was the fatal blow. But if the man was already dying or dead, why skewer him afterwards? It spoke of anger.

Gareth thought back to the last moments of his milk-brother's life. The Danes had backtracked from the first ambush site, perhaps to here, following a different path from Hywel and his men, and then set up the second ambush. According to Bran, they hadn't gotten the seal from Anarawd in the first attack, and thus couldn't prove he was dead. *Prove to whom?* And was that failure why this man was dead?

For about two heartbeats, Gareth thought about throwing the body over Braith, but immediately discarded the notion. Even if the body itself had something more to tell him, he loathed the idea of carrying it all the way to Dolwyddelan.

Instead, Gareth used the man's axe to dig a shallow grave. He dumped the body into it and stacked rocks and stones from the fort over it to protect it from wild animals. Then with the armor and weapons lashed to his saddle bags, Gareth mounted Braith, turned her onto the track, and continued to the site of the original ambush, still evident by the churned up road and darkened blood. It had soaked into the earth by now, but its discoloration was unmistakable. It was helpful that it hadn't recently rained this high in the mountains. But even if it had, and rain had washed all signs of the battle into the creek that ran beside the road, the putrid pile of dead horse flesh would have given the location away.

That had been a long morning. With two truncated shovels Meilyr found in his cart, some of the men-at-arms had dug a ditch in which to pile the horses. While Gwen appeared to carry nothing with her but one satchel of clothing and a small bag of medicines, Meilyr was a packrat.

"What made you bring these all the way from wherever you've been?" Gareth had asked him.

"Some days we camp beside the road—particularly in the summer as we move from one location to another before looking for a winter patron," Meilyr said. "It's quite pleasant, even if it doesn't sound like it to you, and we use the shovels to dig for roots to eat, to carve out a fire pit, or to make a makeshift latrine."

So that explained the shovels, but not the odd mix of broken cookware, bent tools, and discarded clothing that covered the bottom of the cart. Gareth had chided Gwen about it on their walk to Caerhun, before the second ambush.

"I've tried," she'd said. "He won't let me touch his things. But I also won't let him bring any of it into our rooms once we find them. He's accumulated this mess just since the spring."

Even though Gareth wished Gwen were with him now, he was glad she hadn't seen that dead man back at the fort, nor was forced to revisit the location of Anarawd's death. They'd all worked hard shifting the dead horses off the road and preparing the human corpses for transport. Even Gwalchmai had helped once he returned with the carts, straining his thin shoulders and weak stomach.

Gareth dismounted and walked along the edge of the road until he reached the spot where Anarawd had lain, still marked with a trio of sticks. As he'd remembered, there wasn't enough blood here to tell him more. He drifted into the woods, thinking of the man as he'd known him.

Anarawd was a number of years older than Gareth, so had ruled in Deheubarth with his father and brothers long before Gareth had come to know of him. While none of Anarawd's brothers had disputed his ascendancy to the throne upon their father's death, Gareth had never thought much of the man. Like King Owain's brother, Cadwaladr, he covered his lack of acumen with bluster, talked more than he listened, and felt that his hereditary right to the throne should automatically garner the respect that he, as a man, hadn't earned.

At the same time, Gareth had heard no complaints from the people Anarawd governed and one could often tell the kind of person a man was by the opinions of his inferiors. Prince Cadwaladr's subjects could surely give anyone who asked an earful.

Focusing again, Gareth crept along the perimeter of the battlefield, his eyes on the ground. He hadn't been mistaken that Anarawd's murderer had moved his body. He didn't know if he could learn anything from finding the exact spot, but a man could never have too much information. He crouched low near the eastern ditch, and at last picked up the parallel trail left by Anarawd's boots. The killer had held him under the arms and dragged him out of the woods to the road. As Gwen had noted, hauling him by his feet would have been easier, though it would have done damage to his head, which perhaps the killer wanted to avoid.

Gareth backtracked the trail into the woods. The further he went, the more obvious the signs of both the tracks and the blood, which must have poured from Anarawd's body onto the ground. Another fifty feet in, and Gareth found the spot where Anarawd had fallen. The killer had tried to cover the blood stains with leaves, but Gareth removed them with a few swipes of his boot.

What had Anarawd been doing in the woods? Had he run from the battle as Hywel had surmised? And yet, the wound was to his chest. Gareth returned again and again to the indications that Anarawd had to have known—or at least momentarily trusted—the man who killed him. Otherwise, Anarawd would never have allowed him to get so close.

Abandoning the quest for answers for now, Gareth headed the last miles north to Dolwyddelan, marveling at the vagaries of fate. Because he hadn't ridden these miles the other day, he'd failed in his duty to escort Anarawd to his wedding. And yet, because of that same failure, Gareth and Gwen had been thrown together on a joint task that allowed them opportunity to speak and work together as friends. Whatever the cost to Owain Gwynedd, Gareth couldn't feel sorry for that.

Dolwyddelan Castle sat on a rocky knoll, guarding a mountain pass through the Vale of Conwy, one of the greenest and windiest regions of Wales. Dolwyddelan was primitive compared to Aber, but nonetheless, Gareth liked it. He'd first encountered Hywel here and it was here that Hywel had offered him a second chance at honor.

At the time, Gareth hadn't dared travel all the way to Aber to meet the prince, fearing that his reputation had preceded him. It had, but that hadn't been a hindrance in Hywel's eyes. Although he'd never mentioned it directly, Hywel had hinted that they were two of a kind. His father delegated his more unsavory tasks to Hywel, but not all of them could be done alone. Which is where Gareth came in.

The heavy wooden gate was open when Gareth reached the earth and timber wall that surrounded the castle. The guard waved him through.

"Sir Gareth!" A familiar figure trotted down the steps to the keep and across the courtyard to where Gareth waited.

"Gruffydd, my friend," Gareth said, dismounting. "It's a pleasure to see you—a delayed one, I might add."

"We heard what happened to King Anarawd." Gruffydd shook Gareth's hand. "I know you have much to preoccupy you in your service to Prince Hywel, but I'm glad you're here. We've just found a body."

17

"You're doing it again, Gwen!" Gwalchmai strode up to Gwen, his chin jutting out and his expression fierce.

"Doing what?" Gwen sniffed at the mint in her basket, half-listening to him. She'd come to the garden to be alone, but Gwalchmai didn't seem to understand the concept. She couldn't pinpoint the source of his outgoing personality, not even in her temperamental father, from whom he'd gotten his voice. Their mother had been a shy mouse, overwhelmed by Meilyr and hardly ever opening her mouth in company, for all that she loved her children and husband.

"Protecting me," Gwalchmai said. "I'll be twelve soon and in two years I'll be a man."

"I know that, Gwalchmai." Gwen lowered her basket and turned to look at him. "I know you don't need me."

Gwalchmai softened. "I don't mean that. But I'm not six years old anymore. I can take care of myself."

Gwen gazed at him. Gwalchmai had no idea how she held herself back, telling herself it would be to his disadvantage if she continued to mother him as she always had. His future as a bard was clear; hers was much less so. She could continue to travel with them, to cook and clean and nag them, but … did she want that for the rest of her life? By Gwen's age, every other woman she knew was married. Except for Cristina, who'd somehow managed to stave off all other suitors until King Owain noticed her. It looked to Gwen as if she thought him well worth the wait.

"Have I said you can't?" she said. "I've hardly seen you for days."

"And that's exactly the problem," Gwalchmai said.

"What are you talking about?"

"I'm talking about you," Gwalchmai said. "Taking risks, putting yourself in harm's way. Keeping it all to yourself because you think I'm too young to understand what's going on."

Gwen gritted her teeth, damping down her irritation at *his* attempt to mother *her*. Her father did that quite enough, even if she'd long since figured out how not to listen to him. "We're at Aber. It's hardly dangerous here. I let Gareth go south without me, didn't I? Am I worried, even though he's been gone a day longer than he'd said? No. Here I am, pruning the beans in the garden on a sunny afternoon, minding my own business and not interfering in anybody else's."

"Don't tell me what to do, is that it?" Gwalchmai said. "Why can you tell me what to do and not the other way around?"

Gwen took in a deep breath, recognizing this moment as one that had been a long time coming. "When did I last tell you to do something? You've been your own person for a while now."

"This morning you told me to comb my hair," he said.

"Do you resent that?" she said.

Gwalchmai gazed at her, and then flopped onto the bench near the row of beans. "Yes."

"Even if you know it's the right thing to do?"

Gwalchmai dug the toe of his boot into the dirt and she thought he wasn't going to answer, but then he said, "Even if."

Gwen nodded. She'd noticed that Gwalchmai was far less likely to do what she asked, just because she asked. "I can try to stop. Mothering you is a hard habit to break." Gwalchmai was alternately so earnest and sullen, Gwen found herself wanting to laugh. Except that wasn't fair to him either. Putting down her knife, she touched his hand. "Is that really what you came here to say? Or is it something else?"

Gwalchmai looked up, his expression as intent as ever. "I overheard Lord Cadwaladr speaking of Sir Gareth last evening. He was regaling the men crowded around him with the story of how he threw Gareth out of his hall for insubordination."

"Yes," Gwen said. "You were seven when that happened. Do you remember?"

"I remember you crying," he said.

"And you don't want to see me cry again over Gareth?"

Gwalchmai had the courage of youth and didn't even appear embarrassed. He nodded.

That he cared enough to talk to her touched Gwen's heart. "Father didn't refuse Gareth's offer of marriage because Gareth had dishonored himself, as Cadwaladr implies. Gareth refused an order his conscience told him he couldn't carry out and Cadwaladr dismissed him for it. Father respected that. If Gareth had followed the order, how could Father have given me to such a man? But at the same time, he couldn't let me go to a man who had no way to support me. Not at sixteen."

"And now?" Gwalchmai said.

Gwen paused. *Gareth.* How did he really feel about her? What had he done all these years that was so *irregular*? He'd refused to discuss his time as a mercenary and she wondered what his tasks had entailed. He'd done *something* of which he was ashamed. Which he wouldn't tell her. And was that his fault? Surely every man was entitled to his secrets, especially a soldier who followed his lord's orders, even when those orders offended him. As both Gareth and she knew, the alternative was dismissal. Or death.

"I'm not going to marry Gareth," Gwen said. "Even if I wanted to, I don't know that he'd have me. He has a new life with no place for me in it."

"Then he's a fool," Gwalchmai said.

Gwen smiled. "He hasn't hurt me, Gwalchmai. Life hurt me, but I've grown up since then. Still ... thank you. You've grown up more than I've wanted to admit."

Gwalchmai nodded, looked down at his feet, and then raised his head again. "There's something else, too. Something I overheard someone say."

"What is it?" Gwen said, not expecting much of note.

"My friend Dafydd says King Anarawd's brother, Cadell, is going to marry Elen in Anarawd's stead. He was talking to Cristina about it."

Gwen blinked at this upwelling of information. "Cadell was talking to Cristina?"

"Yes."

"Go on." Gwen braced herself, now sure he was going to tell her something she didn't want to hear.

"Cadell said he knew something that would convince King Owain that Gareth murdered Anarawd."

"What did Cristina say?"

"I don't know," Gwalchmai said. "They moved too far away for Dafydd to hear."

Gwen stared into the distance. There was no telling what information Cristina had shared with Cadell or vice versa. She straightened. If Gareth was to hang, it wasn't going to be over this. Not if she could help it.

She turned to her brother, about to smile her dismissal, when she stopped herself. Not only was he older than she'd thought, but he'd brought her good information. She canted her head as she looked at him.

"What?" he said.

"Neither you nor Father have appreciated the work I've done for Hywel," she said. "But you've just done similar work for me."

Gwalchmai's eyes widened. "I—" He stopped himself. "I guess I have, at that."

"How would you like to do a bit more?"

Gwalchmai's eyes brightened and Gwen hastened to head him off before he got too excited. "Nothing dangerous." She pointed a finger at him. "Nothing that draws attention to yourself. Just listening and reporting, like you've just done."

"And what are you going to do?" Gwalchmai said.

"Find Hywel." Gwen stretched, loosening her muscles from too much bending among the weeds, and headed towards the kitchen door.

Gwalchmai called after her. "Don't do anything stupid!"

Gwen raised a hand to indicate she'd heard, though she didn't answer. She hoped she'd done the right thing with Gwalchmai. Maybe if she gave him a small task, it would keep him out of bigger mischief.

She'd passed through the kitchen and hall, looked in Hywel's office, and was coming down the steps into the courtyard by the main gate, still searching for Hywel, when Gareth came through it.

"There you are," she said.

He reined in and dismounted. When she reached him, he caught her around the waist. She gazed up at him, stunned at how natural his greeting felt.

"I have much to tell you," he said, overriding her confusion.

"Did you find something?"

"Lots of somethings." He turned her towards the hall, his hand still resting at the small of her back. It felt *right* there.

But then Cadwaladr and Cadell appeared in the doorway. Cadell pointed his finger at Gareth. "Seize that man!"

"What? No!" Gwen stepped directly in front of Gareth, as if that could protect him from this unexpected onslaught.

Nobody else moved. Even Prince Cadwaladr gaped at Cadell in astonishment.

"I've heard that before," Evan said from somewhere to Gwen's right. "Not going to make that mistake again."

"Not on anyone's orders but the King's," another man said.

The two men-at-arms did move closer to Gareth, to protect him, Gwen hoped. Gareth's arm had slipped around Gwen's waist, and she pressed back against him.

Cadell had his own supporters, however, his own *teulu*, and they moved from all directions, pushing through the men of Aber's garrison, to surround Gareth and Gwen. One of them grabbed her arm and yanked her away from Gareth while two more pinioned his arms behind his back. It was that first evening all over again.

"What are you doing? He's done nothing!" she said.

Madog strode from the entrance to the barracks. "Let go of the girl." His command carried across the courtyard. "And unhand Sir Gareth."

Cadell, however, outranked him, and thundered down the steps. "I've done a complete search of the castle! Moments ago, one of my men found Anarawd's seal among that man's possessions!"

"What?" Gwen spun around to gape at Cadell.

"Let it go, Gwen," Gareth said. "We know why I had Anarawd's seal. And we can prove it. This means nothing."

Cadwaladr caught that this was his opportunity to humiliate Gareth once again, even it wasn't he who had orchestrated it. He strode up to Gareth and put his face right into his. "Nothing?! How dare you! The King of Deheubarth is dead!"

"It is you who are nothing," Gwen said, before Gareth could speak. As soon as she spoke the words, she knew she shouldn't have said them out loud, but she couldn't take them back. To have Cadwaladr assisting Cadell when they were both in the wrong...

Cadwaladr froze, his face a rigid mask. Without responding to Gwen or even looking at her, he threw out his hand, dismissing Gareth. Cadell's men, now augmented by several of Cadwaladr's, hauled him away. Madog watched, impotent, his jaw clenched and his shoulders shaking with suppressed anger. Then Cadwaladr whirled on Gwen. "You would do well to mind your place."

"And what place is that?"

Cadwaladr's eyes bulged. "Silence!" He backhanded Gwen across the face. She staggered, her hand to her mouth and tasting blood.

"I know the truth and so does Prince Hywel. It will come out!" She spat the words, even if they were as far from the truth as it was possible to get, and ran past him, heading towards the stables. She was so furious and hurt she couldn't see straight. Others had described to her an anger that made a red haze before their eyes but she'd never experienced it. That, and the contrast from light to dark as she crossed the threshold meant she didn't see Hywel standing directly in her path until she ran into him.

"Careful." Hywel caught her by the arms.

"Gareth—"

"I heard," Hywel said. "And I heard what you said to Cadwaladr. That was not wise."

"I know." Gwen touched a finger to the corner of her mouth. "A moment ago, I didn't care."

Hywel looked past her to the courtyard. Gwen turned to follow his gaze. Cadwaladr was still glaring at her, his hands on his hips. Then one of his men caught his attention and he turned away, back to the hall. He hurried to come even with Cadell, who stood at the top of the steps to the hall, looking righteous and self-satisfied.

"You should stay out of their way." Hywel dabbed at the corner of her mouth with a handkerchief. "That has to hurt. He wore a ring."

Gwen swallowed. "I've felt worse." And she had, at her father's hands.

Hywel gave her a dark look.

"If you need me, I'll be with Gareth." She made to push past him but he held her arm and pulled her closer so he could look into her eyes.

"I recommend that you do not sing with your brother during dinner tonight."

"The sight of those lords makes me sick anyway."

Hywel released her but didn't leave and she led him past the horseboxes to the rear of the stables. He pulled up short just as one of the guards drove his fist into Gareth's belly. Before Gwen could scream, Hywel clapped a hand over her mouth. "Quiet. Give it a moment."

Gwen pulled away. "How can you stand by and do nothing?"

"You'd have me fire all the arrows in my quiver before the start of battle?" Hywel said. "That is unwise. Gareth has experienced worse. They'll tire of him presently." As he spoke, a guard twisted Gareth's arm and he collapsed forward, just as another guard brought up his knee. Gareth folded in half over it with a moan.

Gwen glared at Hywel for another few heartbeats, hating him in that moment. At his steady gaze, however, she subsided, still in the shadows. She sucked on her lip, half-turned away from where Gareth's guards continued to rough him up. She wanted to clap her hands over her ears. It wasn't that Gareth cried or screamed, but his breathy moans were more than she could bear.

Finally, Hywel's words proved true and Cadell's men threw him face first into the cell. Gareth pushed up on his hands and turned back to them, blood pouring from a gash on his head. "*Dos i chwarae efo dy nain!*" The flames behind Gareth's eyes could have lit the stables on fire.

Then a guard closed the door and the two men who remained settled themselves in front of the door, one leaning against the wall to the left of the door and the second on an overturned bucket.

"We'll give them time to get bored," Hywel said. "Come. We must make a plan."

Reluctantly, Gwen returned with Hywel to his office. She slumped on the bench under the window, unable to think of anything to say.

Hywel plopped into his chair. "Damn." He ran a hand across his brow. "What a day."

"Damn right." King Owain swung around the door frame and halted in the middle of the room. Both Gwen and Hywel stood, though Gwen didn't think the King had even noticed her, so focused was he on his son. She tried to sidle towards the door, but stopped at Hywel's warning look.

"Sir," Hywel said.

King Owain put his hands on Hywel's desk and leaned onto them. "I have put up with your defense of that man for four years, but no more."

"Gareth had nothing to do with Anarawd's death, Father." Hywel said this very calmly, his back straight and his hands resting at his sides.

King Owain went red to the roots of his hair. He pointed his finger at his son. "How dare you defend him!"

"I must defend him. He is my man." Hywel paused. "Besides, in this case, Cadell is quite mistaken. Gareth did not take the seal from Anarawd. Gwen gave it to him."

"Gwen!" King Owain spun on his heel to glare at Gwen. She backed away until she hit the wall behind her and couldn't go any further. She gazed at the King wide-eyed, unable to speak. King Owain turned back to Hywel. "Explain."

"Of course." Hywel flicked his eyes to Gwen and then back to his father. Gwen held her breath, waiting for what he would say. "According to Cristina, who gave the seal to Gwen, Cadell himself had it in his quarters. That is where she found it. It may be that Cadell's accusation of Gareth is an attempt to distract us from his own perfidy."

King Owain pressed up against Hywel's desk, his face nearly purple with anger. "What did you say? How dare you bring Cristina into this!"

"He speaks the truth, my lord."

Cristina stepped through the doorway into Hywel's office and very gently closed the door behind her. She shot Gwen a look that told Gwen not to speak. As Gwen was trembling from head to foot, she was hardly going to challenge her future queen. At the same time, Gwen had to ask herself, what game was Cristina playing?

Owain Gwynedd had no answers either. He stared at Cristina and then scrubbed at his hair with both hands, making the straw tufts stick up on end. "I am undone. My entire family conspires and plots without my knowledge." He collapsed onto the bench that Gwen had vacated.

"Please forgive me, my lord, but I was attempting to help your son in his search." Cristina gave King Owain a look that managed to make her look coquettish, rather than guilty or embarrassed. "King Cadell's room was one of several I examined."

"Why?" King Owain raised his hands and dropped them in his lap in a helpless gesture. "Why would you do this?"

"Because I was the only one who could."

King Owain gazed at her. Cristina didn't back down. Like Hywel, she kept her face calm and unconcerned. Then King Owain began to laugh. He threw back his head and roared at the ceiling. Still standing behind his desk, Hywel grinned at Gwen. She just barely managed to smile back. It really wasn't funny—and the power Cristina seemed to wield over the King certainly made it worse—but for the moment, Cristina appeared to be on their side.

Eventually, King Owain sobered. "Did you tell Cadell what you found?"

"Of course not," Cristina said. "I gave the seal to Gwen, who obviously showed it to Hywel and Gareth, which is how it ended up among Gareth's things. I have no idea how Cadell came to hear of it."

"He would, of course, have discovered it missing," Gwen said.

"That is if he put it there in the first place," Hywel said, "and if he is the perpetrator of all this."

"Ach." King Owain waved a hand. "You're looking in the wrong direction. Cadell is neither smart enough, nor devious enough, to have planned something this complicated. He's been Anarawd's loyal advisor ever since their father died." Owain paused. "I am considering giving him Elen's hand."

"But someone ordered Anarawd's death, my lord," Cristina said. "Who stands to gain the most from it?"

"What about Uncle Cadwaladr—"

"Don't speak his name!" King Owain jutted his chin out at his son. "I have heard your opinion of him and I grant that he might be wrong about Gareth, but he has done nothing to deserve any accusation, especially not one as inflammatory as this."

Nobody replied and King Owain seemed to sense their muted disapproval. He straightened. "I need proof of someone else's guilt, Hywel, before I can free Gareth. You know that."

"I'll get your proof, Father." Hywel glanced at Gwen. "We'll get it if it's there to find."

"I trust you," King Owain said. "You have never failed me." And with that astounding piece of fatherly affirmation, he stood and held out his arm to Cristina, who took it.

Hywel stopped his father, however, before he could leave the room. "Why do you think so poorly of Gareth, Father, when he has served us well?" His tone was genuinely curious. "Back when we first heard the news of Anarawd's death, you referred to something Uncle Cadwaladr told you. What was it?"

King Owain pursed his lips. "I'll tell you. There's no reason not to. Cadwaladr believes Gareth was the spy who revealed our movements to the Normans in the last days of fighting in Ceredigion, before your grandfather died."

Gwen blinked. Whatever she'd been expecting, it wasn't that.

"Why didn't he name him so at the time?" Hywel said.

"He chose not to. We'd won the war; there seemed little to gain and the admission that he'd harbored a spy would have shown weakness just at a time when he needed to show strength. The people of Ceredigion needed a leader, not one who could be fooled by a strip of a boy."

"All I can tell you is that I don't believe it, Father," Hywel said. "It doesn't fit with the man I know."

"Perhaps. For now, I want him where I can see him. It was his brother, Bran, who rode with the Danes," King Owain said. "Perhaps they conspired together."

Gwen's teeth were clenched so tightly she didn't know if she'd be able to pry them apart. That the truth could get so distorted never ceased to amaze her. She wanted to say something, but at a warning look from Hywel, kept her mouth shut.

King Owain narrowed his eyes at his son. "You will do well to remember that the punishment for treason is death."

Hywel swallowed hard. "I would not have forgotten that, Father."

King Owain nodded curtly and left, Cristina on his arm, leaving Gwen and Hywel alone once again.

"That means Gareth stays where he is, doesn't it?" Gwen said.

"For now."

18

Back in the stables, Gwen and Hywel gazed down at Gareth, who lay flat on his back on the hard, dirt floor, rather the worse for this incarceration. "I'm tired of being thrown in here for something I did not do!" His tone was emphatic, but the volume was weaker than Gwen liked. "And now you tell me that King Owain thinks that because Bran was with the Danes, I was too? To what end? Nothing could be further from the truth."

Gwen knelt beside him and felt his head. "Are you much hurt?"

"I'm fine." Gareth grasped her hand. "But what about you?" He touched the redness that spread from the corner of her mouth to her cheek. And then his voice hardened. "Who did this?"

Gwen glanced up at Hywel, who lounged against the doorframe, one hand resting on his sword. He grimaced, but didn't answer.

"Gwen—" Gareth's voice had a warning tone to it.

She sighed. "Cadwaladr."

"Goddamn—" Gareth swallowed whatever else he was going to say, squeezed her hand hard and then let go. He pushed himself up onto his elbows and glared at Hywel. "Nice of you to intervene, my lord."

"I have no obligation to explain myself to you," Hywel said. "But I will repeat what I told Gwen: this is a long game I'm playing and it wouldn't do to confront Cadell—or Cadwaladr—over something that doesn't matter."

Gareth opened his mouth to speak, and then closed it. "Doesn't matter—" He mumbled further under his breath, but didn't openly protest.

"What did you discover on your journey?" Hywel said.

"A couple of bodies." Now Gareth scrambled to his feet, holding a hand to his belly and moving more stiffly than usual. Gradually he straightened and stretched. "A few bruises, Gwen, that's all." He'd read the concern on her face correctly. "As Lord Hywel pointed out, it's a small matter."

Gwen nodded, going over in her head what she'd seen earlier in front of the cell. At the time, it had looked as if Cadell's men had beaten Gareth badly, but maybe her eyes had fooled her. They might have been pulling their punches, wanting to make it look good to please their lord. Gareth had told her that for the years he'd served Prince Cadwaladr, many of his friends had learned to shade their actions so as to not openly violate their orders, but not exactly follow them either. It was a matter of living with oneself afterwards.

Then Gareth's words registered. "More bodies?" she said.

"I found one in the Roman fort near the intersection of all those trails," Gareth said, "and a second at Dolwyddelan. The castellan discovered that death an hour before I arrived. The murderer had stuffed him into the latrine. It was just his bad luck that the slops came to clean it when they did. The body was cold and stiff; it had been in there—or at least dead—no more than two days."

"Do you know the identities of the dead men?" Hywel said, still leaning against the doorframe.

"The first was a Dane. Someone killed him with a knife to the chest."

"The same method as Anarawd," Hywel said.

"Yes, but a different knife," Gareth said, "one that the killer left behind. In addition, the killer drove a spear through the man's middle—after he was dead, mind you."

"How very interesting," Hywel said.

"Why skewer a dead man?" Gwen said.

Hywel turned to her. "Why indeed?"

Gareth nodded. "I brought his effects home to Aber. They'll be in my saddlebags still." He paused. "Someone saw to Braith, I hope?"

"I made sure of it," Hywel said. "And the second?"

"The second was a stable boy at Dolwyddelan Castle."

"Really?" Gwen catalogued the boys she'd seen when she was there with her family. Then she pulled herself up short, disturbed that she could be so calm about so many murders. It wasn't right that she should get used to them. But as it was... "Why would someone want to kill a stable boy?"

"We don't know the answer to that, but he had been assigned to tend King Anarawd's horse," Gareth said.

"That could be important," Hywel said.

Gwen wrapped both arms around her middle, a sick feeling in her belly. "Anarawd's horse died in the ambush."

"Stinks to high heaven, now," Gareth said. "Putrid."

"I can't present any evidence of course, not from here," Gwen said, ignoring him. "But that boy ... could he have been the one who looked after my father's horse?"

Gareth canted his head. "It's possible. Though several boys could have shared the task, just as they do here."

"My father's horse turned up lame the morning King Anarawd left Dolwyddelan." Gwen spoke slowly as she thought it out. "Father was so very angry. The boy was terrified. At the time, I didn't think anything more of it than that the child feared my father's wrath, but what if he'd been instructed to nobble Anarawd's horse, and he hurt the wrong one? What if it wasn't my father he feared, but someone else who'd tasked him with a job he failed to accomplish—someone who killed him?"

"Why would the murderer have wanted to prevent Anarawd from leaving Dolwyddelan?" Gareth said. "That makes no sense."

"Anarawd arrived at Dolwyddelan Castle a day early," Gwen said, "and thus left a day early too. The killer could have wanted to delay Anarawd past a dawn start—which is exactly what happened to us instead. Perhaps he feared the mercenaries wouldn't have time to get into position. As it turned out, it was my father who was forced to borrow a horse and Anarawd who wouldn't wait for him."

"There are too many murders in this," Hywel said. "Too many murderers altogether. It's nonsensical." He pushed off the frame, no longer relaxed. If there had been more room to pace he probably would have. "We've got someone who ordered the ambush; someone who killed Anarawd; someone who killed the servant woman; someone who killed the Dane; someone who killed the boy; someone who poisoned Gareth; someone who moved Anarawd's body."

"Seven someones? Three?" Gareth said. "All the same?" He swiveled on one heel and kicked at the wall. A board split. "And what makes even less sense is that I find myself back in this *cachu* cell!"

Gwen took a step back at his anger. Maybe because he saw it, Gareth stopped himself from aiming another kick at the wall. And then he laughed, though there wasn't much amusement in his voice, and threw out a hand to Gwen—"Sorry. Sorry for my mouth too."

Gwen waved a hand. It was hardly the first time she'd heard profanity. She preferred it to when a man swore by the saints, who might actually be listening.

"I've spoken with my father," Hywel said. "He once again will entertain the notion that you didn't kill Anarawd, but he leaves you here, Gareth—and is happy to do so—because Cadell still has his ear." He paused. "Just be thankful Cadell doesn't have more power at Aber than any other prince, myself included."

"There's something else..." Gwen cast her eyes sideways at Hywel, wondering if she should speak or if he would prefer to tell Gareth the rest of what had passed between Hywel and his father.

Hywel nodded and delivered the bad news: "You should also know that Prince Cadwaladr's latest accusation against you is that you were a spy for the Normans."

"What?" Gareth gaped at him. "When—when was I supposed to have done that?"

Hywel smiled. "He implied that you passed vital information to fitz Martin that allowed him to hold Cardigan Castle against us."

"He's mad!"

Hywel smirked. "I thought you'd say that."

"So you're letting Gareth out?" Gwen said, relieved that at last something was going to go right.

"No. Not until Cadell goes home." Hywel shrugged. "Unfortunately, that might be a while as my father seems set on marrying Elen to him in Anarawd's place."

Gareth's jaw clenched. Then he mastered himself and turned to Gwen. "And that means you have to stay away from me."

"What? No I don't. Why would you say that?"

"I won't have suspicion falling on you."

Gwen stared at him, so irritated she couldn't respond. Then Hywel tugged her arm. "Come. Gareth's right." He shot Gareth a grin. "Not for the first time, but don't get used to me saying so."

19

"**G**wen! Gwen!"

Gwen eyes popped open. It was almost as if she'd been expecting someone to come and wake her up. She couldn't say that she'd had a full night's sleep since she left Dolwyddelan.

She sat up, clearing the last of the sleep from her mind. Then, the voice came again. *"Gwen! Gwen!"*

"Hywel?" She whispered his name and then thought better of how loud it sounded in the quiet room, fearing she'd wake the other women. One rolled over as Gwen waited, breath held, and then stilled. Wrapping a blanket around her shoulders, Gwen got to her feet, tiptoed to the door, and slipped out of the room.

Three men waited for her, none of whom were Hywel. She had a flash—only an impression really—of cloaks and hoods before one of the men put a hand over her mouth, pulled her to him, and whispered, "Come with us quietly or Hywel dies."

Gwen tried to swallow but her mouth had gone dry. She wanted to ask what they had done to him, and if they realized what kind of trouble this would bring them, but couldn't speak around the man's hand. And then she had to focus on her feet as he urged her down the stairs, through the sadly deserted kitchen, and towards the postern gate. Once outside, in the narrow space between the kitchen garden wall and stables, the man removed his hand. She opened her mouth to scream, but before she could, he shoved the open end of a flask between her teeth and poured.

She choked and coughed as the liquid sloshed into her mouth. "What is this?" She tried to twist away, but another man held her head with a forceful hand to the back of her neck. The man holding the flask grabbed her jaw and cheeks and forced her teeth apart. He upturned the flask and she swallowed. And then swallowed again.

By the time the third man grasped her around the waist and hauled her towards the postern gate, the drink was taking hold of her. And by then she knew what it was, too, not that it mattered except it implied that they meant to subdue her, not kill her. *Poppy juice*, she said to herself, and then didn't remember anything more.

* * * * *

Gwen groaned, her hand to her head. The room in which she found herself was plain, with an unlit fireplace, wooden beams that supported the roof, and little else. It wasn't the room in which she slept at Aber. Gwen blinked—and then remembered. *I'm not at Aber!*

That she was alive, Gwen considered to be something of a miracle, given the bodies that Anarawd's murderer had no apparent qualms about strewing across Gwynedd. It was why she was alive that concerned her. Not that she wasn't happy about it; obviously the man who ordered this had his reasons. She didn't know—and didn't really want to find out—what a man might think a credible reason for abducting her.

Or *a woman*, Gwen supposed, though the notion that any woman, even Cristina, was behind her captivity seemed vanishingly remote. She lay as they'd left her, on her side and curled into a ball, in a room that was entirely empty except for her. Her head and stomach hurt so badly, just the thought of standing made her nauseous. She tried to piece together the course of events since Aber, but couldn't recall more than passing emotions and vague shadows.

At least they hadn't put her at the back of the stables where Gareth had found himself. Wherever she was, she was in a house of some kind, and a well-kept one at that, given the fine wood floor on which her pallet rested. She also, now that she could feel her body better—and see it—wore a finely woven blue dress over the night shift she'd worn to bed. She really didn't want to know how they'd gotten her into it while she'd been unconscious.

What troubled her most about her imprisonment was the extent to which none of this made any sense at all. Where had she gone wrong? To whom had she given the false impression that they were near to finding the killer? Neither she, Hywel, nor Gareth had come close to discovering who'd murdered Anarawd, much less killed all those other people.

Gwen amused herself with the idea that multiple people had worked at cross-purposes, running into each other in their attempts to cover up their crimes and cast blame on someone else, until she remembered that the 'someone else' in question had been Gareth. *Worse and worse.*

She couldn't help Gareth, not from wherever she was now, so she forced thoughts of him to the back of her mind and refocused on her own predicament. For now, she needn't concern herself about all those potential villains. She just needed to worry about the one who'd stolen her away.

From the quality of the light leaking through the cracks around the shuttered window, the day had faded into late afternoon. She tried to marshal the requisite energy to open the window but just as she had convinced herself she could stand, footfalls outside her door stayed her. The bar came up and the door opened.

"I know you're awake." It was Prince Cadwaladr, striding across the floor to the window and opening it for her.

Gwen put a hand to her head, cursing herself for not controlling her temper better with him. But had Cadwaladr really killed the stable boy, attempted to poison Gareth, and stolen Anarawd's body? She couldn't see it. He'd have had to get his hands dirty himself and usually he ordered others to do his most unsavory tasks. How many men could he have who would murder a stable boy and a servant woman? How much money was one man's soul worth and what would he take in trade?

"You might as well sit up and pay attention."

Gwen did as he bid, blinking her eyes against the sudden light. The scent of the sea that she'd noticed earlier was stronger now on the breeze. She filed that away in the back of her mind for future thought. "Why am I here? Why have you taken me from Aber against my will?"

"Against your will?" Cadwaladr swung around to look at her. "Why would you think that? No, my dear. I took you from Aber to keep you safe, since you were in great danger there."

"What are you talking about?" she said. "In danger from whom?"

"From Gareth, of course," Cadwaladr said. "Even in his cell, he could harm you as long as he has Hywel's ear. That might not have been evident to your lover, but it was clear as day to me."

"To ... my lover?"

Cadwaladr made an impatient motion with his hand. "Men in love are blind. Naturally, Hywel wanted to keep you with him, but it wasn't the wisest course. As his uncle, I had to take action when he would not."

Gwen gaped at Cadwaladr. Her throat closed on any comprehensible thing she could possibly put forth. Cadwaladr gazed at her with such condescension and certainty, any contradiction of his beliefs was impossible—and probably unwise. She looked away, her hand at her head. It ached and she didn't know if it was from the poppy juice, or the surprise of hearing him get this so drastically wrong. But as it appeared to be the only reason she was alive, she didn't dare deny it.

"Since it was clear my nephew was incapable of seeing the truth, I acted. After my brother hangs the traitor, we will return." Cadwaladr turned to look out the window. "We don't have long to wait. Last I spoke to him, King Owain promised me Gareth's death would occur at dawn tomorrow."

Gwen struggled to rise, the desire to throw herself at Cadwaladr and choke him so strong, she felt she'd actually have the courage to do it. Seeing her movement, Cadwaladr put out a hand. "Now, now. Easy. You shouldn't move quickly in your condition."

Gwen subsided, settling for shooting daggers at him with her eyes. Truth be told, now that Cadwaladr had her here, Gwen had the feeling he wasn't quite sure what to do with her. He was very confident as he spoke to her, but he twitched more than usual and so far hadn't looked her in the eye even once. "Where are we?"

Cadwaladr tsked under his breath—exactly like her father often did—and returned to the doorway. "I'll send food and water." He closed the door behind him.

Gwen rested her head against the wall of her prison, pulled a thin blanket over her legs, and closed her eyes. She'd obviously slept the day away. She opened her eyes again and looked towards the open window. Pushing through her exhaustion, Gwen rose to her feet, stumbling almost as if she'd been on a boat instead of lying on a pallet on dry land. Her hands clutched the window ledge.

The sea! Cadwaladr had been playing games with her not to give her the name of the castle. He must have known that one look out the window would tell her. She'd been here before. Another glance around the room with clearer eyes told her she'd even been in this room before. Owain Gwynedd had only two seaside castles within a day's range of Aber that Cadwaladr might think to use: Criccieth, south of Caernarfon, and Aberffraw to the north. How she could have missed a ride across the Menai Straits she didn't know, but she had. Cadwaladr had grown up here, as had she and Hywel.

They were at Aberffraw.

She pushed the shutter wider to better illuminate the room. Turning back, she studied the empty fireplace, the mantle, and the box that held the extra firewood, empty today since it was August. Crouching down, she traced the faded lettering that Hywel had carved into one of the box's slats, long ago. She'd been there when he'd done it and been appropriately shocked at the time: *Meilyr is an ass.*

She laughed.

They'd taken their lessons together here. Her father had included her, with King Owain's permission, more to keep Hywel company than because anyone thought it appropriate she learn to read. Even then, however, she'd the sense that Meilyr himself thought he would personally benefit from teaching her. Thus, every morning for two years, she and Hywel sat together in this very room, learning their Latin and Welsh from Meilyr. Along with their letters, he taught them figures, and, most importantly, music.

In those years, it was music that had governed their lives, far above the hated Latin. Even King Owain, who paid far less attention to his second son than his first, had recognized Hywel's capacity as a musician and acknowledged that to give him anything less than the best and most thorough instruction and guidance would be doing Wales—and by extension, King Owain himself—a disservice.

Hywel had asked her to listen to the first song he'd ever composed. Just her initially, to help him gather his courage to show it to Meilyr. He'd said it was *to* her, as well, though almost immediately she doubted it as she overheard him telling one of the serving wenches the same thing three days later. He was only twelve and she ten at the time, but every woman in the room was fair game to him, even then. Meilyr had approved the meter and rhyme, if not the actual content, and Hywel's career as a warrior-poet was born.

Not long after, Gwen's mother had died birthing Gwalchmai, and Gwen's lessons ended, replaced by caring for the baby. Hywel, too, began splitting his time more between his swordplay and his lessons. He might be the second, bastard son of the second son of the King of Gwynedd, but to all concerned the 'warrior' part of 'warrior-poet' was ever the most important.

As fate would have it, King Owain's older brother, Cadwallon, died the next year. All of a sudden, Hywel was far more important to his father than he'd been before. King Owain might dote on Rhun, he might not understand this second son, who was both wildly creative and physically bold—and exactly like his father—but he needed him, just as King Owain's father had needed Owain himself when Cadwallon died. It wasn't hard to see the parallels between King Owain's growing up and Hywel's, even if the idea of Rhun dying prematurely was horrifying.

But in a royal family, these things must be acknowledged. Just as the possibility of treachery of one brother towards another needed to be accepted as well. Hywel would make an extraordinarily capable King of Gwynedd, perhaps more so than Rhun because he was so much more intelligent and devious. But he'd been born second. Gwen was too old now—and she and Hywel had grown too far apart—to ask him if he minded. Purportedly, King Anarawd had gotten along with his brothers too, and it might well be a smooth transition for Cadell to step into his brother's shoes as King of Deheubarth. If that was the case, such an outcome was rarer than it should have been.

The food came and went, served by a wide-eyed squire. He'd brought a fresh loaf of bread, some cheese, and mead, but it left Gwen unsatisfied. It wasn't that she was hungry, but the room was empty of everything and everyone but her and her memories—and regrets. All she could do was stare out the window to the sea and wonder when, and if, a rescue would come.

She understood that if nobody came for her, it wouldn't be because Gareth didn't want to come. If he knew of her absence, despite their five year separation, he would move heaven and earth to get to her. If he didn't come for her, it was because he couldn't—whether because the King still imprisoned him in his cell at Aber or because King Owain had hanged him, as Cadwaladr hoped. Gwen prayed that Hywel, in playing his great game, would think that was more than a minor issue, even if in the end he might not be able to stop his father from building a gallows for Gareth or might feel that saving Gareth's life wasn't worth his father's supreme disfavor.

Hywel, too, should notice Gwen was gone. What his assessment of her value might be, Gwen didn't have the confidence to judge. As with everything, he'd calculate the costs and benefits of coming after her and come down on the side that gave him the strongest position. If he wasn't willing to save Gareth, he certainly wouldn't be willing to rescue her. She didn't lie to herself that she prayed he'd do both.

Gwen continued to gaze out the window. The drop to the ground was at least twenty feet—far more than she could ever hope to jump, and the exterior of the castle was otherwise smooth. It wasn't even built in stone with commensurate handholds. As the sun fell lower in the sky in front of her, its light reflected off the water in the distance. She lost track of how long she stood there.

Then, her gaze sharpened and her heart caught in her throat. She'd never seen Danish warships before, but she'd heard them described. She knew enough to understand what she was seeing: three ships, their decks stacked with men, rowers working in unison, plowing through the calm waters of the estuary towards Aberffraw.

It was right out of a nightmare. For hundreds of years, the Danes—or the Irish or the Vikings, it hardly mattered which and for the purposes of the Welsh, there were few distinctions among them—had ravaged the coast of Wales, either from their homes to the north or from Ireland, a portion of which they'd conquered before the Normans came to Wales. And rumor had it, the Normans had Viking ancestors too, which Gwen couldn't help but believe. From their Dublin seaport, the Danish invaders had sacked churches, raped women, and kidnapped any number of people to bring them home as slaves. Their ships were fast and sleek, capable of riding right up to the beach and casting off at a moment's notice.

Gwen, Gareth, and Hywel had known that whoever had paid to have Anarawd killed had hired Danes from Ireland to do the job, but that more mercenaries might come to Aberffraw, now, was almost beyond Gwen's comprehension. Everyone knew that Danes would do anything and everything for a profit. No act, no matter how heinous, was beneath them. If Cadwaladr paid them, they would do his bidding, regardless of what that bidding was. And there wasn't a single thing that Gwen could do about it.

20

"I don't understand it." Gareth paced around the confined space of his cell, intentionally kicking at the wooden bucket in the corner as he passed it. *Pace, pace, pace, kick; pace, pace, pace, kick.* If he kept it up much longer, Hywel would have his head, but the crunch of the wood under Gareth's boot was eminently satisfying just now. "I knew it wasn't like her to keep herself away from me all day, despite what I told her. Has nobody seen her?"

Hywel braced his shoulder against the wall just inside the door to Gareth's cell and folded his arms across his chest. He watched Gareth pace with what looked like amusement on his face—perhaps at Gareth's admission of his and Gwen's friendship—though, admittedly, that was Hywel's usual expression. Hywel rarely showed his true thoughts to anyone, much less to Gareth.

"Nobody," Hywel said. "I didn't see her at breakfast, though I didn't notice that I hadn't until later. My men and I rode out before noon and we didn't return until just before the evening meal when I went looking for her."

"And you've questioned the garrison?" Gareth said, knowing that it wasn't his place to tell Hywel his job but unable to help himself. "Nobody saw her leave?"

"No," Hywel said.

"The castle isn't very big; she can't have gone far. Is she in the bath? Could she have slipped and fallen?"

"It's not running today," Hywel said. "But yes, I looked there."

Gareth pursed his lips, taking that as Hywel meant it: he, himself, along with his men and squires, had looked thoroughly throughout the castle. None had found her and if Hywel hadn't found her, she wasn't here to be found. Gareth cursed himself for his blindness, for not seeing that something like this could happen if Gwen continued to pursue the murderer without him. "This tells me she got close to the culprit without knowing it."

"I would have to agree," Hywel said. "Although you have to admit that she could have left on her own, without telling anyone."

"Gwen wouldn't—" Gareth stopped. He and Hywel studied each other and Gareth guessed Hywel's thoughts mirrored his: *She wouldn't leave Aber without telling me, would she?*

Hywel nodded. "We are in agreement that she could have left without telling one of us—even both of us—but I don't believe she would have left her family overnight without their knowledge."

Gareth eased back against the wall, mirroring Hywel. "She cares too much about Gwalchmai to want him to worry. She might have lied, but she would have told him something."

"And she did not." Hywel stepped to the open doorway, looked through it, and motioned to someone beyond that Gareth couldn't see.

"Yes, sir?" *Evan.*

"We're done here." Hywel held out his hand for the key.

With a wary expression on his face, Evan handed it to Hywel, who pulled the door shut behind him, locked it, and handed it back. He strode away. Gareth poked his nose through the small window in the door.

"You're not the only one who's angry, Gareth," Evan said, his voice low. "Your friends are with you. You've done no more than your duty, as we all have."

"I know that," Gareth said. "I don't blame you. I've been as much blindsided by these events as anyone."

Evan stepped closer so their faces were a foot apart, albeit separated by the door. "That's the problem isn't it? Nobody could have foreseen Gwen's abduction." He gestured helplessly. "Nobody but the killer."

Gareth nodded to appease his friend, even though Gareth knew the truth was far more complicated than that. It wasn't as if he'd forgotten that someone could hurt Gwen. He hadn't considered it at all, which made the whole situation far worse. It was one thing for the killer to attack Gareth—to poison him—it was quite another for him to abduct her. *And for Gwen herself...* Gareth's mind shied away from what might be happening to her.

"King Owain's anger has lost its fire," Evan said. "He's gone cold—cold even to Cristina."

"You think that's better?" Gareth said with a laugh. "It doesn't sound like it."

Even snorted. "To my mind, the King is much more manageable when he's hot. Frozen as he is, he's likely to hang you at dawn because he can."

Gareth stared at Evan, waiting for his assurance that Hywel wouldn't let that happen. It didn't come. Instead, Evan said, "If I find Gwen, I'll let you know."

"Thank you," Gareth said.

Let me out of here!

Unconsciously, Gareth's hands fisted and his body coiled to launch himself at Evan's throat. He would have, too, if the window hadn't been too small to admit him. Evan gave no sign that he'd read Gareth's thoughts. He shrugged, turned away, and settled onto a stool beside the door with his arms folded across his chest and his legs stretched out in front of him.

Gradually, the noise from the courtyard died down and the castle quieted. Horses shifted in their stalls, easing into more comfortable stances for sleep. One whickered. Then nothing. Gareth leaned against the far wall of his cell, watching the play of light and shadow coming through the crack he'd made in the side wall. He was studying the damaged board, contemplating kicking all the way through it and taking his chances in the courtyard, when Hywel came back.

Praise be to God!

"Come," Hywel said, as if he'd been gone only a moment instead of hours. He unlocked the door and pushed it open. "My men have Braith and extra provisions for you." He held out a cloak to Gareth who took it and swung it around his shoulders.

"Do you have my sword?"

"Here." Hywel handed it to him.

Without haste, though his hands trembled, Gareth buckled the belt around his waist and loosened the sword in its sheath. Hywel hadn't brought his knives, but Gareth wasn't going to test his luck by asking for them. He could overlook their absence as the price to pay for freedom. Silently, Gareth followed Hywel from the stables. He didn't ask why or wherefore, just accepted that Hywel had made a move in his so-called game.

Nobody guarded the postern gate, which told Gareth that Hywel had used his considerable influence to arrange things the way he wanted them. The door didn't even creak when Hywel opened it. They filed silently through it, walked alongside the curtain wall until they reached the southern corner, and then headed across the cleared space that surrounded Aber. No shout came from the walls, though that might have had less to do with Hywel's planning and more to do with the pitch-black night and heavy cloud cover. It had rained while he'd been in the cell—he'd known of it because of the dripping in the corner, and thus the need for the bucket that Gareth had enjoyed kicking.

Now, the grass and dirt in the field squished under his boots and he trod carefully so as not to slip. Once through the field, they entered the trees to the west of the castle. It was even darker than before, if that was possible, and he struggled to keep up with the still-silent Hywel. Soon, they reached a trail that led northwest. And at last, Hywel began to talk.

"After I left you, I circled the wall, looking for any sign that a member of the garrison, rather than simply workman, had left the castle on foot. We found boot prints outside the postern gate— the one we just came through. One pair of shoes had sunk so heavily into the mud that the man either weighed double me or carried something heavy."

"You're thinking it was a man carrying Gwen?" Gareth said.

"Could be," Hywel said. "The guards on the wall had no answers for me, nor did the men working on the wall, as they don't use the postern gate. Nobody saw anything amiss and I had no one left to question."

"So you talked to Madog," Gareth said. That's what he would have done, every time.

"Of course," Hywel said. "It just so happened that I found him in the presence of my father, who swore that he'd given none of the lords permission to leave Aber and that it was inconceivable that any of them would have defied him."

Even in the darkness, Gareth recognized the tone Hywel's voice took on when he knew something that others didn't and that he'd accompanied the knowledge with a smirk. "Go on," Gareth said.

"Madog begged to differ—and begged is not too strong a word in this case as my father's sentiments are well known. He hates being contradicted or proved wrong... Anyway, Madog told my father that Prince Cadwaladr had left before dawn with all of his men."

Gareth halted abruptly, stunned. "And nobody noticed? King Owain didn't notice?"

Hywel had walked another pace before realizing that Gareth had stopped. He paused and turned back. "The next Council meeting isn't until tomorrow—or rather, today," Hywel said, with a quick check for the moon, which the clouds still veiled. Gareth, for his part, had no idea what time it was. "Too many people are staying at Aber right now to keep track of them all. Apparently Cadwaladr told Madog he would return before the evening meal, which, of course, he did not."

"How did your father take this information?"

Hywel paused, choosing his words carefully. "Not well. Coming hard on my assertions of my faith in you—and Cristina's admissions—it made him fear that his trust in Cadwaladr has been misplaced." Hywel continued walking. Gareth fell in beside him. "It does not please my father to find himself in error."

"I can imagine," Gareth said.

"Did you know that Gwen cursed Cadwaladr when he ordered your imprisonment?" Hywel said. "I warned her to stay away from him."

"You should have warned him to stay away from her." Gareth's sudden anger threw him off his stride and he took a deep breath to calm himself.

"Cadwaladr wouldn't have listened to me," Hywel said. "If he spirited her out of Aber without anyone seeing, it implicates him in Anarawd's death far more than anything else he could have done."

"I have no doubts, now," Gareth said.

"But you are biased," Hywel said, matter-of-factly. "I still think Cadell is good for it."

"Is that because you don't want him marrying your sister?" Gareth said. It was impertinent, but Cadell's excessive effusiveness rubbed Hywel the wrong way too, and Gareth had seen the disgust in Hywel's face when he'd looked at him at table.

Hywel didn't dignify that with a response. "Be that as it may, I'm coming around to your way of thinking." He put a hand on Gareth's arm. "You have to be prepared for what he might have done to Gwen, Gareth."

Gareth clenched his fists. *Rape? Murder?* "She's not dead," Gareth said. "I would know it."

Hywel didn't contradict him. "It may have been her dead body that got carried through the postern gate, but somehow I doubt it. It would have been far easier for her to die in any of number of ways—even smothered in her sleep—than for Cadwaladr to kill her and hide the body."

"We've one missing body as it is," Gareth said. "Surely that's enough."

"Anarawd," Hywel said. "But he was dead to start with."

Gareth nodded, glad to move on from Gwen's demise as a topic. "Does your father—"

"—know I've released you?" Hywel said. "No."

"Was that wise?"

"Who cares for Gwen more than you?" Hywel continued walking up the trail. "Besides, you know how to track and fight. And you know Cadwaladr, perhaps better than I do."

"I've fought with him, or rather, for him," Gareth said.

Hywel smirked. "Never did much fighting himself, did he? Much like Anarawd. That ambush must have been a shock."

"What did you say?" Gareth said, confused. "Anarawd didn't like to fi—"

"Never mind," Hywel said, interrupting and changing tack again. "We'll leave it that King Owain tasked me with finding Gwen and that I will do, using whatever means I believe necessary."

Gareth nodded to himself. That was the metal that lay beneath Hywel's open-hearted façade—and the part of him he'd gotten from his father.

"When I tracked the footprints from the postern gate, they entered the woods just as we did," Hywel said. "Then they disappeared, replaced by dozens of hoof prints. My guess is that whoever took Gwen met up with the rest of his company."

"Just as, I hope, we will?" Gareth said.

"Ahead," Hywel said.

Good as his word, after another quarter mile of walking, the trail came out on the road that headed west from Aber to Bangor and Caernarfon. When they reached it, half a dozen of Hywel's men stood in a clearing to the side of the road. Relieved to know they wouldn't be doing this alone, Gareth clasped Evan's forearm in greeting.

"They've been waiting for you," Hywel said. "These were the ones who most objected to seeing you locked up in the first place."

"In truth, a dozen more wanted to ride with us, but my brother settled for six." Rhun grinned, his bright hair gleaming gold in the torchlight.

Evan laughed. "Madog told me if our young prince here didn't break you out before the King hanged you, he'd do it himself. He'll be glad that he didn't have to test his resolve."

"I told Evan it'd be good for you, being locked up," another man piped up, this one named Alun. Like Evan, he was of an age with Gareth, in his late twenties, though he'd been part of Hywel's guard since Hywel became a man ten years before. "Teach you patience."

Gareth laughed. "Thanks, gentlemen ... my lords," he said, touched by their concern. "I'm none the worse for the experience. I *am* worried about Gwen."

Immediately, everyone sobered. Here they were, past midnight, on the road half-way between Aber and the village of Bangor, and Gwen had been missing since before dawn.

"We have every reason to believe that she's alive," Hywel said. "Perhaps he thinks he can use her as a bargaining chip."

Hywel didn't say who *he* was, but they all were thinking *Cadwaladr*. The evilness of the deed made Gareth sick to his stomach. As long as Cadwaladr believed Gwen to be useful to him, she would be safe. At the same time, while she meant something to Gareth himself, he still didn't see why Cadwaladr would place value on her life. He obviously thought she knew enough to indict him, thus the abduction. But why not simply kill her? Gareth kept his fears to himself. Better for his friends to view this as a rescue rather than as a quest for revenge.

Since he'd left Cadwaladr's service, he hadn't often had cause to think about the man himself—had, in fact, avoided thinking about him and what he'd done for him—but even after his dismissal, Gareth wouldn't have guessed Cadwaladr would go as far as this. Still, a man never knew what was in another man's heart, even his own brother's. It seemed clear now that Gareth's milk brother, Bran, had betrayed Anarawd. At Cadwaladr's behest? It sickened Gareth to think on it.

21

The small company rode through the early hours of the morning, stopping every now and then for Gareth to dismount and ensure they still followed the proper path. Even though much of the stonework of the old Roman road remained, grass and dirt had made headway between the rocks and revealed traces of a recent passage of men and horses. Cadwaladr's company hadn't tried to disguise their route. Like the act of killing Anarawd itself, it revealed a disturbing overconfidence.

At Caernarfon, some fifteen miles west of Aber, the trail ended, along with the road. Gareth dismounted to crouch beside the last traces of hoof prints, embedded deep in the sandy soil ten feet from the edge of the swift-flowing waters of the Menai Straits, which were just visible beneath the light of the waning moon that had finally managed to peek through the clouds. The other men stopped beside him and stared across the Straits to the opposite shore. Anglesey, the bread basket of Gwynedd, lay before them.

The water slopped at his feet, about half-way between high and low tide. The rest of the footprints had washed away. Cadwaladr's company, if they'd had any sense, had taken the ferry across the Straits nine hours before, when the tide was at its lowest.

"It's Aberffraw, isn't it?" Gareth said to Hywel, who trotted his horse close to where Gareth stood.

"That's my guess as well," Hywel said. "I've thought so all along."

I've thought so all along. As Gareth stared across the Straits, his prince beside him, Gareth understood Hywel as he never had before. Unlike most men, Hywel never lied to himself. He might not know what was at stake with every task he undertook, but he was clear-eyed about what he knew and what he didn't know.

His stance and tone told Gareth that this particular venture was only beginning and that Hywel was prepared for it going *bad* to a degree that surpassed anything they'd ever experienced. It wasn't that people were going to die, though they might, but that Hywel understood one true thing: that by bringing Cadwaladr to justice—if indeed that became necessary—he would break his father's heart. By doing so, he would put himself, as the bringer of bad news, in a more precarious position than any he'd ever been in before.

In that light, Hywel's choice to bring Rhun with them, or rather, to allow him to come along, was no longer odd. Rhun was always ready for adventure—in many ways he was more reckless than Hywel—but he'd not taken part in any of Hywel's tasks up until this night. King Owain protected his eldest son, and thus he rarely participated in the less savory aspects of ruling Gwynedd.

But he was here, now, because Hywel knew that if Rhun told King Owain that Cadwaladr had stolen Gwen; if Rhun told his father that Cadwaladr had been behind the murder of Anarawd and his men, his father would believe him when he couldn't bring himself to believe Hywel.

For Gareth's part, he no longer had any doubts.

Evan sighed. "I'll see about waking the ferryman."

"Best to cross once it's light. I'd say we have three hours to rest." Hywel made a small motion with his hand to settle the men. "If we wait for the slack water before the turn of the tide, the water will be at its calmest and lowest."

Nodding their acquiescence, the rest of the men dismounted. Gareth continued to stare across the Straits. A light flared in the distance. Perhaps it came from a fire burning in an open pit and he imagined Gwen sleeping beside it. He measured the distance from shore to shore, wishing he could ride to her immediately. But Hywel was right: he couldn't rescue Gwen single-handedly and it would be foolhardy to try to swim the Straits in the dark. The Menai Straits were not something a man should take lightly.

Strong men and too many ships to count had foundered in its waters—at times deceptively slow and at others, moving so fast the current could pull a man under and out into the Irish Sea before anyone could save him. That was not a fate that any of them wanted to share.

Besides, if Gwen was still alive, she wasn't sleeping next to a fire pit but was already at Aberffraw. The castle lay on the western shore of Anglesey, only five miles from where Gareth stood. Aberffraw had always been the seat of the Royal House of Gwynedd. Its construction dated back to Rhodri Mawr, who ruled Gwynedd two hundred years before, and possibly even earlier to the great Cunedda, the legendary founder of the kingdom of Wales.

The castle had been decimated at various times: by Viking raiders from the north and west; by Normans from the east—the last before King Owain's father had retaken Anglesey from them over twenty years ago. When King Owain succeeded to Gwynedd after the death of his father, he began reconstructing Aberffraw anew, quarrying stone from the east coast of the island and bringing slate from Snowdonia. Meanwhile he lived primarily at Aber, which if nothing else was a more convenient location for his many subjects to find him.

"Rest easy, Gareth." Evan stopped at Gareth's right shoulder to look across the water with him. "Cadwaladr will not have harmed her."

Gareth turned to look at him. "Why do you say that?"

"He had plenty of opportunity between Aber and here to kill her and dispose of the body," Evan said. "Did he?"

"No," Gareth said. "We would have seen the signs."

"Exactly," Evan said. "That means she still serves a purpose—and it's not to warm his bed. I'm not saying he's above that, but I've never heard that Cadwaladr enjoys forcing women, for all his other faults."

Gareth clenched his teeth, but nodded and returned his gaze to the water moving in front of him. Come Owain Gwynedd's wrath, prison cell, or the very gates of hell, he was never letting Gwen out of his sight again.

22

"**J**esus! I wish he would hurry!" Rhun cursed from beside Gareth.

"Only a little while longer, my lord." Gareth eyed the ferryman's placid poling. "We'll soon reach the other side."

As Hywel had planned, it was half an hour before low tide, the best time to cross the Straits. They all had to get across within that half hour, however, because once the tide turned, the current would shift so suddenly, it could capsize the boats. Unhindered, Gareth could swim (and had swum) the Straits, but that was as a youth. These were grown men—heavier, worried, out of practice— and in some cases, afraid of the water. The bards sang of the Welsh being caught between the mountains and the sea. But for the some of these men—those raised inland—the sea was as foreign as Ireland or London.

The fog had risen to coat the trees, the shoreline, and the company in damp cobwebs of mist. Normally, that would have bothered Gareth, because it meant an enemy might sneak up on them unawares. In this case, however, it allowed them to cross the water unseen. He thought it unlikely that Cadwaladr had left scouts to watch the shore. The arrogant prince wasn't a good enough soldier for that, even if some of his men knew better. It was one of the problems Gareth had encountered in serving in his company: Cadwaladr's bravado wouldn't let him admit when he didn't have all the answers.

It might even be that Cadwaladr had yet to admit that he'd done anything wrong in taking Gwen from Aber. His highest moral imperative was his own well-being. Anything that ensured it, Cadwaladr believed, was for the greater good of all.

At last, the men gathered on the opposite shore, all in one piece. Gareth fought down shivers from the cold wind that blew from the west and checked his belongings before mounting. Then, Hywel and Rhun led them away from the Straits, down a narrow pathway that led to a wider road a half a mile from the shore.

Once away from the water, the fog dissipated, revealing a remarkably beautiful day. Anglesey as a whole was comprised of flat farmland with rich crops, which upon harvest, were shared—sold, bartered, tithed—with the people of mainland Gwynedd. Now in mid-August, the wheat was nearly ready to harvest and the land was a patchwork of green, blue, and gold.

The road went north-west from the Straits, through a region with farmland to the east and extensive mudflats to the west, interspersed with stands of well-leafed trees that thrived in the marshy land. Aberffraw had been built on one of the few hills on Anglesey.

The Welsh had occupied that hilltop since before the Romans came. The foundations, then, were older than even the

Roman fort that superseded it. Many other Welsh castles had been built the same way, on older foundations, rather than building from scratch. That was how Aber was blessed with an entire room devoted to bathing, not to mention two narrow tunnels leading from the main building, one heading south, towards Aber Falls, and the second to the beach.

Another half a mile and the castle rose before them, the top of the gatehouse just visible above the trees that lined the road on either side. Although Rhun outranked him, it was Hywel who raised a hand to stop the company. Rhun had (delightedly) made clear from the start that this was Hywel's task while Rhun was just along for the ride. Obeying Hywel's unspoken order, the company turned off the road and into the woods to the west of it. The men circled around Hywel, expectant.

"What now?" Rhun said. Then, at Hywel's uncharacteristic silence, he threw back his head and laughed in perfect imitation of their father. "No wonder you've been so silent for the last five miles. You don't actually have a plan, just now, do you?" Hywel had the grace to smile sheepishly. His brother was one of the few who could get away with that kind of comment. Rhun slapped Hywel on the shoulder. "Never mind. You'll think of something. You always do."

"I was waiting to see if Aberffraw was truly our destination before formulating one," Hywel said. His words didn't come out defensive, just matter-of-fact. "I need to know what we're dealing with." He pointed a finger at Gareth. "Three of you circle around the fort to the south and west, three to the north. Feel free to draw their attention—and their arrows. I want to know what we're up against. Alun will stay with me and watch the front gate. If my uncle means us no harm, this will be like singing scales. If he orders his archers to shoot..."

"He's not that much a fool," Rhun said, ever the optimist.

Hywel met Gareth's gaze with a skeptical one of his own. "We'll meet back here in half an hour. At that point, I'll need to speak with Cadwaladr, if he is, indeed, here. We must know if Gwen is his prisoner."

"If he's here, he has Gwen," Gareth said.

"Likely," Hywel said, "but I owe it to all of us—and to my father—to be sure."

With a chorus of "my lords," the men dispersed to their tasks. Gareth had the luck to partner with Rhun and Evan. They surreptitiously crossed the Ffraw River before it opened into the estuary, and, a quarter mile from the entrance to the castle, slipped from tree to tree, careful not to give the watchers on the wall of the castle above them any glimpse of their passage. Not yet anyway. Gareth didn't expect Cadwaladr to leave sentries down here. The view from the castle walls would provide him with all the warning he needed if anyone got too close.

At one point, Gareth thought he caught a glimpse of a face in an upper floor window and stopped. "Evan, your eyes are better than mine. What do you see?"

Evan peered through the trees to get a better look. "A woman. Could be Gwen."

A few dozen yards further, the forest could hide them no longer. It hadn't been thick to begin with, but the closer they got to the beach, the more scrub-like the trees became. Once they petered out entirely, grass and sand were all that stood between them and the ever-widening Ffraw River. On one side, it wended it's way the last half-mile to the sea, while on the other, the castle sat on its higher hill above the north bank of the river.

It was Gareth's job to protect the trio's southern flank and he scanned the grass, looking for archers or traps. Consequently, he didn't see the threat on the other side until Rhun grasped his shoulder and pulled him down into the grass.

"Watch out!"

A heartbeat later, an arrow slammed into the sand where Gareth had been standing a moment before. Scrambling behind a scrubby bush, the three men crouched among the cheat grass, thankful they'd tied their horses a hundred paces away, out of sight and arrow range.

"So much for finding a peaceful solution," Gareth said. "Cadwaladr doesn't mean well."

"It gets worse," Evan said, looking around the bush, first at the castle and then at the water behind them.

"How so?" Rhun said, his back to a too-small dune.

Evan jerked his head. A hundred yards away, on a half-moon of sand created by a bend in the river, three Danish ships rested. Six men guarded them—two to a boat. Bad enough that the Danes outnumbered them two to one, but each ship was big enough to carry an additional fifteen men. Those were odds that would give even Hywel pause. Knowing it, the Danish guards smirked at them, not even bothering to stir from their posts. Instead, they had the look of men watching an archery contest from a ringside seat.

"We have to get back," Gareth said. "This is already more than we bargained for."

Rhun took in a deep breath and tipped back his head, gazing at the wispy clouds above their heads. "Uncle Cadwaladr," he said, hissing through his teeth. "Why are you doing this?"

"It won't please your father, that's for sure," Evan said.

"The real question is what has Cadwaladr gotten himself into—and does he know how to get himself out of it again?" Rhun said. "Danish allies are not to be taken lightly and if my uncle reneges on any deal he's made, they'll kill him and sleep untroubled afterwards, even if he is Owain Gwynedd's brother."

"He'll be telling himself that it seemed like a good idea at the time," Gareth said.

"That's where all bad ideas start, don't they?" Evan said.

"And end the same way too," Gareth said. "He'll expect that King Owain will get him out of whatever trouble he's made."

"He'll have to surrender to Hywel," Rhun said. "He can't possibly believe he'll get away with this."

Oh yes he can, Gareth said, but only to himself.

Rhun peered over the top of the bush. He was rewarded for his efforts with another arrow that just skimmed off the top of a dune and over their heads.

"If they're meaning to miss, it's not by much," Evan said.

"I'm worried about our friends on the other side of the castle," Gareth said.

"We've only a few men," Rhun said. "We're not a threat—out here or at the gate—and Cadwaladr knows it. He's playing with us."

"That may be," Gareth said, "but these arrows aren't shot from toy bows."

"For the love of Christ, my lord," Evan said. "See reason. Cadwaladr's men are *shooting* at you, the heir to throne of Gwynedd!"

"He doesn't know—" Rhun stopped and shook his head. "Uncle Cadwaladr would know better than to harm one of King Owain's sons."

"Well he damn well should know it," Evan said. "But he doesn't, else he wouldn't be shooting at all. Who does he think we are? Normans?"

"Perhaps he's too scared to think straight?" Rhun said.

"Scared?" Gareth gestured towards the castle. "Maybe Cadwaladr is frightened beneath all that bluster, but if I had forty-five Danishmen at my back, I wouldn't fear much. Certainly not us when we're out here and he's in there."

"I could come back here with an army in a day," Rhun said. "Cadwaladr has to understand that."

As Rhun spoke, Gareth caught a flash of color from the trees. It was Alun, waving for them to come in. "It's time to find out what's going on," Gareth said.

With a glance among themselves for reassurance and a *one, two, three*, the three men dashed across the grass to the cover of the trees. They reached it before the assailants on the wall loosed any more arrows. Stopping to look back up at the castle from the safety of the woods, Gareth strained to see Gwen's face again but couldn't.

"I saw her too," Alun said, without having to ask for whom he was looking. "She's gone now. Whatever we've started, it's pushed Cadwaladr into action."

23

The companions trotted through the woods to the spot to which Hywel had retreated, still under the cover of the trees, some hundred yards from the castle gate. A good archer was easily accurate at that distance, which was why Owain Gwynedd had cleared the trees around the castle to that extent. The sea air and wind had kept stunted the plants that tried to grow back.

As Gareth and Rhun rode up to him, Hywel acknowledged them with a nod. "Stay in the woods at first. If I show either of you to Cadwaladr, he'll realize the game is up. I can't decide if I want that or not."

"Whatever we do, we can't play the same game Cadwaladr is playing," Gareth said. "He will set a trap for us. We must avoid it."

"No doubt." Hywel turned his head, studying Aberffraw's façade. "He doesn't know my father well if he thinks he'll let the murder of Anarawd and his men pass."

"We still don't know if we can lay that at his door," Rhun said. "He has taken Gwen. That is all we know."

"Then we must force him to admit it," Hywel said. "He has something up his sleeve, something that worries me. Taking Gwen is far too confident a move for a man who has plotted against the King of Gwynedd, even if he and my father are brothers."

"What he has, brother," Rhun said, "are three dozen Danes in the fort with him. Their boats lie on the beach, guarded by six more."

Hywel turned his attention to Rhun, his face expressionless, but then his eyes twinkled and a smile hovered around his lips. "So that's it. Cadwaladr has mortgaged all of Ceredigion on this venture. We'll have to make it so he can't pay."

Gareth took in a deep breath, glad that Hywel saw the presence of the Danes as positive news. He couldn't agree. "If we show Cadwaladr our numbers, which he may have already guessed, he'll know that King Owain hasn't sent an army just yet. Nor had the time to put one together on the off chance Cadwaladr came to Aberffraw."

"Let him know we want to see Gwen and we just want her back," Rhun said.

"She's a bargaining chip," Hywel said. "He'll use her as a hostage to gain safe passage to the boats on the beach."

"Are you going to allow that?" Gareth said.

"I want Gwen back too," Hywel said. "If we let Cadwaladr go now, we can deal with him later on our terms. Or my father can. Ceredigion is not so far from Gwynedd that we can't pen him in there. And if Cadell learns of his treachery, that he was behind Anarawd's murder, Cadwaladr will have nowhere to turn."

"Unless Cadell conspired with Cadwaladr," Gareth said.

Rhun's eyes widened at the idea, but Hywel laughed. "With the plot discovered, do you think Cadell would admit to it? No, he'll stand with my father in that event."

While Gareth and Rhun watched from the trees, the remaining five men mounted their horses and urged them to a spot fifty paces from the front gate. That they were on horseback would give them an opportunity to flee if Cadwaladr ordered his men to shoot. For all Cadwaladr's perfidy so far, Hywel assumed it wouldn't come to that.

After some shouting and a short wait, Cadwaladr appeared above the gatehouse, resting an arm along the top of the wall. "Hello, nephew. You asked to speak to me on some matter?"

Gareth had no trouble hearing the exchange, even from a distance.

"I would like you to return Gwen ferch Meilyr to me," Hywel said.

"I'm afraid I can't do that," Cadwaladr said.

"And why is that?"

"I took her from Aber to keep her safe from the man who murdered Anarawd." Cadwaladr said. "When Gareth hangs, I will release her."

Gareth's mouth twisted at Cadwaladr's confidence and the smile that accompanied his words sent chills down Gareth's spine. "Did I hear that right?" Gareth asked Rhun. "He actually said that he took Gwen to protect her?"

"It's a reason that could be believed, if we didn't know more than he thinks we do," Rhun said.

Hywel was unmoved. "I can't leave—I will not—until I have Gwen beside me."

"I'm afraid I can't give her up to you," Cadwaladr said. "It's too dangerous for her."

"Let me be the judge of that," Hywel said.

Cadwaladr gave an exaggerated sigh. "The perils of youth. So tragic... ."

"Uncle—" Hywel said, his tone a warning.

Cadwaladr straightened. "Are these all of your men?" He gestured casually with one hand. "You brought so few."

"Not all," Hywel said. "What of the Aberffraw garrison?"

At Hywel's words, Gareth's eyes snapped to the top of the wall. Hywel had noticed what he had not—that everyone along the top of the wall belonged to Cadwaladr in some fashion, rather than men who'd sworn allegiance to King Owain.

Cadwaladr shrugged. "No harm has come to them. Has my brother hanged the traitor yet?"

"Not yet." Hywel canted his head to one side, as if curious, and tried again. "Give Gwen back to me, Uncle. She doesn't need to stay here to be safe. I can protect her."

"I don't agree," Cadwaladr said.

"Why do you care for her so?"

"Ah." Cadwaladr smiled. "It is not I who cares for her, but you."

"So you didn't take her to protect her from Gareth, but to hurt me?" Hywel said. "How can that be?"

Silence. Gareth nodded, recognizing that Cadwaladr had said something he shouldn't have and was now uncertain as to how to continue. Hywel studied his uncle, letting him think for another few heartbeats, but it was Rhun who spoke next. He walked his horse forward, out from under the trees. Cadwaladr's eyes widened at the sight of him. He had to know that Rhun's presence was not a good sign for him.

"My father knows now that you ordered the death of King Anarawd," Rhun said, showing an aptitude for bluffing for which Gareth wouldn't have given him credit. "That you refuse to give up Gwen only deepens your predicament, not aids it. Release her and give the Danes with whom you are in league leave to return to their boats. If you do these things, now, without hesitation, I will speak to my father on your behalf."

"I did not kill Anarawd," Cadwaladr said.

"Nobody said you killed him," Hywel said, "but you paid mercenaries from Ireland to do the job for you." He tipped his chin towards the men on either side of Cadwaladr. "Danes such as these. We have enough evidence to convict you with what has happened here, but were we to cage you at Aberffraw while Rhun and I traveled to your seat in Ceredigion, do you think I wouldn't find more?"

"And yet you come here with only six men," Cadwaladr said, the sneer back in place. "You're still guessing at the truth."

"I'm not." Hywel waved a hand in Gareth's direction, indicating that he should join them.

Marveling at the case Hywel had built out of nothing, Gareth obeyed, urging Braith forward. He came into view and Cadwaladr paled. "You! But—"

"I have not been hanged, as you can see," Gareth said, closing the door on the trap Hywel had set. "Nor will I be. I am free and in the company of King Owain's sons. You cannot hide the truth from us any longer, Cadwaladr."

But that impertinence, coming from someone he'd dismissed for disobedience and reviled in the years afterwards, was too much for Cadwaladr. The prince cursed, shook his fist once at Hywel, and shoved his way past his men on the walkway. He raced away along the balustrade to where it connected to the upper floor of the hall.

"Uh oh." That was Evan.

"Damn," Hywel said. "What now?"

"We need another plan, brother," Rhun said. "And quick."

24

They came for me.

Gwen had screamed Gareth's name when the first arrow flew at him, though fear had constricted her lungs and the sound hadn't traveled all the way down to the beach. She'd felt a change in the atmosphere in the fort—whether it was the running feet and shouting in the courtyard below her, or simply the sense of urgency permeating the castle—such that when Gareth, Rhun, and Evan had appeared on the edge of the river, and then dived behind the bush to avoid that arrow, she hadn't been surprised. Terrified for them, but not surprised.

And it wasn't going to be just them either. If Gareth was out of prison, with Rhun beside him, then Hywel was here too, proving yet again that he was completely reliable when it mattered most.

Gwen waited, listening for footsteps outside her door that would tell her change was coming. She didn't yet know what that change was going to be, or if she would survive it, but she felt that anything was better than spending any more time alone in this bare room. She'd spent so many years here, alone or with Hywel. If her father hadn't fallen out with Owain, she might have been born, lived, and died at Aberffraw.

Just as Gareth and the others raced back to the cover of the trees, thankfully unharmed, one of Cadwaladr's men entered her room. Gwen spun around at his approach, but all he did was elbow her away from the window and latch it. "Prince Cadwaladr's orders," he said.

Then he grasped her arm and walked her out the door to a low stool in the corridor. "Sit."

Gwen sat. The guard propped himself against the wall, his arms folded across his chest. She studied him for a moment, and a new coldness swept through her when she realized that she'd seen him before—at Aber, of course, but more importantly at Dolwyddelan Castle, before all of this started.

"What are we waiting for?" Gwen said, when she couldn't stand the silence any longer.

"New orders," he said.

"Where is Cadwaladr?"

The man glanced at her, his expression unreadable.

Frustrated, Gwen tried a new line of attack. "I saw you talking to that stable boy at Dolwyddelan," she said, even though she hadn't. "Given that he ended up dead, your role in all this seems clear. Maybe you killed the servant at Aber too, after she failed to murder Gareth."

The man stared at her hard-eyed, and then looked away, still not answering. Time crawled by as Gwen tried to imagine what was happening outside. At least in the hallway she could more easily hear what was going on inside the castle. Footsteps pounded below her, echoing through the walls, but why the men were running and where they were running to, she couldn't tell.

Maybe they're abandoning the fort? A woman would be a needless hindrance on a sea journey, and since Hywel had obviously followed Cadwaladr from Aber, Cadwaladr could surely gain nothing by keeping her prisoner. "Are you going to let me go? Surely there's no sense in following Cadwaladr in this?"

Irritation—and something else, disbelief?—crossed the man's face, but still he didn't speak and time stretched out with every beat of Gwen's heart. Then, finally, the man straightened, looking towards a door at the far end of the hallway that led to the battlements and Gwen focused on it too. A moment later, the door burst open. Cadwaladr himself bounded into the building. He reached her in three strides and lifted her bodily off her stool.

"Let me go!" Gwen hadn't fought when his men had taken her from Aber, but now she instinctively resisted. She kicked at him and tried to wrench away.

"You will do as I say!" Before she could speak again, Cadwaladr had her pressed against the wall, his fingers around her neck. "Do as I command or you will die."

Gwen struggled for breath, staring into Cadwaladr's face. He held her there for a long count of ten before releasing her and stepping back. Her neck stung from where his fingernails had bit into her skin and she gagged, holding her throat with one hand and breathing hard.

"Will you obey?" He stared down at her, his hands on his hips, as she bent over, still gasping.

"I will," Gwen said. Better to give in now while he still seemed to want her alive, on the chance she could escape later.

Cadwaladr grabbed her arm. "Damn right you will."

He half-dragged, half-carried her down the hall to the far door that he'd just come through. Men, both Danish and Welsh, lined the battlements leading to the upper storey of the gatehouse. The Danes with their smirks and long, untied hair were a contrast to the Welshmen, many of whom had hair shorn short and trim beards. At Cadwaladr's appearance and the sight of Gwen's struggles, they wore expressions ranging from a completely blank face, for those who'd spent more time in Cadwaladr's service, to outright horror—quickly suppressed as Cadwaladr and she approached.

Gwen, for her part, once they were outside, stopped dragging her feet and walked with him, since there was no way for her to escape with so many of his men about. Cadwaladr urged her along the wall until he stood with her at the top of the gatehouse. He placed himself directly behind her, using her as a shield. The wind had picked up since Gwen first stood in her window and the flag above her head streamed full out, pointing east, towards Aber. Below them, Gareth, Hywel, Rhun, and four others—all Hywel's men—sat astride their horses. She tried not to be disappointed that they weren't backed by more soldiers, though three had their bows up and arrows nocked.

"Release those arrows and the girl dies," Cadwaladr said.

Nobody moved. Hywel kept his face impassive. Gareth swallowed hard. Rhun opened his mouth to speak, but then closed it as Hywel made a slight movement with his hand to stay him.

"In truth, why should I care?" Hywel said. "We have bowmen and knights among us. Properly positioned, we can cut down any who attempt to leave Aberffraw. In a day, the King will be here with an army. Kill the girl or not. Our orders will not change."

"You can't fool me," Cadwaladr said. "You don't mean what you say. Not when Gwen carries your child."

Jaws dropped on both sides of the wall. Gwen hastily closed her mouth before Cadwaladr became aware of her shock, but even Hywel couldn't keep the surprise out of his face. He stared at Cadwaladr, transferred his gaze to Gwen who tried to stare stonily back, and then turned to speak to his brother and Gareth. They pressed close in brief consultation. Gareth became animated, gesticulating with one hand and stabbing a finger towards Cadwaladr.

Cadwaladr's decision to kidnap instead of kill her now made a lot more sense. For all Hywel's liaisons, he'd yet to father a child that lived, mortality among infants and mothers being what it was. Rhun, too, had produced no children. Although he was two years older than Hywel—approaching twenty-five—he was more circumspect in his liaisons. If Gwen was genuinely pregnant, it would be King Owain's first grandchild. Cadwaladr was right to think that Hywel—and the King—would take that very seriously.

"Who told you?" Gwen said. The revelation explained everything, and yet was so stunning, she could barely get the words out, much less call down to Gareth to tell him that that it wasn't true. Of course, Hywel knew it wasn't true.

"Cristina."

Gwen choked on a mixture of hysteria and laughter at the name. Cristina appeared to be a meddler and a trouble-maker of the worst sort, playing both sides against the middle as she saw fit. Her gambit with the seal still left Gwen gasping, since it was only through her that King Cadell could have known Gareth had it; at the same time, convincing Cadwaladr that Gwen was Hywel's mistress may have saved Gwen's life, but it also had drawn his attention to her in the first place. Who knew if it was this knowledge that had given him the idea that he could use her? If Gwen ever saw Cristina again—if she lived through the next moments—she had a mind to throttle her.

Hywel faced forward again. "Let her go, Uncle. Using Gwen as a shield will gain you nothing."

Cadwaladr lifted his chin and his voice, defiant as ever. "So you are beginning to see reason." He smiled his satisfaction, while at the same time tightening his grip on Gwen's waist.

"Let her go, uncle," Rhun said. "You don't want to do this."

"I think I do," Cadwaladr said. From a sheath at his side, he produced a knife and slipped it under Gwen's chin. Gwen strained to lift herself out of its range, but of course Cadwaladr just moved with her. She hoped that those on the ground could see it well enough to know if the blade had a notch. She couldn't get a close look. At the sight of it, Gareth gave an audible gasp and Hywel put out his arm to stop him from speaking, or throwing himself at the gate.

"As you wish," Hywel said. "You win this round." He fisted his hand at the men behind him, who lowered their bows.

With that, Cadwaladr seemed to decide something. He sidled along the top of the wall, still hiding behind Gwen's body, which she held as stiffly as she could to avoid the knife. When he reached the stairs that led to the courtyard below, he couldn't hold the knife to her throat and get her down the stairs at the same time, so he put it away. Then he twisted Gwen's arm behind her back and force-marched her down them, his grip so tight it would leave a bruise. In that formation, they crossed the courtyard, heading towards the postern gate.

"Faster, you fool!" Cadwaladr stabbed the finger of his free hand at a man who ran in front of them so he could open the door. Pulling up, Cadwaladr allowed the host of Danish raiders to file past him first before following with Gwen. A glance behind her revealed that Cadwaladr's own men would remain at Aberffraw. She caught the glances of two of them, including the one who'd guarded her in the hallway. His face, as before, told her nothing.

Cadwaladr manhandled her through the door and into the midst of the three dozen Danishmen. Moving faster than she would have thought possible, yet still silent, the Danes escorted them at a run along the pathway that led from the postern gate to the beach. Gwen blinked her eyes against the sun which now blazed down unrelieved by clouds. Noon had come and gone. The boats on the shore a quarter of a mile away drew nearer with every heartbeat.

Gwen struggled against Cadwaladr now, anger conquering her fear. Though her dress hampered her movements, she kicked out, connecting at least once with his shin and forcing him to slow. She made him drag her weight and Cadwaladr cursed and shook her. She hoped he'd fling her aside and leave her behind, even if it meant a fall and a broken arm. Anything would be better than continuing as they were.

Well, almost anything.

"I'll take her," a giant of a Dane said in heavily accented Welsh, though there was a hint of amusement in his voice. He slipped his arm around Gwen's waist.

"No!" Gwen flailed at him with her fists but he batted her hands away, lifted her from Cadwaladr grasp, and threw her over his shoulder. Her arms and head hung down his back and she continued to beat on him, for all the good it did her. His grip around her legs was so strong she couldn't even kick him properly. She certainly couldn't penetrate his leather armor. The tears that had threatened to overwhelm her for the last hours pricked her eyes, though they were more out of frustration and anger than sadness.

Gwen bounced on the Dane's shoulder as they ran down the slope, through the thick grass, to the strip of sandy beach beyond. He crossed the yards to the three ships in three or four strides. Though Gwen arched her back, craning her neck to see where they were going—or even where they'd been—it was a lost cause. Men shouted all around her, mostly in Danish which she didn't speak at all. The men the Danish leader had left to guard the boats must have moved into action the instant their company spilled from the postern gate because by the time the Dane and Gwen reached their designated craft, they'd already pushed off and the boat was in two feet of water.

Gwen still on his shoulder, the big Dane surged into the river and caught the rail of his ship with his right hand. Now that she understood that they really planned to take her away from Aberffraw, Gwen shrieked and beat on the Dane with both fists. She tried to wriggle off of his left shoulder, shifting her hips, but his grip was as strong as ever. Again she tried to kick out with her feet but the best shot she managed only caught her foot in his cloak.

The Dane had started out muttering under his breath at her resistance, but now he laughed and unceremoniously dumped her into the boat. She landed on her rear and fell backwards. Her head glanced off a bench. She lay sprawled as he'd left her, her eyes squeezed shut, catching her breath. She hadn't even gotten her feet wet.

It took hardly any time at all for the rest of the Danish mercenaries to clamber in after her. Her Danish captor himself stepped over the side, his boots shedding water into the bottom of the boat. He reached down, hooked her under her arms and plopped her onto one of the seats set in the middle of the boat so she wouldn't interfere with the rowers. She tried to push up, to better see the shore, but the Dane kept one hand on her shoulder holding her down. Heavily laden, the boat put to sea.

It had all happened so quickly, Gwen hadn't had time to develop any kind of plan. When the Dane moved off to direct one of his men, perhaps thinking her no more of a threat, Gwen spun in her seat. *I have to get out of here!* The panic that accompanied that thought rose in her chest and she swallowed it back down. As with the Dane, the other men were going about their business, not paying attention to her. She scooted towards the side of the boat, peering around the shifting men so she could see what was happening at Aberffraw. The oarsmen bent their backs into their task, chanting out the count in unison.

Beyond the bank, figures appeared around the southern end of the castle. Gwen's heart lifted. *They were coming!* Gareth rode flat out, bent over Braith's neck and racing her down the slope from the castle to the river.

One of the Danes to the rear of the boat shouted a warning and the big Dane raised a fist. His men obeyed and the pace of their strokes increased.

"Pull!"

This came from Cadwaladr, and the order could have been repeated in Danish, or the men might have been muttering *idiot* for all she knew. Certainly the order was unnecessary, as the Dane had gotten his men moving without even having to open his mouth. Gwen hadn't imagined boats could move as quickly. The rhythm was unrelenting and the boats swung into the faster current in the middle of the river. Within a count of ten, Gwen's ship lay fifteen yards off the shore and a good fifty from where they'd entered the water.

Gwen shot one look behind her to see what Cadwaladr was doing. He gazed away from her, west towards Ireland. Grey clouds hung on the horizon, obscuring any view but of the sea. The middle of the Ffraw River was calm but soon they'd leave the safety of the estuary and enter the surging waves at its mouth. Afraid that she'd already hesitated too long, Gwen launched herself from her seat.

She placed one foot on the edge of the boat, pushed upwards with the other, and dove into the water.

Except she never made it. A thick arm caught her around her waist, hauling her back, and a low chuckle sounded in her ear. "You've got spirit," the big Dane said as he spun her around. "I'll give you that."

"Not so fast, my dear." Cadwaladr accepted her weight in his arms and pulled her away from the ship's rail.

And it was from that position, with Cadwaladr's sickening touch around her waist, that Gwen watched the ship leave the estuary and enter Aberffraw harbor. Tears tracked helplessly down Gwen's cheeks as her view of the shore, and her friends, receded into the rising mist.

25

Gareth could only stare, horrified, as the fog and distance obscured Gwen's boat from his view. He slowed Braith, allowing the others to catch up to him. Why hadn't it occurred to him that Cadwaladr would flee so precipitously, and in that direction? It should have. He'd seen the ships. But for him to have left his entire Welsh garrison behind, along with all of their horses, was wholly unexpected. Gareth, Hywel, and Rhun had wasted precious time in front of the gate, dithering, waiting for Cadwaladr to return or for more information, before they'd realized that he wasn't coming back.

Hywel pulled up beside Gareth. For a moment, Gareth couldn't look at him—couldn't bear to look at him—and then he couldn't contain the rage any longer. The blood thrummed in his ears. Even so, he managed to control his voice. "We must know where they're going."

Hywel nodded. "If that ship is bound for Dublin, there's nothing we can do for her. You know that."

"I know it," Gareth said.

"Either way, Cadwaladr's lands in Ceredigion are forfeit," Hywel said. "If we get there and she's there, we'll roust him out. If not… ."

"If not, she's in the hands of the Danes, for as long as they wish to keep her." Gareth gazed out to sea for a long count of three and then turned his head to face his lord. "You haven't denied it."

"You know so little of me that I have to?"

"Yes." The word hissed through Gareth's teeth.

Hywel put a hand on Gareth's arm and Gareth just managed not to twitch away and brush him off. "I swear to you I've never touched her. I think of her as a sister."

Gareth's jaw was so tight he wondered that he hadn't ground his teeth to the nubs. Then his shoulders fell. He'd known it, but it was better that Hywel had said it. "As far as I know, Cadwaladr has it completely wrong. She belongs to no one and isn't carrying any man's child."

"She's smart enough not to admit it to Cadwaladr—or to anyone," Hywel said. "She has time before they discover the deception. Weeks maybe; they'll be back before then."

"Why do you say that?" Gareth said.

Hywel tipped his head to one side. "So many years in Cadwaladr's company, and mine, and that's not clear to you either?"

Gareth felt like the words could have been mocking, but they weren't. Hywel was merely curious. "Tell me," Gareth said.

"Cadwaladr is a child in a man's body," Hywel said. "He was thinking only of himself when he gave the order to murder

King Anarawd—certainly not of the consequences were he caught—and that's all he's still thinking about. He cannot put himself in another's shoes long enough to understand how seriously my father will take this betrayal."

Gareth nodded as this piece of Cadwaladr's character slid into place. "You think he'll come back just as soon as he can. That he honestly doesn't believe your father is angry and will punish him as he deserves."

"He deserves hanging," Hywel said. "But Cadwaladr has calculated correctly in this at least. My father's bark is usually worse than his bite."

Gareth nodded again. He'd viewed Cadwaladr as a bully, which he was, but he was more like a five-year-old searching for attention—and any kind of attention was better than none. "That doesn't mean we can condone what he's done," Gareth said.

"Of course not," Hywel said. "Cadwaladr isn't a child but a middle-aged prince of Gwynedd. *He* might excuse his own actions, rationalize them away, but the rest of us can't. Not even my father will be able to, this time."

This time. Hywel had recounted to Gareth his confrontation with his father when he broached the subject of Cadwaladr's potential treachery. But King Owain had claimed that Cadwaladr had been loyal up until now. Hywel hadn't contradicted his father but that didn't mean that what the King said was true. Perhaps Cadwaladr wasn't the only one who'd been lying to himself. For Gareth's part, this time he was even more of a pessimist than Hywel. King Owain would do what he pleased as it suited him. Far from hanging Cadwaladr, he might pardon his brother's crimes, no matter how heinous, if he had a good reason.

Hywel gathered the other men who'd ridden to the beach and led the way back to Aberffraw's main gate. They arrived to find Rhun observing two rows of Cadwaladr's men—all of whom were men-at-arms. Tellingly, Cadwaladr hadn't chosen any knights to accompany him to Anglesey.

Though not peasants, these men had achieved a similar station to that which Gareth had held before Cadwaladr dismissed him. A knight, especially an older one, wouldn't have lost his reputation along with his position for opposing Cadwaladr as Gareth had with his small act of defiance. Unlike knights, who had their own lands and authority, these men were dependent on their lord for their living. This was, of course, why Cadwaladr had chosen them to assist him in his treachery.

The men-at-arms comprising Aberffraw's garrison stood sentry behind Cadwaladr's men, blocking their retreat to the castle. They were weaponless: Rhun had made them stack their weapons by the gatehouse. Now he paced, his hands behind his back, in front of the watching men-at-arms.

"You have all served Cadwaladr for long enough to recognize the truth about my uncle," Rhun said.

At this preamble, Hywel dismounted and waved the rest of the men off their horses. While Rhun continued speaking, enumerating Cadwaladr's crimes, Hywel tapped Gareth's shoulder and signaled him closer. "I wonder how many of them wish they'd followed your example."

"Honor is lost a day at a time—a year at a time—not all at once. Rarely is the moment for defiance as clear as it was for me," Gareth said. "Cadwaladr chips away at you until it's hard to remember what it was like when you stood on your own two feet."

"And yet," Hywel said, "honor, even once lost, can be regained. There is hope for these men."

"And for me?" Gareth said, not quite looking at his prince.

Hywel shot Gareth a rare smile instead of a smirk. "Oh yes."

"That's the fine line, isn't it?" Gareth said. "It's easy to say *I did what I had to do* but there are lines a man shouldn't cross—shouldn't be asked to cross—even if we've all done it more times than we can count."

"I'm not worried about you," Hywel said. "You are not your milk-brother."

Gareth turned his attention back to Rhun's lecture, Hywel's confidont '*oh ycs*' still echoing in his ears. Such was the basis of loyalty; Gareth would die to protect his lord and at times like these, he believed Hywel might do the same for him. That trust and loyalty were not the same thing was something Cadwaladr had never understood.

A few of Cadwaladr's men appeared unmoved by Rhun's speech.

"The one on the far left," Gareth said. "Maredudd."

Hywel nodded. "I noticed. You know him?"

"He's stood with Cadwaladr for thirty years," Gareth said. "He's seen it all. He could be Madog, if Madog would have served Cadwaladr."

"Which he wouldn't," Hywel said.

Rhun was as aware as they of the effect—of lack of effect—of his words on Cadwaladr's men. He glanced at Hywel, who flicked his finger *one, two, three* in their mutual code. *Three men.* Hywel shifted, glanced at Gareth, who nodded his understanding. Then Hywel tipped his head at two of his archers.

Without seeming to move, all of Hywel's men eased into more ready stances. Rhun gave each of Cadwaladr's men a long look and then stepped close to Maredudd, who'd found a position at the end of the first row of men.

"Have you heard anything I've said?" Rhun said.

"All of it, my lord." Maredudd looked straight ahead, over Rhun's left shoulder.

"To whom do you owe your allegiance?"

"To Prince Cadwaladr, my lord."

"Do you understand that he is foresworn? That he will be stripped of his lands? That he has abandoned you?"

Maredudd's lips tightened. "I pledged my allegiance to him the day I became a man. I have never broken my vows." His eyes flicked to Gareth and then away again.

And then, in a move Gareth had been expecting but for which he still wasn't entirely prepared, Maredudd coiled and leapt at Rhun. He barreled into the prince, knocking him over, and then raced past him, heading towards the woods to the north of the castle. Hywel pointed and the archers released their arrows at the same instant. Two found their mark and Maredudd fell forward, dead, both arrows sticking straight up in the air from his back.

Rhun lay sprawled where he'd fallen. None of Cadwaladr's men, who were closer, moved to assist him so Gareth stepped forward, his hand out. Rhun grasped it, levering himself to his feet, and brushed the dust from his clothes. Hywel hadn't stirred, beyond that initial motion ordering his men to shoot.

Rhun pulled out his sword and stood with it loose in his hand. "Anyone else care to follow that man's example? Does anyone else refuse to acknowledge my father's authority?"

Silence.

While Rhun was speaking, Hywel moved without haste to the back row of Cadwaladr's men. Gareth watched, having no idea what his lord was doing, other than that it demanded a grim set to his jaw. Rhun shot a quick glance at Hywel that told Gareth he was in on it too. They'd come to some sort of agreement that needed no conversation.

Hywel paused, as if he was counting to himself, and then stepped behind and just to one side of the second of Cadwaladr's men he didn't trust. The man shifted from one foot to the other, trying to see Hywel's face out of the corner of his eye. Rhun had been speaking—more of his lecture about Cadwaladr—but cut off his words in mid-sentence, coming to a halt in front of the last man whom Hywel had pointed out. In the same instant that Hywel grasped the second man around the head and shoulders, Rhun shoved his sword through the third man's stomach.

Rhun's man fell to his knees, his hands clutching his belly. Hywel, meanwhile, had wrenched his man's neck and broken it.

His face expressionless, Rhun pulled out his sword, reached down for the end of the man's cloak, and wiped off the blood with it. The remaining soldiers fell as one to their knees. One shouted, "My lord!"

"That's better." Hywel moved to the front of the company to stand beside his brother.

"We should kill them all," Rhun said, his tone matter-of-fact. "We can trust none of them." Coming from him, the words were far more daunting to Gareth's ear than if Hywel had spoken.

A voice piped up from near Hywel's fallen victim. "I will swear! I will swear allegiance to Owain Gwynedd!" The boy was probably no more than sixteen. His face was deathly pale and his hands gripped his knees so tightly his knuckles stood out white.

The remaining men looked left and right. One of the problems with having a ruler such as Cadwaladr, was that he didn't take kindly to men who carried their own authority and whom he couldn't bully. Thus, none of the men left were leaders; without Cadwaladr and the three men-at-arms already dead, Cadwaladr's company had no head.

Rhun pursed his lips. "For those of you who didn't choose your allegiance, but allied yourself with Cadwaladr through birth or circumstance, I will spare your life. For those who chose him, and when you discovered your error, could not escape his clutches, I will spare your life. But for those of you who chose to serve Cadwaladr, even when you knew what he was, I tell you now that if you ever waver in my father's service, if I sense one moment of hesitation on your part for your changed circumstance, I will kill you myself."

"Do you hear my brother?" Hywel said, his voice soft but carrying over the heads of the kneeling men. "And if you hear him, do you listen?"

"Yes, my lords," the men murmured, all ten of them.

The boy practically slobbered on the ground at Rhun's feet. Gareth felt for him. It could have *been* him, six years ago. Gareth was just thankful that he'd escaped before something comparable had happened to him. He'd never known where the certainty had come from, but one day he'd woken up with the courage to walk away. It had already been too many years of service in which he couldn't stomach his allegiance, but he hadn't known how to get out. Overnight, he'd resolved not to commit one more crime, not to perform one more heinous deed, at Cadwaladr's behest.

Perhaps the boy, like Gareth, would survive long enough to recover the honor and courage he'd lost. Gareth was glad, too, that Rhun was in charge and not Hywel. Hywel's eyes told him that he would have killed them all—and would probably have been right to. They couldn't trust these men, not even the boy, because unlike Gareth, none of them had had the courage to walk away.

26

Gwen hung her head over the side of the Danish ship, emptying her insides into the sea for the twentieth time. The chop of the waves was such that she had to grip the rail tightly just to stay upright and not spew the contents of her stomach—what little remained of them—on herself or in the boat. Part of her thought that would serve the others right, but the smell would probably only make her more ill. The moment of spite wouldn't be worth it.

The big square sail flew above her head and men scrambled all over the boat as they maneuvered the rigging, tacking their way towards Ireland. As soon as they'd left the immediate vicinity of the shore, the leader—the same man who'd carried her—had ordered his men to hoist it. It puffed out now—satisfactorily it seemed from the looks on the sailors' faces. In addition, the wind hadn't lessened since they'd left Wales, which seemed to please them all no end.

Watching it, the leader turned to Gwen with an enormous smile. "A good wind. If it keeps up, we will reach Dublin before two full days have passed."

Gwen stared at him, horror churning in her gut instead of fear. She rested her forehead on the rail, feeling the coolness of the sea spray blowing into her face, but overcome by despair that with the disappearance of the shore behind them, she had no choices at all. She had to continue with the Danes.

And Gareth... she shivered. Surely he knew that Hywel hadn't touched her—had never touched her for reasons that had never been entirely clear to her, but by now were set in stone. Hywel would tell him so, but sometimes men didn't think clearly when it came to women. And with that, she acknowledged that she loved Gareth—and wanted him to love her. Maybe when she saw him again she'd have the courage to tell him. She fingered his cross which she still wore around her neck. The time had never seemed right to give it to him. As it had every day for the last five years, it comforted her to have something of his always with her.

Whatever August heat had warmed her on shore had disappeared the moment they'd pulled out of the bay. A new guard hung onto her waist—this time, a young one named Olaf. He grinned through perfectly white teeth and spoke no Welsh, nor any other language it seemed. His grip tightened as her shoulders shuddered, as if he feared she would throw herself overboard even though they were in the middle of the sea. She couldn't even see Mt. Snowdon anymore. As they tacked towards the setting sun, the direction of the wind confirmed what she'd feared: they'd continued sailing directly west, towards Dublin, and not south to Ceredigion as she'd initially hoped.

It had been a faint hope anyway, with Cadwaladr on the run from his brother and in the company of four dozen Danishmen. He would be as safe as he could be in Ireland. Ceredigion was another matter and he knew it. She wondered how his wife would react, knowing she had a coward for a husband. Then again, she probably already knew.

Finally, Gwen had nothing left in her stomach to come up, so her guard left her with her eyes closed, curled on a blanket near the stern of the boat so she'd be out of the way of the oarsmen and the rigging. Her illness gave her two advantages: one, they left her alone, and two, it perpetuated the myth that she carried Hywel's child.

She hoped she could keep up the façade long enough for them to either lose interest in her, or take her back home, though that thought in and of itself was enough to make her gag. It was only because she'd left her family behind—and Gareth—that she could even contemplate a return journey. Gradually the sun lowered in the sky until it shone directly into Gwen's face. She shut her eyes, feeling the warmth on her eyelids.

All of a sudden, the sun disappeared. Gwen opened her eyes to find the big Dane blocking the light. He gazed down at her, his hands on his hips. Gwen curled up tighter, not wanting him to look at her, speak to her, or touch her. The Dane didn't appear to get the message.

"No sea legs, eh." He crouched in front of her and reached a hand to her shoulder.

Gwen twitched away.

"You're afraid of me?"

"Shouldn't I be?" Gwen said. "You'll do whatever Cadwaladr says and I know of what he's capable."

The Dane snorted. "I don't take orders from Cadwaladr."

Gwen had been staring at his boots so as not to look into his eyes, but the disgust and assured tone in his voice made her chance a glance at his face. "What do you mean?"

"You think us barbarians," he said, "but I reckon my Latin is better than yours."

Despite herself, Gwen smiled. "Don't tell my father that."

"See," the Dane said. "Already your fear leaves you. I am Godfrid mac Torcall, descended from Brian Boru, like your Hywel, eh?"

Gwen opened her eyes fully, finding that her fear was fading, as he'd said. "I am Gwen, a bard's daughter."

His eyes lit at that, although whenever she'd looked into them they'd been bright—as if he found the world deeply amusing. Maybe he was like Hywel in that, though in Hywel, that amusement came out with more than a touch of cynicism. "You will sing for us when we reach my father's hall."

"Is he the King of Dublin?" Gwen said.

A shadow crossed Godfrid's face. Apparently, this was the one thing that could dampen his mood. "He shares power with Ottar."

Gwen didn't know who Ottar was, nor Torcall for that matter. The politics of Wales were so complicated that she'd never had time to learn anyone else's, though she'd met men from

Ireland before in southern or western Wales. "And Cadwaladr? Does he have plans for me?"

Godfrid glanced behind him to where Cadwaladr stood near the prow of the boat, one foot up on a box of cargo. He rested his hip on the rail and looked towards Ireland. "He may not realize it, but you are *my* hostage now, not his. You carry my cousin's child. He should not have taken you from Hywel."

Cousin. And that eased Gwen's fears even more. The Danes were no less fierce about kinship than the Welsh, for all that brother murdered brother just as in Wales. Gwen had learned enough about Hywel's ancestry growing up with him to understand what that tie meant to the Royal House of Wales.

As Godfrid promised, they reached Dublin just after noon on the second day out from Anglesey. Though pale, having not kept anything down except a few sips of water in two days, Gwen was able to sit up once they reached the calm harbor below the city. She'd never seen so many ships in one place, from the larger warships like the one in which she'd sailed, to the smaller, more agile craft that hugged the coast.

These Danes didn't seem to be fisherman as much as traders, bringing goods from all over the world into Dublin. She wondered how much of it was stolen. The Danes hadn't raided Welsh shores for a hundred years, but that didn't mean they hadn't moved farther afield. Well ... unless Anarawd's murder counted as a raid. And that wasn't random, since Cadwaladr had invited them in.

Dublin was a place unlike any she'd ever seen. In all their travels in Wales, her family had never passed through a town with more than a thousand people. The Dublin streets wended around a maze of thatched cottages. As at home, they'd been built in wattle and daub with thatched roofs, all crammed in together. They also appeared to have been planted anywhere the owner liked. Interspersed among them, equally haphazardly, were craft halls, stalls, churches, merchants, and small greens.

Church bells rang from all directions. She'd thought the Danes heathen, but according to Godfrid, who held her elbow as he helped her off the ship, that was no longer the case, not since the great Sitric of the silken beard had converted to Christianity and later died on pilgrimage to Rome. That was the same Sitric from whom Hywel descended, though not Godfrid as it turned out. He'd explained the genealogy that made him and Hywel cousins, but Gwen had soon lost track of the odd-sounding names and the multiple marriages and divorces that connected them. Besides, as she really wasn't carrying Hywel's child, it could hardly matter to her.

Solid ground felt like heaven, even as the barrage of sights and sounds overwhelmed her senses. "Five thousand souls live in Dublin," Godfrid said, and Gwen could well believe it. The smell of refuse, excrement, and humanity almost made her vomit yet again, but she held onto her stomach with one hand and Godfrid's arm with the other, weaving on her feet but still upright. Godfrid handed her off to the mute Olaf, who guided her through the streets, passing houses, merchants, and an open air market. At first she couldn't grasp what was being sold, until she saw the men, women, and children bound together in a long line. *Slaves.*

Gwen shivered, though not from cold this time. Regardless of Godfrid's present friendliness, if Cadwaladr or the Danes discovered that she wasn't carrying Hywel's child, that could be her fate too. The company wended its way deeper into the maze that was Dublin until they reached Godfrid's father's home on the edge of the city.

Prince Cadwaladr was there before her, smiling and condescending, as if by bringing her here he'd achieved a great victory instead of fleeing Wales with his tail between his legs. The hall rose before them, also unlike anything she'd ever seen. Because Dublin was unrelievedly flat, there was nothing to indicate they'd reached a special residence, other than the size of the hall, which was four times larger than any other place she'd seen so far.

"The true king of Dublin lives over there," Cadwaladr said, waving his hand to indicate the way they'd come. This didn't help her to orient herself, as she'd gotten turned around in the maze of streets. It was confusing enough that the sea lay to the east, not the west, as in Wales.

Danish halls, or at least this Danish hall, wasn't rectangular in shape as she might have expected, but was bowed outwards in the middle, tapering to a third less wide on both ends. It had timber walls, a great thatched roof, and was set on a laid-stone foundation that also served as the floor.

The entrance doors, with two men in full armor to guard them, sat at one of the narrow ends. At Cadwaladr's approach, both men bowed, not particularly low but enough to acknowledge his higher rank, and moved aside. Cadwaladr had lived in Dublin for a long time and these men probably knew him. She shuddered at the thought of making that crossing from Wales more than once, much less willingly, as Cadwaladr had. She held more tightly to poor Olaf's arm, trying to contain her exhaustion, and staggered up the stairs after the Welsh prince.

27

Hywel and Rhun returned to Aber with Cadwaladr's men—without Cadwaladr and Gwen, of course—and King Owain accepted all with glittering eyes. Cold, for now, not hot. The king assigned one loyal man-at-arms to each of Cadwaladr's wayward men, with the express intent of getting them drunk and hearing each man's story. King Owain, like Hywel, might have preferred to kill them all, but somehow Rhun's earnest objections persuaded him to defer that fate. As Hywel remarked to Gareth later, it would be easy enough to kill them later, if the need arose.

To Gareth's surprise, King Owain appointed him as one of the 'trusted' knights, although his assignment was the poor boy, Tudur, who'd been the first to fall to his knees outside Aberffraw. Gareth watched him drink, not even trying to keep up with his consumption of mead after the first two flagons, which the boy downed before touching his meat. Once he got started, he just kept going, talking through his turnips and onions and roast chicken about how his father had died and he'd inherited his station.

"I was so proud to serve a prince of Wales," Tudur said.

"Even this one?" Gareth said.

Tudur tried to shake and nod his head at the same time, and almost fell out of his seat. "Who was I to know the man he was? I'd seen the times my father had come home not willing to talk about what he'd been doing, but..."

Gareth studied the boy, waiting, knowing as only he could what was coming next.

"... the reality of service was something entirely different."

Gareth couldn't mistake the anguish in the boy's voice.

"We sacked a village, you see," Tudur said.

As Tudur went on at length about how the peasants had screamed, Gareth's confusion grew. Raping and pillaging were part and parcel of the internecine warfare that predominated in Wales, though he couldn't think of a particular lord with whom Cadwaladr had been at war at that time. Then, as Tudur talked more, it dawned on Gareth what Tudur was saying. Gareth put a hand on his arm to stop him talking and grasped his chin with the other hand. "You pillaged one of Prince Cadwaladr's own villages?"

Tudur nodded, so drunk now he didn't even try to stop his tears from falling. "In Ceredigion."

"Why?"

Tudur just blubbered. Money? Disobedience? What could possibly be the reason a lord would murder his own villagers who were the source of his income, whatever their crimes? Cadwaladr's rationale might not have been clear to Tudur either. Or at least he couldn't articulate it after five cups of mead.

Gareth looked around for someone else who was still sober, but as he observed his friends at the other tables, he realized that they were drinking as steadily as their counterparts. He glanced towards the fire where Hywel sat, still as a stone, his chair pushed back and the sole of one boot planted on the edge of the table. Hywel caught his eye, held it, and then looked away again. Gareth went cold. Hywel already knew.

By now, Tudur was sobbing into his drink. Gareth rose, patted him on the shoulder, and crossed the hall to where his lord waited.

"Sit." Hywel kicked at the rung of the chair next to him so it skidded out from under the table.

Gareth took the chair and sat. He gripped his knees as he thought of what to say.

But Hywel spoke first. "Gareth, tell me when a man's actions require redress from his lord?"

"When they endanger the alliances of his sovereign," Gareth said, "or threaten the stability of the realm."

Hywel nodded. "I am aware of the stories these men are telling. Until Cadwaladr ordered the death of Anarawd, he had not crossed the threshold from reckless to treason." Hywel nodded towards the men in the hall. "Cadwaladr is a royal brother. He could do what he liked with his own lands."

"And if your father took him to task or brought him up short, it might send Cadwaladr into the arms of an enemy, someone who would look the other way," Gareth said. "Even the King of England."

"How many Welshmen would die if Cadwaladr brought an English army into Wales?" Hywel said.

Gareth knew his face held a stony look. He could admit that Hywel's assessment of the political situation was accurate, even if he didn't like it, but he couldn't accept it. Still, he answered Hywel. "Far more than a little village in Ceredigion."

"When a prince is trying to preserve his country, he doesn't have the luxury of worrying about the small things."

The small things. Not for the first time, Gareth was glad he wasn't a prince of Wales, continually forced to choose between two unacceptable alternatives. He took leave of his prince and was just leaving the hall when Meilyr stopped him on the steps, Gwalchmai a pace behind.

"You saw her?" Meilyr spoke around a clenched jaw and hands so tightly fisted it was a wonder his nails didn't draw blood.

"I did," Gareth said.

"What can you tell me?"

"Not much more than King Owain already has," Gareth said. "She left Aberffraw by boat, Cadwaladr's captive."

"If he harms her—"

"He thinks she carries Hywel's child," Gareth said. Meilyr's already red face turned purple. Before he expired on the spot, Gareth put a hand on his arm. "Cadwaladr has been misled. But for now, it keeps her safe from him or any man."

"How dare you patronize me—"

"I love your daughter, Meilyr," Gareth said. "I would have her hand if you will give it, when we get her back and if she agrees."

Meilyr's mouth opened and closed like a landed fish and then he snapped it shut. "Find her. Return her safely to me and we will see." He brushed past Gareth and into the hall. Gareth wondered if Meilyr would be able to speak civilly to Hywel and hoped for his sake that he could.

Gareth looked at Gwalchmai, who'd remained behind, and rested a hand on his shoulder. It looked to Gareth like he was close to crying. "I won't tell you not to worry, but this is a long way from over. We'll find her. I swear it."

* * * * *

The next morning, King Owain stood in the center of his hall, his nobles surrounding him. He held a staff in both hands. "My brother, Cadwaladr, ordered the death of King Anarawd, my friend and the man who would have been my son." His voice carried throughout the hall. "Rather than face what he has done, and the choices he has made, he has fled, we believe, to Dublin."

The majority of the people listening had heard some of this before. Nobody gasped in horror or dismay. "Most here already knew what kind of man Cadwaladr was," Rhun said, *sotto voce*.

Gareth turned to find the prince at his right shoulder. But Rhun was only repeating Gareth's own thoughts: that even if someone hadn't heard the news, it shouldn't have come as a surprise. And that thought gave Gareth pause too, for if everyone had known what Gareth himself had faced in Cadwaladr's service, why had so few understood and forgiven Gareth for his summary dismissal?

Rhun gave him a smile. "Do you know why I knighted you?"

Gareth shook his head. "We'd won the battle…"

Rhun didn't wait for him to finish. "It was time." He tipped his chin towards the crowd of men listening to King Owain. "It isn't that men couldn't forgive you for disobeying Cadwaladr, or at least, that's not the full story. Your very existence revealed to them their compliance and dishonor. They shunned you because you had more courage than they, even if they prettied it up with talk of loyalty."

Gareth swallowed hard. Rhun smiled again and returned to watching the room.

"I hereby strip my brother of his inheritance; I reclaim the lands in Ceredigion, Anglesey, and Lleyn that I gave him." King Owain took the staff, split it over his knee, and tossed the smaller half into the fire. "Henceforth, I have no brother." He turned to Hywel, who unlike Rhun had stood with his father throughout the ceremony, his hands behind his back. "Go."

Hywel did as he was told. By noon, he'd gathered half his father's personal guard (his *teulu*) along with all of Hywel's own men and every other knight or man-at-arms the remaining nobles at Aber could spare.

King Cadell planted himself in front of Hywel. "I will ride with you to Ceredigion before continuing to my own lands."

Hywel turned to him, surprise etched in his face. "Aren't you staying for..." His voice trailed off, one of the few times Gareth had ever seen Hywel nonplussed.

"I will marry your sister in a year's time, if all goes well," Cadell said. "It is unwise to be hasty in these matters and I would prefer to clear up the details of my brother's murder first." He paused, his eyes narrowed at Hywel. It was the first time Gareth perceived the steel behind Cadell's smarmy façade. "I would like to know that no suspicion falls on me in this matter."

"It is all my uncle's doing, as far as we know," Hywel said.

Thus, the company of two hundred, Hywel and Cadell in the lead, left Aber and rode east to Caerhun and then south. It was a distance of some twenty miles to Dolwyddelan, a journey Gareth knew well, and then a further fifty to their ultimate destination: Aberystwyth Castle, Cadwaladr's seat in Ceredigion. From the look of determination on Hywel's face, they'd be resting little and pushing the horses, even in the mountains.

The company spent that first night at Dolwyddelan and a second in a rough camp near Machynlleth. To reach Ceredigion, they then followed the Roman road to the west of the mountains that took up much of central Wales—a road that was difficult to traverse with an army and which slowed them considerably.

So it was just after noon on the third day when they reached the ford in the river below Aberystwyth and gazed the quarter of a mile—straight up—to the castle. As one of the few large fortresses in Ceredigion, it was well positioned to guard the entire coast of Wales.

It sat at the crest of a large plateau, a hundred feet above the floodplain. The castle was larger and better defended than a manor house, more on the scale of Dolwyddelan than Aber, but with no stone to protect it. Anarawd's father had burned the original castle in 1135, and Cadwaladr rebuilt it in earth and wood.

Ditches surrounded the wooden palisade, making a siege difficult, not that any army had a hope of getting close to it in a frontal assault. It wasn't any easier from the rear: the plateau dropped off sharply behind the castle, straight into the sea.

Hywel pulled his horse close into Gareth's. "I expect you to accompany me when I speak to Cadwaladr's wife."

"Yes, my lord," Gareth said. "But what about King Cadell?"

"He has chosen to remain in the background." Hywel cast a glance to where Cadell had dismounted in the midst of his men.

Gareth followed his gaze, still not sure what to make of this new king. He turned back to his prince. "You don't believe that Cadwaladr is here, do you?"

"No," Hywel said. "Although I suppose he could still surprise me. I certainly didn't anticipate him taking Gwen, nor that he'd believe she carried my child." He gazed into the distance for several heartbeats, before seeming to shake himself out of the brief reverie. "Let me do the talking."

"Of course," Gareth said.

"Will Cadwaladr's wife surrender the castle, do you think?" Evan reined his horse in on the other side of Gareth.

"No, she won't," Gareth said. "Not necessarily for his sake, but for hers. Alice believes she has as much—if not more—right to Ceredigion as her husband does."

Cadwaladr, in one of those strange, royal alliances, had married Alice de Clare, the daughter of the man whom Owain Gwynedd, Cadwaladr, and Anarawd had defeated for control of Deheubarth back in 1137. At least her father had died near Abergavenny, fighting against the men of Gwent, rather than by Cadwaladr's own hand. Still, it was a stretch to think theirs was a love match.

Gareth had left Cadwaladr's service shortly thereafter. Alice, for her part, was not a beauty, though purportedly far more intelligent than her husband. To Gareth's mind, that wouldn't be difficult.

"Come to within two hundred yards—no further—and aim to stay in the trees by the river," Hywel said. "They've seen us coming but right now she doesn't know why we're here or how many men I've brought. I'm just her nephew, traveling through Ceredigion. Right now her greatest concern is how she's going to feed us all."

"We could deceive her," Gareth said. "Enter the castle and take it from the inside."

"We could." Hywel gave Gareth a piercing look. "And if her garrison refuses to surrender? It will be hand to hand in the courtyard. I value my men more than that—and Cadwaladr's for that matter—far more than he does."

Choosing six other men he trusted, Evan among them, Hywel led the way up the road to the castle. The path doubled back on itself twice before coming out on the flat area in front of the castle gate. The portcullis was up as they arrived, but Hywel hesitated on the threshold.

"Please ask my aunt to come to the gate," he said to the guards. "I have news she should hear."

The guards murmured among themselves and one of them ran for Alice who appeared shortly thereafter. She was in her late twenties—and heavily pregnant. Gareth blinked at that. Fighting this woman was surely not what they wanted. At the sight of her, Gareth and Hywel dismounted and walked forward to greet her.

"Why is it that you do not come inside?" Alice spoke in French, which both Gareth and Hywel understood—though Gareth couldn't speak it as well as his lord.

"I am here on a less than pleasant mission, Aunt." Hywel took her hand and bowed over it. "I would speak to your lord husband."

Alice looked bewildered and Hywel did not release her hand, even as she tried to tug it away without seeming to. "He's not here, Hywel. He—" she hesitated as she looked from Hywel to Gareth, perhaps searching for some kind of reassurance, which she didn't find in Gareth's eyes. "He went to Aber for your sister's wedding."

"He has left Aber, Aunt," Hywel said.

Alice shook her head. "I've not seen him."

"Then I ask you to call your son, and come with me," Hywel said.

Now Alice backed away—just one small step, but enough to show that she didn't necessarily trust Hywel or his motives, even if she'd been polite up until now. "Why?"

Hywel moved with her, still clasping her hand. "My lord father, the King, has sent me to seize these lands, including this castle. Your husband has fled to Dublin."

Alice's face paled. Her control was good, however, because the expression lasted only for a heartbeat. Then she whirled on one heel, dragging Hywel with her. "Close the gate! We must defen—"

Hywel didn't let her finish. He grasped her around the shoulders and pulled her against him, his sword suddenly unsheathed. He pointed it at her guardsmen who'd been slow to react behind her. Perhaps they hadn't understood French enough to grasp her conversation with Hywel. She'd screamed her orders in Welsh, however.

Holding Alice, much as Cadwaladr had held Gwen, Hywel backed away from the gate. Unlike Cadwaladr, however, he held no knife to her throat and didn't threaten her men with her death. "I will not hurt her but I will take her with me if you do not do as I ask. She has commanded you to defend the castle but it is your choice whether you do so or not. Do you yield? I am sent by Owain, King of Gwynedd and my father. His seal is on this action."

The captain of the guard, an older man named Goronwy whom Gareth knew from his days in Ceredigion, skidded to a halt just on the castle side of the wooden gates, which the guards had half-closed at Alice's warning. They wouldn't have wanted to drop the portcullis until she was safely back inside.

Goronwy flicked his gaze from Alice to Hywel, and then past them to Gareth. His eyes widened. Gareth canted his head in acknowledgement of an old friendship but didn't say anything, since Hywel had asked him not to.

"We defend," Goronwy said.

"Send out the boy," Hywel said. "Now. For his own safety."

"Why do you do this?" Alice said. "We've done you no harm."

"Your husband paid mercenaries to murder Anarawd, the King of Deheubarth, and all his men," Hywel said. "As Cadwaladr has fled and left you and his men to face the consequences of that decision, my father has disowned him."

Alice stared straight ahead, absorbing this news without apparent emotion. She believed Cadwaladr had done exactly as Hywel said; she had to know him well enough for that. Perhaps she knew of his numerous other crimes. This time, however, he'd been found out and there were consequences in that for her.

Hywel saw it too. "Cadwaladr thinks only of what he wants and getting it, whether or not his wants are good for him or Wales," Hywel said. "I'm sorry you've been caught up in it."

"Mama!" A boy of five raced out the gate, which Goronwy then closed behind him. Gareth scooped him up before he could reach Alice and carried him to Braith. Hywel, meanwhile, boosted Alice very gently onto his horse.

"Then why did you not let me defend Aberystwyth as I intended?" Alice said. "Surely your father wishes that Cadwaladr and I should share the same fate."

Hywel gave a derisive laugh. "Do you know my father as little as that? We will take your castle, but I would not do it with you and the boy in it."

And that, right there, was all anyone needed to know about the difference between serving Hywel and what Gareth's time had been like under Cadwaladr.

28

At that first feast, Gwen scared her captors when she threw up everything she'd tried to eat. She should have known better than to consume anything more than broth after her illness on the ship, but nobody had suggested it. She'd eaten until she was full, and then thrown off the grasping hands of her guards in order to lose it all in the grass outside the hall. She'd been given leave to go to bed after that, and slept all of the next day and night. Two days in Dublin, nearly a week since she'd been at Aber, with how many more before they could return home?

Gwen sat on her pallet combing her hair with her fingers. She'd slept near the main hall in a small hut which comprised the women's guest quarters. She was glad the Danes were civilized enough not to make her sleep in the hall. She wished she had other clothes to put on but so far none had been forthcoming.

A young woman appeared in the doorway of the otherwise deserted room, blinking in the transition from sunshine to the darkness within the hut. "Godfrid says to come out now."

Gwen looked up at her as she stood silhouetted in the doorway. "Excuse me?"

"Come out now," the girl repeated. Then she added, "Godfrid says."

"Thank you." From the girl's accent, Gwen didn't think she knew much more Welsh than that. Gwen pulled on her boots, straightened her filthy dress and followed the girl outside.

"Food and drink," Godfrid said without preamble.

"No, 'how are you?'; no, 'I'm sorry this has been so rotten'?" Gwen tossed the conversation back at him. "No, 'I'm sorry to have taken you away from your home?'"

Godfrid coughed and gave Gwen a quick bow. "How are you, Gwen?"

"Filthy and hungry, thank you for asking," she said. "What's to become of me?"

Godfrid allowed the smile that was in his eyes to show on his lips. "Food first."

"Godfri—" Gwen swallowed the rest of the name at Godfrid's quizzical look. This was a man used to giving orders and having them obeyed. Just as with the girl, who ran off at a gesture from him. Gwen bit her lip and looked down at her scuffed boots.

"This way." Godfrid headed back to the hall.

Two dozen other people—men, women, and children— gathered for the meal. Gwen would have liked to sit with a family, to remind herself that she had a father and brother back in Wales—and a man who just might love her—but Godfrid nudged her towards an empty table and sat across from her.

A different girl, this one with a collar around her neck indicating her slave status, laid a full cup of beer and a bowl with the needed broth inside it.

"Eat," Godfrid said.

"Thank you," Gwen said to the girl, who didn't meet her eyes. Gwen took one sip, hesitated, and then took another. The broth warmed her stomach and for the first time in a week she didn't feel ill.

"Wait." Godfrid put a finger on the rim of the bowl and forced Gwen to set it down.

"It's all right," Gwen said. "I won't eat too much this time."

Godfrid nodded. He turned sideways on the bench, leaned against the pillar that buttressed it, and crossed his arms. "Cadwaladr is not here."

Gwen looked at him over the top of the bowl, and then gave a quick glance around the room. "Where's he gone?"

"To Ottar," Godfrid said.

"And that upsets you?"

Looking even more pensive, he drummed his fingers on the table. "A company of Ottar's men went to Wales ten days ago and have not returned."

"Oh." Gwen took another sip of her soup and then swallowed hard, feeling a bit sick again.

Godfrid caught the nuance beneath that short utterance. "You know of it?"

"Yes," Gwen said. "It's why Cadwaladr is here. I suppose it's not surprising you don't know the whole story, given what followed."

"Tell me." Godfrid swung his legs down from the bench, braced his elbows on the table, and hunched over them. "I must know." His blue eyes glared at her beneath his bushy blonde brows.

Gwen sighed, not feeling like she had a choice but to tell him the whole story. "Cadwaladr hired your people—or rather Ottar's people—to murder the King of Deheubarth. A man named Anarawd. Anarawd was to marry Owain Gwynedd's daughter—Hywel's sister—and was on his way to the wedding when he was murdered."

"Ho." Godfrid pushed off his elbows and gazed at Gwen with a stunned expression. He tsked through his teeth. "That is a tale." Then his eyes narrowed. "Why did Cadwaladr do this?"

"I couldn't tell you why," Gwen said, "except that he saw an advantage in it for himself."

"If the money was good, such a proposition would tempt Ottar, though I find it distasteful myself," Godfrid said. "What went wrong?"

"They killed Anarawd and all his men, as Cadwaladr intended," Gwen said. "But later they attacked the company bringing King Anarawd and his dead companions to Caerhun for burial." She shrugged. "They underestimated their opponents."

"You mean Ottar's men are all dead," Godfrid said.

Gwen nodded. "Owain Gwynedd is very angry. He didn't take kindly to Anarawd's death and even less to Danish mercenaries being hired to see to it."

"I see," Godfrid said, and Gwen knew he really did see. On one hand, Godfrid may have participated in any number of similar acts, but as a prince himself, he understood that King Owain couldn't condone what his brother had done under any circumstances. "And what will Owain Gwynedd do?"

"I don't know yet," Gwen said. "Cadwaladr abducted me from Aber before the King knew that Cadwaladr was behind Anarawd's death."

"And now he does know," said Godfrid. "I overheard the conversation between Cadwaladr and Prince Hywel."

"I imagine so," said Gwen.

"Does it seem to you that Hywel will come to Ireland, to rescue you from his uncle?" Godfrid said. "He came to Aberffraw for you."

"He did," said Gwen. "But that was his own country. Hywel won't know what bargain Cadwaladr has made with Ottar or your father. Or even if it's with them at all. Ireland is a big country. Besides, we don't have ships like yours."

"Where does Cadwaladr rule in Wales?"

"Ceredigion," Gwen said. "Lands that Owain gave him."

"So Hywel might think he took you there?"

"It's likely," Gwen said. "Hywel's responsibility will be to secure those lands for his father and root out any who remain loyal to Cadwaladr, not to chase after me."

Godfrid held Gwen's eyes, his gaze steady. Gwen held her breath, not sure what he was seeing. And then... "You don't love him," Godfrid said.

Gwen looked away, unable to lie that well. "It's not like that. You don't understand."

"Ah, but I do." Godfrid pointed a finger at her. "Not only do you not love him, but you are not his lover either."

Gwen blinked. "I..." Her mind worked furiously to think of how to answer without giving the game away. "Yes, I am."

Now, Godfrid laughed. "You are a very bad liar." He leaned back from the table, a look of satisfaction in his eyes. "I am right. You thought you could pretend that Cadwaladr spoke the truth as long as nobody asked you about Hywel directly. Nobody has asked you directly before this."

"No—" Gwen said.

Godfrid wagged a finger in her face. "I watch my men when they lie. You lied to me now. You are not his lover and you don't carry his child." He peered at her. "You don't carry any child. That you've been sick from the voyage gives cover to your lie."

"I never lied," Gwen said. "I never said anything to Cadwaladr about this at all. I just didn't deny what he so firmly believed. Besides, he stole me from Aber and once he'd done that, he would have killed me if he knew the truth."

Godfrid folded his arms across his chest, still looking satisfied. "You survived."

Gwen straightened in her seat, relieved that he wasn't angry. "I did."

"And what about everything else?" he said. "Is that untrue also? What do you do in Wales when you are not captured by princes?"

"I am a bard's daughter," Gwen said. "I told you the truth about that. And I may not be Hywel's lover, but I do know him well. My father was his tutor and we are of an age." She smiled. "We learned our Latin together."

"So that is why he came for you," Godfrid said.

Gwen tipped her head to acknowledge the possible truth in his words. "Perhaps. But while I may not be his lover, I am his spy."

Godfrid gazed at her for a count of five, and then he threw back his head and laughed. The sound echoed throughout the hall. Several of the other diners looked at him, but then turned away, smiling themselves. They were probably used to his laughter.

"Now that you tell me, I find I am not surprised," Godfrid said, sobering. "There's a story here you must tell me someday."

"Someday." Gwen paused, and then dared ask, "When did you first suspect that something was wrong with Cadwaladr's assumptions?"

"On the battlements at Aberffraw, I noted your shock when Cadwaladr told Prince Hywel you carried his child," Godfrid said. "Hywel himself couldn't hide his surprise, but I assumed that your reaction and his was a response to Cadwaladr's unveiling, not that it wasn't true. Later, I thought back to the scene and realized that you were as surprised as Hywel. And also that you were not attached to him in that way."

"We were that obvious?" Gwen said. "I need to work on my lying."

"Oh no, you don't." Godfrid barked a laugh again, but turned serious almost instantly. "Remember, I don't speak your language as well as I would like. I've learned to watch your faces."

"Does anyone else know, do you think?" Gwen said.

"Not Cadwaladr anyway."

"That's a relief," Gwen said. "What will you do now? Will you tell your father or Ottar? The longer I stay here the more obvious it will become that all is not as Cadwaladr believes."

Godfrid tapped a finger on his upper lip. "I will not reveal your secret. It pleases me to keep it." He paused. "But I don't see how Cadwaladr could not learn of it eventually. He has spies everywhere too."

"I will pretend as long as I can," Gwen said.

"Cadwaladr thinks only of himself," Godfrid said. "That makes him dangerous. He will become even more so if he learns of the deception."

"I can't avoid his company," Gwen said. "I am a prisoner here—whether yours or his—does it really matter?"

Godfrid pushed back from the table, preparing to stand. "I am offended."

Gwen bit her lip. She closed her eyes, marshalling her thoughts. "I need to go home," she said, even as she gagged at the idea of the voyage across the sea and what it would do to her. "You need to let me go home."

"I would let you," he said. "But I have no plans to return to Wales. It may be that you will have to wait for Cadwaladr."

Gwen rubbed her face with both hands, repulsed by the idea but with no counter to it. "If I must, I must."

"What if I said you did not have to?" Godfrid put his hands flat on the table and leaned his weight on them. "What if I set you free, but then you stayed in Dublin. With me."

Gwen dropped her hands. Godfrid was looking at her as if she was the only person in the room. When she didn't answer, he touched her chin with one finger. "Think on it."

He straightened, the reckless grin again on his lips and his eyes alight. Stunned, she watched him greet several men on his way down the central aisle. Then, with only one look back and an insouciant wave, so reminiscent of Hywel, he was gone.

29

"Gareth will take care of you," Alice said to the handful of boy in Gareth's arms, surprising Gareth with her vote of confidence. "Just don't pepper him with too many questions."

She turned away, back to Hywel, and Gareth whispered, "That means you can ask some."

Gareth boosted the boy, Cadfan, onto Braith's back and made sure he held the reins tightly. Braith wasn't a warhorse as Alice's Norman ancestors understood them, but was still far too big for Cadfan.

"Where's my father?" Cadfan said—probably the toughest question he could have chosen to ask.

"I don't know," Gareth said. "Maybe Ireland."

"Why'd he go there?"

"You've heard of something called 'politics'?" Gareth said.

Cadfan nodded.

"That's why," Gareth said. "Best left well enough alone by both you and me."

For her part, Alice perched on Hywel's horse, her hands in her lap. Normally, Hywel's horse was more nervy than this, but he seemed to understand that prancing was not allowed today. Sedately, with Gareth and Hywel walking and leading their charges, they made their way back down the hill to where Hywel had left the rest of the men.

"You truly mean to take my castle?" Alice gazed back up the hill where it squatted, as yet undamaged.

"Yes, Aunt," Hywel said. "I have no choice."

"We always have a choice," she said, tartly.

"Tell that to Cadwaladr," Hywel said. "And ask Anarawd how he felt about it."

That silenced her—and everyone else. Hywel pulled Gareth aside. "I didn't expect her to be pregnant. What do I do with her?"

"Ask her," Gareth said. "If any woman knows her own mind, she does."

Hywel glanced again at Alice, who glared at him. "I would go to my mother but her home is too far for me to travel in my condition," she said, having evidently overheard their exchange. "A convent lies just north of the castle. I can stay there until the baby is born. My midwife lives in the village and she will help me."

"When is the baby due?"

"Not for two months."

That eased Hywel's concern, and with a few terse orders, he had three of his men escorting Alice and Cadfan back across the ford of the Ystwyth River, and then north towards the village.

Cadfan, now seated behind one of the men-at-arms assigned to him, twisted in his seat to look back at Gareth. "Goodbye, sir knight."

Gareth saluted and bowed, "Young sir." Once the two were out of earshot, he turned to Hywel. "She was prepared to defend the castle herself. She could still be a threat."

"But not today, I think," Hywel said. "Her men remain in the castle and unless she incites the village against us, I find it unlikely we'll hear from her again. At least not soon."

"Your father may hear from her," Gareth said.

Hywel laughed. "No doubt. Nonetheless, my men will see her safe and then guard the Abbey until I deem such precaution unnecessary. What I don't want is for her to send a message to a nearby ally who might interrupt my plans."

"And what are those plans, my lord?" Gareth said.

Hywel jerked his head to indicate Gareth should follow, and walked under the trees to where his other captains gathered. His two hundred men and horses had scattered among the woods along the river, mingling to some degree, but mostly coordinated according to which lord they served. Soon, ten men—the leaders among them—gathered around Hywel.

"My father does not want a long siege," Hywel said. "I will speak with Cadwaladr's captain one more time, and if his response is the same as before, we'll burn the castle to the ground today."

"Today, my lord?" one of the men, Maelgwyn of Rhos, said.

Hywel stepped out from under the trees and checked the sky. "We've a few hours until sunset. Plenty of time."

"But surely such a move is—" Maelgwyn stopped speaking at Hywel's hard look.

"Tell me you weren't going to say, 'without honor'?" Hywel said.

"Of course not, my prince." Maelgwyn accompanied the denial with a slight bow. "Although I have to admit that I am uncomfortable with our task."

Hywel studied the man, eyes piercing, but Maelgwyn's reservations had the other lords murmuring among themselves.

"Have you forgotten what Cadwaladr did?" King Cadell said, his voice quiet, but loud enough so that they all heard him.

Maelgwyn looked down. "No, my lord."

"Cadwaladr is a prince, but he murdered a king—one with whom he himself was allied, and whom Owain Gwynedd planned to bring into his family as a son," Cadell said. "If Cadwaladr could do it to Anarawd, he could do it to anyone. Any of you."

This discussion was making Gareth impatient and he stirred beside Hywel, thinking to speak. Maelgwyn cleared his throat, as if to say something more as well, but Hywel gave neither of them the chance.

"Get your men ready," he said. "The time for action is now. I will accept the surrender of the garrison, should they choose to surrender, but I will not back down." And then he paused to look into the face of each man in turn. "It is not I who orders this, but my father."

Maelgwyn straightened his shoulders, seemingly putting aside his doubts. "Yes, my lord."

"If there are Danes in that fort, my lord," said Alun, who'd come as Prince Rhun's representative, "they will have already left by the postern gate. We should have sent men to the beach to stop them."

"Alice did have Danes among her men," Gareth said, "though that they were Danes didn't register until just now. Alun is right."

"I saw them too," Hywel said. "I deliberately let them go."

"Why is that?" Color rose in Cadell's cheeks. "They are bloodthirsty killers; they'll go back to Ireland, get reinforcements, and continue to plague our shores."

"The only good Dane is a dead one," Maelgwyn said.

"That's what the English say about the Welsh." Hywel's eyes narrowed. "You may recall that I have Danish blood, Maelgwyn."

Maelgwyn paled. "Yes, my lord." This wasn't turning out to be a good day for him.

"We cannot kill every Dane in Ireland," Hywel said, his voice full of patience. "I am letting them go because I want to encourage Cadwaladr's return to Wales. The sooner my father confronts him in person, the better. The Danes will tell Cadwaladr that I've taken Aberystwyth. It will anger him."

"I don't understand—"

Hywel cut Maelgwyn off. "Obviously. This move is part of a greater whole, which I hadn't realized I had to explain to you. My father wants his brother back in Wales, under his control, not inciting animosity and wreaking havoc among our Danish allies. If I let these Danes go, they'll tell my uncle what has happened here at home. He won't be able to resist doing something about it."

A few of the men nodded.

"Regardless," Hywel said. "As Alun pointed out, they've probably already gone and there's nothing we can do about it. I don't care if the entire garrison of Cadwaladr's Welsh men-at-arms departs and disperses, though I would rather deliver them to my father as we did the men from Aberffraw. But if we spare all of them and yet take the castle, my father will consider this endeavor a victory. We will send a message to Cadwaladr that he must pay for his actions. I want that castle!" He punctuated this last sentence with a fist into his palm.

"Besides," Gareth said as the men dispersed to their appointed tasks, even Maelgwyn, "Cadwaladr still has Gwen and I want her back. If he doesn't bring her home, I may never see her again."

"I haven't forgotten Gwen, Gareth," Hywel said.

Gareth bit his tongue, holding back the words he wanted to say. As with the villagers whose deaths Cadwaladr had ordered—at the hands of his own men—the loss of Gwen was not a matter that King Owain could allow to trouble him. If pressed, he might say that it was an unfortunate happenstance, but to wager a kingdom on one girl? No, Gwen's well-being was Gareth's responsibility. And so far, he hadn't done his job in seeing to it.

For now, however, his duty to his lord forced Gareth to push the thought of Gwen, along with the image of her wearing a slave collar around her throat, to the back of his mind where it had sat and festered all this last week. That her captors thought she was pregnant with Hywel's child was a life-saving grace, but how long could that last before they discovered it was a lie? And what would happen to her when they did?

Despite their blood-curdling reputation, Danes were no different from any other men—which was both good and bad. They were, in fact, no more or less cruel than the men who surrounded him now, but they were also men, and despite the fact that she often seemed to care little for her appearance or what men thought of her, in Gareth's opinion, she was lovely. And he wasn't the only one who thought so.

As Goronwy's answer was the same as before, over the next hour, Hywel moved his force south to higher ground, though still some fifty feet below the elevation of the castle. He planted those men-at-arms and knights who could double as bowman within striking distance of the castle, two hundred yards away, sheltered behind their long shields. He then arrayed the remaining one hundred and fifty men in a ring around the castle, out of arrow range, but within sight of the walls so Goronwy would see what he faced.

Cadwaladr couldn't have left more than twenty men in the garrison, though if Danes were among them, that number might be doubled. Even so, forty could hardly charge out to attack two hundred with hope of success. And if they did, that would leave the castle empty. Hywel could take it intact in that case, or burn it down empty, just to show Cadwaladr his father's power.

The men hastily rigged regular arrows with knotted bits of cloth, ready for lighting moments before being loosed. Others scoured the woods for firewood, more easily found in August than at other times of year. Two men went into the village of Aberystwyth to garner oil with which to soak the cloth and make the fire more difficult to put out. The tied cloths would make the arrows wobble in the air, but Hywel wasn't interested in accuracy, or even in killing anyone. He wanted to burn the wood and thatch that comprised the interior of the castle.

"Loose!"

The first flight of arrows blazed into the sky just as the sun began to set behind the castle. The day had been a bright one and the night promised to be more beautiful still. Some of them fell short, falling to the ground outside the walls, but Hywel didn't move his men any closer for fear of the archers on the battlements. Still, one of the opposing arrows, surely loosed from a mighty bow, reached their lines and hit an archer in his right shoulder. He screamed and Gareth raced forward to drag him from his place.

"Move! Move!" That was Alun, directing another archer to fill the downed man's spot.

"Fire at the men on the wall!" Hywel said. "Regular arrows! Force them to keep their heads down!"

Flight after flight arced into the air, with more and more finding targets. Fire blazed over the top of the wall. This was how Owain Gwynedd and Cadwaladr had defeated this very castle in their battle against the Normans six years before, after which Anarawd retook the title of King of Deheubarth. It was how Hywel would take the castle now, and why King Owain had started the process of rebuilding all of his bastions in stone.

"It will soon be done." Hywel folded his arms across his chest and gazed with satisfaction at what he'd wrought. He turned to Gareth. "Take Evan and some others. Circle around to the north. I want to know what's happening with the men on the other side."

"If Cadwaladr's men flee, should we stop them?"

"Not at the cost of your lives," Hywel said. "In truth, they have nowhere to run. Between what we accomplish today, and what King Cadell plans in the coming weeks, we'll deprive Cadwaladr of all his holdings."

Gareth gathered a half dozen men and led them along the bank of the Ystwyth River. They followed it west, passing between the castle hill and Pen Dinas. Before they reached the beach, they rode upwards towards the plateau on which the castle sat. Now that the sun had fallen into the sea, they'd be safe enough in the growing darkness, and certainly Goronwy and his men would be too busy trying to contain the fires to worry about who and how many were coming against him from the rear.

A moment later, however, they found a downed man-at-arms lying in the grass. He was one of the scouts Hywel had sent to survey the area an hour earlier.

"What happened?" Gareth sprang down from Braith.

"Danes." The man moaned and held his side as blood seeped through his fingers. "They ran from the postern gate not long ago. Me and some others thought to stop them, even if Prince Hywel said we needn't."

"Which way did they go?" This came from one of Gareth's men.

"They carried heavy goods towards the beach," the man said.

"And you couldn't stop them?" Evan pressed a cloth to the man's wound before giving way to another soldier who knew more of healing.

"They just kept coming—twenty at least," he said. "We couldn't move out of the way fast enough."

Gareth pointed at a man-at-arms, still mounted on his horse. "Ride to Prince Hywel. Tell him what has happened. For the rest, find our other scouts and see how many more are down. Evan and I will follow the Danes. At a minimum, we can make sure they're gone for good, back to Dublin as Prince Hywel intends."

Gareth threw himself on Braith who navigated the descent to the beach far more fluidly than Gareth could have on foot. As they raced down the hill from the plateau, the figures of two dozen Danes coalesced out of the murk. They were already at the water's edge, loading their goods into two boats. At the sight of Gareth and Evan, several moved to intercept them, giving the remainder time to stow their loot.

A man in one of the boats waved an arm and called something in Danish. The six men broke out of their intimidating stance and returned, climbing awkwardly over the rail since the boats were already pushed back from the shore.

"Wait!" Gareth shouted one of the few words he knew in Danish and spurred Braith faster. "We mean you no harm!"

"Are you out of your mind?" Evan said, trying to keep up.

At Gareth's call, one of the Danes put up a hand and his rowers stopped pulling on the oars. He stood in the stern, his hands on his hips, defiant. He'd cropped his hair and beard so short he looked less like a Dane than a Saxon. Fortunately, he also spoke some Welsh.

"What do you want?" he said. "Why do I not kill you?"

Gareth reined Braith at the water's edge. "You sail for Ireland?"

"We did not come to defend a castle without Cadwaladr in it," the man said. "We take his gold and go home."

"And the men on the bluff that you harmed?" Gareth said.

The man shrugged. "They were in the way. That is all."

Gareth nodded, the reply within the realm of the expected. These Danes had no feelings about harming his men one way or the other. *They were in the way.* "I have a message for someone in Dublin."

The man didn't reply, just waited, impassive, not promising anything.

"A girl. Her name is Gwen. She's Welsh. Cadwaladr stole her from Aber. He left our shores with three longboats. The captain who commanded them was larger than average, blond."

The Dane nodded. "Godfrid. My brother."

"Tell Gwen that Gareth said he will come for her."

"Tell her yourself. Come with us if you dare." He grinned and gestured to his ship. "As guest." He thumped his chest. "I am Brodar, and I will take you to Dublin."

Gareth stared at him. Evan had come up beside him by now and grasped his arm. "What did he say?"

"He challenges me to come with him. To Dublin."

Gareth gazed out over the water. He desperately wanted to go with Brodar, to see to Gwen's safety, but his duty lay in Wales, serving his prince. He also, deep inside, feared that if he went to Dublin, he would not return.

"Go." Evan flicked the reins in a sort of dismissal. "I will explain to Hywel what has happened."

Evan's urging was all Gareth needed. He dismounted, threw Braith's reins to Evan, and then walked into the water that slapped around the stern of Brodar's longboat. He heaved himself over the rail.

A grin split Brodar's face. "Brave man."

Brodar roared at his men, something again in Danish that Gareth didn't catch, and they picked up the oars again, falling almost instantly into a unified rhythm.

Brodar pushed at Gareth's shoulder. "Sit there."

Gareth obeyed, finding a place at the prow. He settled onto a wooden seat and faced east. Evan remained as Gareth had left him, Braith's reins in his hand and her empty saddle a stark reminder of Gareth's impulsive choice. Gareth lifted a hand and Evan returned the salutation.

Once out of the bay, the wind rose and the Danes hoisted sail. They'd have two days of hard sailing before they'd reach Dublin. And Gwen. If she still lived.

30

Over the next few days, Godfrid didn't mention his suggestion that Gwen stay in Dublin. Her lack of answer for him didn't seem to interfere with the ease with which he spoke with her either. He remained attentive, even springing questions on her about her life in Wales, her family, and her music, which she'd sung to great applause—and apparent surprise—that third evening in Dublin. When she'd walked off the dais, Godfrid had looked at her as if she was a creature he'd created especially himself. It was flattering, if nothing else, but...

She couldn't delay talking to him about herself, and about them, if such a union would ever work, any longer. Across from him at the evening meal, she touched his hand. "I've thought about what you said to me. About what you asked."

Godfrid had been taking a sip from his cup and now set it down. She had his full attention.

"You've offered me something that I've wanted since I became a woman: a life that includes a man who cares for me, and children," she said. "And maybe even more than that, it seems likely you've offered me the freedom to be my own person."

"I meant it so," Godfrid said. "Yet, I see in your eyes that you do not accept."

"I cannot," Gwen said. "Please believe me when I tell you that it's not because of you."

"There is another," Godfrid said, and Gwen could see him thinking it through. "Though not Hywel."

"Not Hywel. In Wales—" Gwen paused again, trying to think it through herself and explain it in a way that would make sense to him, even if it meant talking around the subject first. She shrugged. "I think it's much the same here. One's family confines and constrains you in ways you don't even understand until you are away from them."

"It is thus with me and my father." Godfrid gestured to the front of the hall where Torcall sat, holding court. Shorter and darker than his son, he projected an aura of power that Gwen couldn't quite put her finger on or explain. It was enough that when he spoke, the hall quieted, and people walked more softly in the space around him.

"You are a grown man and yet, you do his bidding," Gwen said.

Godfrid smiled softly. "That is true." He touched her hand with one finger, mimicking what she'd done to him. "You were not speaking of my father."

Gwen smiled, shy now that it came to it. "My father has turned down every contract for me that has come his way. I've cared for him and my brother, Gwalchmai, since my mother died at Gwalchmai's birth."

- 263 -

"He doesn't want to let you go," Godfrid said. "He is clever but not wise."

Gwen tipped her head, acknowledging the distinction. "Part of me wants what you are offering, but I cannot stay here, Godfrid. It's possible that I could go home and then come back, but I am Welsh and my feet are dug deeply into that soil. I can't allow Cadwaladr—and all of you—to return to Wales without me." She gestured to the room at large. "Your coming will not be good for my people."

Godfrid studied her face for a long moment, and then nodded. "Cadwaladr will want my father and Ottar behind him when he faces Owain Gwynedd."

"And that is only one of a long list of his mistakes," Gwen said. "Your presence will have the opposite effect of the one he inten—"

The doors burst open at that instant, cutting Gwen's sentence short. Cadwaladr strode through them, at the head of a crowd of Danes. A grin split Godfrid's face and for a moment Gwen feared it was the sight of Cadwaladr that cheered him, but then a man walking just behind the Welsh prince lifted a hand to Godfrid, who waved back. He was a shorter, squatter version of Godfrid himself, so Gwen wasn't surprised when Godfrid said, "My brother, Brodar, comes."

Cadwaladr and Brodar were followed by ... *Gareth.*

Gwen stared, her heart in her throat. *Has he been captured too?* But his hands weren't tied and his sword still rested at his waist. He walked ahead of some of the Danes as a not-quite-trusted equal rather than a prisoner. His head swiveled this way and that and instinctively she knew he was looking for her. She stood, and then found that her feet had started moving of their own accord. She ran towards him. "Gareth!"

"*Cariad.*"

Gareth caught her and buried his face in her hair. Gwen had her arms around his neck, hanging on for dear life, thankful for how solid he felt. She only had a moment of him, however, before he pulled back, remembering propriety before she could. "You're all right? You're not hurt?"

"This is the one?" Godfrid loomed over them both, for though Gareth was a taller man than average, Godfrid dwarfed him.

Gwen clutched Gareth's hand. "Yes." A wave of relief swept through her at the admission. *Yes, he is the one.*

Godfrid stuck out his hand to Gareth. "She's in one piece. Keep a better eye on her next time. Don't let her be fair game for murderers and Danes."

Gareth eyed Godfrid and then to Gwen's relief, clasped Godfrid's offered forearm. "Your brother, Brodar, invited me to your hall, over the objections of Prince Cadwaladr. I am Gareth ap Rhys, a knight in Hywel ap Owain Gwynedd's company."

"Welcome," Godfrid said.

Gwen didn't even detect a hint of a growl in his throat, which later might be disappointing, but now was pure relief that she wasn't going to be caught between these two men.

"We must sit and drink," Godfrid said. "I sense that my father and Ottar will speak to everyone after they've conferred."

"Ottar's here too?" Gwen said as she and Gareth followed Godfrid back to their table. Gareth's arm remained firmly around her waist as he steered her across the room.

Godfrid canted his head towards his father's chair. Cadwaladr had found a seat on Torcall's left, with Ottar on the right, and the three huddled together, deep in conversation.

"Long odds that this conference bodes well for my king," Gareth said.

Gwen almost cried aloud, so glad was she to hear that subtle mockery again. The only person with whom she'd been able to converse had been Godfrid, but his Welsh wasn't sophisticated, though perhaps in his own language he was just as clever as Gareth.

Godfrid, for his part, still had other things on his mind. "How is it that Cadwaladr was able to abduct Gwen?" He accompanied his query with a belligerent set to his chin.

"I can't answer that." Gareth eyed Gwen. "I still don't know exactly what happened because I've not had a chance to speak to her since he took her from Aber."

"Wasn't your fort protected?" Godfrid said, not yet backing down. "Don't you look after your women?"

Gwen put a hand on Gareth's arm in hopes it would stop him from throttling Godfrid in frustration and turned to the big Dane. "Cadwaladr's men-at-arms threw Gareth in prison and Owain Gwynedd allowed it. King Cadell, Anarawd's brother, had false information pointing to *Gareth* as the killer of Anarawd, instead of Cadwaladr. Prince Cadwaladr, of course, supported him."

Godfrid's eyes flashed to Gareth, who still glared at him, and then he barked a laugh, the sound coming from that constant well of amusement inside him. "That sounds so much like Cadwaladr, it's a wonder you didn't see it coming yourselves. I had to put up with him for years in my father's hall when he lived in Dublin. Still, coupled with the other things you've told me, it is clear he has become more devious since he returned to Wales. That, I wouldn't have expected."

"Nor I, to tell the truth," Gareth said.

"How is it that you got free?" Godfrid waved his hand to encompass the space Gareth took up. "You are not imprisoned now. You stood with Prince Hywel at Aberffraw when he confronted Cadwaladr."

"Prince Hywel released me from my confinement, once it was clear that Gwen was missing," Gareth said. "Owain Gwynedd had instructed Hywel to track down Gwen—along with Cadwaladr if indeed it was he who had taken her—and my lord deemed me necessary to the task."

Godfrid's eyes lit again at that. "I see. And here you are in Dublin, and you have my brother to thank for it." He gestured towards Brodar who broke away from another table to come to theirs.

"That is true," Gareth said, though Godfrid wasn't listening anymore.

Godfrid stood so he and his brother could clasp hands. They slapped each other on the back. "How is it that you are here?" he said, still speaking in Welsh, even though both men would have been more comfortable in Danish.

"Ahh," Brodar said. "He hasn't told you yet? Prince Hywel came to Aberystwyth and burned us out."

Gwen turned to Gareth. "Is that true?"

Gareth nodded. "King Owain stood before the nobles of Wales and disowned Cadwaladr for acts beyond forgiveness."

"So what happens next?" Gwen said.

Gareth nodded towards the three lords at the front of the hall. "Cadwaladr plans to return to Gwynedd at the front of a horde of Danes."

"Horde?" Godfrid caught the derogatory term.

Gareth held out a hand. "Company. Army. Contingent. I spoke without thinking."

"But it is what King Owain will be thinking, Godfrid," Gwen said. "You must know this. Your people raided our shores for centuries before Gwynedd and Dublin made peace. King Owain's father sought asylum with you, much as Cadwaladr has, but his was a rightful claim to the throne of Gwynedd, not the shameful retreat of a man disgraced and honorless."

"I know it." Godfrid glanced over his shoulder at Cadwaladr, laughing now beside Torcall. "Anarawd was to be King Owain's son-in-law?"

"Yes," Gwen said.

Brodar took a drink. "Cadwaladr has got us all in a right mess this time, hasn't he?"

Nobody could argue with that.

Gwen leaned close to Gareth. "What did Cadwaladr say when he saw you?"

"He went for his sword, but Brodar told him to put up, since I'd come to Dublin as his guest." Then Gareth grinned. "He cast aspersions on my antecedents."

"And you—" Gwen was almost afraid to ask.

"I am a better man than he," Gareth said. "He'll get his comeuppance soon enough."

Those in the hall ate and drank in merriment, and as the meal came to an end, Torcall stood to silence the crowd and speak to his people. Gwen didn't understand his words, but Godfrid leaned in and translated quietly underneath his father's speech: "I have spoken with my friends, Cadwaladr of Gwynedd, and my fellow ruler of Dublin, Ottar. They tell me that Cadwaladr has been dispossessed of his lands in Wales."

"How do we know this is true?" This came from one of the men near the front.

Torcall looked to Brodar, who raised a hand. "I saw it myself."

Torcall continued: "Prince Cadwaladr has informed me that he will pay us two thousand marks to come with him to Gwynedd and persuade..." Here, Torcall paused, allowing for general laughter around the room, "... his brother to reinstate him."

Cadwaladr nodded sagely, still seated at the table on the dais.

"I say we go!" Ottar raised a fist into the air.

"So say I," Torcall said, in a more level voice. "We leave in two days' time."

Two days. Gwen glanced at Cadwaladr, expecting him to look expansive and satisfied as before, but now he glared at their table. He wasn't looking at her, however, so much as at Gareth, who was talking to Godfrid and Brodar and didn't notice. Still not looking at her, Cadwaladr stood, excused himself from the two kings, and strode towards Gwen's table. All three men looked up at his approach, and all three rose to their feet.

"The girl stays with me," Cadwaladr said. "Now that we are returning to Wales, I insist upon it."

"You gutless bastar—" began Gareth, but Godfrid had already stepped in front of Gwen, his hand to Cadwaladr's chest.

"You will not touch her," he said, all amusement gone.

Cadwaladr snorted. "What would I want with her? She's Hywel's whore, not mine."

Before the debate grew even more heated, Torcall and Ottar appeared on either side of Cadwaladr. Torcall edged between Cadwaladr and Godfrid, his eyes on his sons. "We agree with Cadwaladr that she was part of his protection," Torcall said, and then added something in Danish that Gwen didn't understand. Godfrid, at least, eased away from both his father and Cadwaladr, who reached forward to grasp Gwen's arm.

"Let go of me!" Gwen jerked her arm, trying to twist it out of Cadwaladr's grip.

Gareth had his arm around her waist again, looking daggers at Cadwaladr.

Cadwaladr put his hands up. "Torcall. See to this bitch."

Gareth's hand went to the hilt of his sword but before he could draw it, Godfrid had his forearm in a tight grip while Brodar tugged at the back of Gareth's hair.

"She goes with him," Torcall said, not looking at Gwen but at his sons and Gareth.

"You're going to let her go? Just like that?" Gareth said to Godfrid.

Godfrid, for his part, let go of Gareth in order to grab Gwen's chin so he could look into her eyes. "My father assures me that you will be safe."

Gwen shook them all off. While some part of her couldn't be unhappy that men were fighting over her, it would only get Gareth in trouble. "All right; all right. Heaven forbid any of you come to grief because of me. I will go." Her stomach roiled at the thought of leaving Gareth so soon after reuniting with him, but Cadwaladr had proven to be a fearsome, yet fickle, foe. If her going could protect Gareth, she could bear his presence for a while longer.

"Gwen—"

Gwen grasped the edges of Gareth's cloak. "Stand down." And then softened her words by going up on her toes and pecking Gareth on the cheek. "I'll be fine."

Torcall tugged her away from Gareth. With a last glance back at the three men, all of whom looked murderous, she allowed Cadwaladr to lead her out of the hall.

31

Gareth didn't see Gwen again until they were loading the boats for the voyage to Wales. The martial nature of the expedition was immediately obvious. The Danes took on supplies, although by Gareth's estimate, only food for the journey and the initial day or two in Wales. Either the Danes were assuming this would be over quickly, or that they could plunder the countryside. As it was late August, the pickings would be easy.

"You will sail with me," Godfrid said to Gareth, as they heaved crates and satchels into the ship, to be stored in the prow or stern.

Danish ships had no below-decks, since their keels were so shallow. It allowed them to pull right up to a beach and push off just as easily, but meant that pillaging—or foraging, as Godfrid preferred to call it—was a way of life. Two dozen men settled easily into their rowing positions. As this was a fighting ship, even though it was large enough to cross the Irish Sea, there was no space for men who couldn't do double-duty. Or triple. Warriors rowed as easily as slaves and it kept them busy through the long days and nights of travel.

Godfrid stood on the edge of the dock and gazed out to sea, his eyes tracing the clouds that were rarely absent, even in August.

"What is it?" Gareth stepped forward to look with him.

"Rain and a little wind," Godfrid said. "Nothing with which to concern yourself."

Gareth's thoughts went to Gwen and her fragile stomach and his own clenched. Many Welsh were fishermen, but he was not and though he'd travelled to Ireland and back twice now, he'd not fallen in love with sea journeys as some did. Perhaps if Gareth had spent his life on the sea as Godfrid had, he'd be as familiar with its moods as he was with the mountains of Snowdonia. There, he could find a trail or track a deer across woods, moor, and fields. Here, all he saw was water.

Gareth had been given no chance to speak to Gwen, though he'd tried. He'd caught a glimpse of her a moment ago, standing in the prow of Cadwaladr's ship. She'd looked over and lifted a hand to him, though she didn't smile and he supposed he couldn't blame her.

"She's all right. I made sure of it." Godfrid grunted as he set down the last sack and shot him a glance from under his bushy eyebrows. "She sleeps in a room with Ottar's women. No one has touched her."

Gareth nodded his thanks. Fear for her had sickened him throughout the last two days. He'd had to force back thoughts of storming into Ottar's hall and demanding her return. But Gwen herself would have been angry at him for that—for calling attention to himself and putting himself at risk over nothing. Or what she might call nothing. To Gareth's mind it was nothing short of torture.

Godfrid raised his fist and the ship got underway. As when they'd sailed west, the men rowed until they reached more open sea, and then hoisted the sail. Their ship was one among eight, nearly two hundred and fifty men in all, bought with Cadwaladr's promise of money.

"Has he paid anyone any gold yet?" Gareth asked Godfrid. He was watching Gwen, three boats over, and noted the moment she sank to her knees by the rail. She faced away from him, probably on purpose.

"Brodar took gold from Aberystwyth before it burned," Godfrid said. "Cadwaladr promised us two thousand marks this time, but according to Brodar, the five hundred he took from the castle was all Cadwaladr had."

"The men who attacked Anarawd's company carried no gold either," Gareth said. "Cadwaladr must not have paid them yet."

"As he has not paid us." Godfrid eyed Gwen's boat. Cadwaladr stood proudly at the helm.

"He will double-cross you too, if it suits him," Gareth said.

"We won't let him."

Gareth shrugged. "I'm not sure you'll be able to stop him, especially since he appears to have Ottar's trust."

"Let's just say that my father is not Ottar," Godfrid said. "I spoke to him of Cadwaladr's treachery, of the murder and Owain Gwynedd's reaction." Godfrid glanced at Gareth. "What troubled my father the most was the sloppiness of Cadwaladr's plans. He is more unreliable than we'd thought."

"I've been doing some thinking myself these last few days," Gareth said. "About that murder, and the aftermath."

"Tell me." Godfrid's eyes flicked from one aspect of his domain to another in rapid movements—to the oarsmen, to the cargo, to his men working in the rigging of the ship—but he was listening.

"Anarawd left Dolwyddelan a day earlier than he'd originally planned," Gareth said. "It wasn't by design but because he was impatient to reach Aber and his bride. As it turns out, Cadwaladr's mercenaries were ready for him anyway. This you know."

Godfrid nodded.

"Later, however, three more people died: a servant at Aber, a Dane, knifed and skewered through the belly in an abandoned fort not far from the ambush site, and a young stable boy at Dolwyddelan Castle."

Now, Gareth had Godfrid's full attention. "And Cadwaladr killed all these too? Or had them killed?"

"It's hard to see that Cadwaladr was actually at the ambush, even if he paid for it. He's never been fond of getting his hands dirty—but the others? I don't know." Gareth shook his head.

Godfrid sniffed. "Anarawd was dead. That was all that mattered. Cadwaladr should have been satisfied with that."

"Cadwaladr has never been one for measured thinking," Gareth said.

"Were you numbered among Owain Gwynedd's men who killed the mercenaries?" Godfrid said.

"Yes," Gareth said. "As was Gwen, though she was caught up in all this innocently enough, since her family was traveling the same road as Anarawd for the same reason—to attend the wedding. They were to provide the entertainment."

"Huh," was all Godfrid said.

"The stable boy and the servant are different matters. Their deaths were clearly designed to cover up wrongdoing: the servant because she was paid to poison me, and the stable boy because he was paid to sabotage Anarawd's horse, whether to delay him until the mercenaries had readied their ambush, or to make him an easy target when they came upon him. But he nobbled the wrong horse."

"And you know this—how?" Godfrid said.

"The horse he hurt belonged to Gwen's father."

"And why do you think this is something I should know?"

"Because you must understand that once Cadwaladr has what he wants, or feels close to getting it, it's highly unlikely you will ever see your two thousand marks," Gareth said. "What is the point of bringing you to Wales except to force King Owain to accept him back and restore his lands? And once he has done that, why should Cadwaladr pay you for your services? He won't need you anymore because he'll be back in the king's good graces."

"He will pay us because we will ravage his lands if he doesn't," Godfrid said, a growl forming in his throat.

"But by doing so, you risk King Owain's wrath and the full weight of his armies against you," Gareth said. "I'm surprised your father didn't think of this already."

Godfrid let the silence drag out while he stared over the water, towards Wales, though they couldn't yet see it. Finally, he nodded his head. "We did think of it. My father spoke with me before I left about the possibility of changing course, should it become necessary."

"Changing course—you mean going back to Dublin? What about Gwen?"

"Not to Dublin, to Aber," Godfrid said. "Through me, my father would have a word with your king."

Gareth stared at him. "You would go against Ottar?"

"You object to the idea?" Godfrid said.

"Of course not." Gareth adjusted his expression. "I'm delighted. King Owain has no wish to fight the combined might of the Kings of Dublin."

Godfrid grunted and folded his arms across his chest. Gareth had told Prince Cadwaladr's son, Cadfan, that politics were best left to others, but in this matter, it seemed Gareth himself couldn't avoid them.

They'd left at dawn, in hopes of reaching Anglesey before nightfall on the second day out, given that the winds were from the west (thus behind them), unlike when they'd sailed west and had to tack against them the whole way to Ireland. High winds rocked them that first night, however, with rain and storm so severe it was only the direction of the wind that told them which way to sail.

Godfrid claimed the storm was a blessing from God on his course of action. Gareth couldn't argue with that, since he didn't want Godfrid to have second thoughts about betraying Cadwaladr, even if Gareth had to spend the entire time fearing for Gwen. But he would have done that anyway.

The storm blew the boat off course—all of the boats, in fact—such that they lost track of the fleet in the night. Each captain put a lantern in the prow, but between the high waves and the wind, by midnight, Godfrid's ship was alone in the Irish Sea.

At one point, Godfrid found Gareth cowering in the prow of the boat, trying to shield his face from the rain. "We'll steer to the north and sail around Anglesey. God smiles upon us. He approves of this new plan."

Gareth didn't know about that. "And the other boats?"

"Cadwaladr's intent was to land at Abermenai, at the mouth of the Menai Straits, on Anglesey."

"He might have already reached shore, given these winds," Gareth said.

"Or he too could have been blown off course," Godfrid said. "His boat could be just on the other side of the next wave for all we know."

"If we don't want him to discover us, we should douse the lantern," Gareth said.

Godfrid cursed, having forgotten it. He shouted to a man in the prow, who extinguished the light, plunging the boat into darkness.

Dear God. Keep Gwen safe.

The waves rolled on and eventually Gareth fell into a fitful sleep. The storm gradually spent itself, and by first light, Gareth woke to find that not only were none of the other boats in sight, but they were already skirting the northern tip of Anglesey.

The rain subsided to a drizzle and, tugging his sodden cloak closer, Gareth staggered to the stern where Godfrid addressed several of his men. He was speaking in Danish but turned as Gareth approached.

"At present rate, we'll reach Aber before another two hours have passed," Gareth said, by way of greeting.

"What will your king think when he sees a Danish ship riding up on his beach?" Godfrid said.

Gareth laughed, his dark mood lifting as they neared the Gwynedd shore. "He won't be happy. But he should be wise enough not to shoot first and ask questions later."

Godfrid guffawed and clapped Gareth on the back. "I like the way you think. I leave this in your hands."

"At the very least, I should ride in the prow," Gareth said. "If Hywel returned from Ceredigion in good order, he will know that I went to Dublin."

"Prince Hywel will forgive you the impulse?" Godfrid said.

"I hope so," Gareth said. It didn't matter so much if Hywel forgave him or not at this point, unless it meant that Gareth was out on his ear again. For Gareth's part, he knew going to Dublin had been the right decision, though that would be small comfort when his purse was empty.

Gareth watched the shoreline with some apprehension. The watchers on Aber's battlements saw them coming long before they reached the shore. They had time to organize a company of men. One Danish ship wasn't as much of a threat to Aber as many more would have been. It was only as they neared the beach that Gareth spared a thought for the uncertainty involved and that he hadn't had time to think this through thoroughly before facing a potentially angry king.

The soldiers came on at a trot, and Gareth's heart lifted to see Hywel's banner streaming above the cavalry. It was Hywel himself, with two dozen men arrayed behind him. Exactly as Gareth had hoped.

While the others waited in the boat, which Godfrid deliberately did not beach, Gareth leaped out, soaking himself to his knees, and waded into shore.

"My lord." Gareth bowed his head.

"I'm glad to see you in one piece, my friend," Hywel said. "What have you brought us?"

With that, Gareth understood that it was going to be all right. This one sentence that acknowledged Gareth's absence might be all Hywel ever said of Gareth's decision to leave Wales without permission.

"Godfrid ap Torcall." Gareth waved a hand behind him for Godfrid to come forward. Still, Godfrid didn't beach the boat. He stepped over the rail as Gareth had and trudged the short distance to Prince Hywel's stirrup.

He held out his hand in greeting, as one king's son to another. "I am pleased to meet you, Hywel ap Owain Gwynedd. I bring you greetings from my father, King Torcall of Dublin."

Hywel leaned down to clasp Godfrid's forearm. "If you come in friendship, you are welcome."

"I do," Godfrid said. "May I invite my men ashore?"

"Certainly," Hywel said. "You are my guests."

"I believe your father will be interested in what I have to say."

"I will take you to him," Hywel said.

Godfrid gestured to his crew and with one stroke, the oarsman had them on the beach. Godfrid left two men to guard the ship and the rest paired off to march behind him. The mounted Welshman surrounded them, but since Hywel himself had dismounted so as to continue on foot with Gareth and the Danes, Gareth hoped it didn't make them feel that they were prisoners, any more than he'd felt like a prisoner in Dublin. Hywel had even allowed them to keep their weapons.

"Was your venture in Ceredigion successful?" Gareth asked his prince.

Hywel glanced at him out of the corner of his eye, a smile quirking the corner of his mouth. "Successful enough. We will speak later."

Gareth nodded, understanding that Hywel didn't want to talk in front of Godfrid. "Yes, my lord."

When they reached Aber, Godfrid looked with interest at the gates, their accompanying towers, and the work being done on the wall. "Stone, eh?" he said to Gareth in an aside.

"You may note that it doesn't burn like wood," Gareth said.

Godfrid barked a laugh. "You have the right of it."

Then they were through the gate, across the courtyard, and into the great hall. Godfrid and Hywel, with Gareth a pace behind, marched between the tables to where King Owain sat. He was arrayed as a king in preparation for greeting Godfrid.

The two princes came to a halt in front of King Owain's seat and both bowed lower than usual. "Father." Hywel moved to stand just to the right of the king's throne, "May I present to you Godfrid ap Torcall, prince of Dublin."

King Owain bowed slightly in greeting. "Welcome to Aber, Godfrid. I am always happy to greet a royal cousin at Aber."

"Thank you, my lord," Godfrid said. "I come to you with some urgency, with news that cannot wait."

King Owain leaned forward. "I would hear it." His glance took in the entire company of Danes—and Gareth—who also bowed his head in greeting.

"No doubt you have heard that your brother fled to Dublin, to my father's seat, when he left Anglesey," Godfrid said.

"That was my understanding," King Owain said.

"He comes to Wales at the head of seven ships—eight if you count mine, which you shouldn't. King Ottar himself commands one of the boats."

"And what is his intent?" King Owain's voice had not changed, but Gareth felt the temperature of the air drop. If Godfrid noticed it, he didn't alter his stance.

"Far be it from me to convey any man's true thoughts," Godfrid said, adding a bardic flourish to his words, "but it is my understanding that Prince Cadwaladr hopes you will gaze on the fleet, see that he is a powerful lord in his own right, and reinstate his lands."

"And he thinks that threatening me with two hundred Danes will make me bend?" King Owain pushed to his feet, his voice rising along with him.

Godfrid canted his head in acknowledgement of the righteousness of King Owain's anger. "Two hundred and fifty men, though fewer now that he doesn't have mine at his back."

"And why are you here?" King Owain said. "What do you hope to gain?"

"Cadwaladr promised King Ottar two thousand marks," Godfrid said. "Gold is a pleasure, but my father and I seek a greater treasure—something that Cadwaladr cannot give us."

King Owain studied the big Dane through several heartbeats before easing back into his chair. "Something from me," he said, not as a question.

"We share blood," Godfrid said. "Your father sought sanctuary with mine, once upon a time, and support when he needed it to regain the throne of Gwynedd. My father and I—and my brothers—ask the same of you when our time comes."

"Against Ottar."

Again, Godfrid tipped his head. "As you say, my lord."

Owain tapped his finger on the arm of his chair as he thought. Then he nodded. "Where did Cadwaladr hope to land?"

Godfrid gestured to Gareth, who stepped forward to speak. "Abermenai, my lord. He must feel safe on Anglesey."

Hywel directed his gaze at Gareth. "You believe what Godfrid says?"

"I do," Gareth said. "He protected Gwen in Dublin, if that brings favor in your eyes. The only reason she didn't return to Wales in Godfrid's boat is that Cadwaladr wouldn't let her. He kept her beside him for the return journey."

"She was well when you saw her last?" Hywel said.

"Yes, as far I know. A storm broke apart our fleet in the night."

Hywel grimaced. "She gets very seasick."

"She does," Gareth said. "It was good luck for us, however, since it meant that by dawn, we sailed alone." Gareth found his shoulders tensing at what she'd endured at sea—and might be enduring now. He forced his mind away, finding the thought of her among the Danes without a protector unbearable.

King Owain stepped off the dais. "I want my *teulu* assembled and ready to ride to Abermenai within the hour." He spun on his heel to look at his steward, Taran, a man who'd also served Owain's father. "When does the tide turn?"

"Noon today," Taran said. "We must hurry if we want to cross the sands before then."

King Owain swung back to the crowd of men before him. "You heard him! Move! We will provision ourselves at Aberffraw." Then King Owain put out a hand to Godfrid. "Thank you for your warning. If we hurry—and our luck continues—we can beat them to the shore. Your crossing was quicker than I've ever heard a ship—even a Danish one—make the journey."

"Prince Godfrid kept the sail up," Gareth said, unable to keep the glint of amusement out of his eye that perhaps only Hywel and Godfrid caught. "About killed us."

King Owain strode to the door of the hall and looked out. A light breeze blew and the sun was halfway up in the beautifully clear sky. "If they survived, they should have clear sailing for the rest of the day. Would they still make for Abermenai, even if they were blown off course and lost time?"

"I don't know." Godfrid came to stand beside the king. "I expect so, provided most of the ships survived the crossing."

"Anglesey is familiar territory to Cadwaladr," Hywel said, "more so than Ceredigion. Home, if you will."

"He'll come, then," King Owain said. "We'll have to risk it." He directed his attention to Godfrid again. "Thank you for your warning, but what of you? Shall you remain with us, or maintain a façade for King Ottar that you support him? It isn't too late to rejoin your fleet."

Godfrid studied his men, all of whom stared back at him impassively. He waved his hand and they broke ranks to huddle around him, speaking rapidly in Danish. Gareth, meanwhile, left the hall at a run to saddle Braith, though not before embracing

Evan who stopped him in the middle of the courtyard. He'd been among the men who'd come to the shore with Hywel, but Gareth hadn't had the opportunity to greet him before this.

"I never thought to see you again," Evan said. "I assumed they'd toss you into the water when you were halfway out to sea."

"Truly?" Gareth said. "You thought I couldn't survive a trip to Dublin?" When Evan just smiled, Gareth added, "Besides, Brodar gave me his word. As odd as it sounds, a Dane has honor. It's just that sometimes that means something different to him than it does to us."

Evan clapped him on the shoulder. "I'll never doubt you again."

Reunited with a saddled and nominally provisioned Braith, Gareth rode out of the castle with forty men before an hour had passed. They had so few because Hywel had left many in Ceredigion to clean up after Cadwaladr and maintain a presence there for a time. King Owain had given the rest leave to visit their homes, thinking Cadwaladr wouldn't return so quickly, even though Hywel had counseled against it.

Godfrid and his men trotted quickly behind them, making for Aber beach where they'd left their boat. Godfrid had decided that open warfare was not in his best interest, not yet. He would return to his fleet, circling far around Anglesey instead of sailing down the Menai Straits, so as to disguise the true direction from which he was coming.

"I should be returning with you," Gareth said.

Godfrid shook his head vigorously. "You are a warrior. If it comes to battle, your life would be forfeit. You will do better with your own people."

Gareth ground his teeth, but had to give way before the determined Dane. "Please tell Gwen that I love her. Tell her it was better not to come myself this time."

"I will tell everyone but her that you drowned in the night; that you were a foolish sailor. You stood up when you shouldn't have and we lost you overboard."

Gareth laughed despite himself, and waved the Danish prince—and unexpected friend—away. He had a feeling they would meet again before this was over.

32

Gwen moaned. She lay as she'd been thrown by the storm. The morning after the storm had brought sunshine with it and Gwen had fallen asleep at last, her cloak over her face to protect it from the sun.

Gradually, Gwen came more awake. The boat wasn't rocking as badly as before and her stomach was more settled than at any time in the last two days. In fact, the boat seemed hardly to be moving at all. Hesitant, hardly daring to believe they'd really arrived at their destination and half afraid that they'd suffered another disaster, this time no wind instead of too much, she lifted her head to look over the side of the boat.

The craft was pulled onto the beach far enough to keep it secure but with the stern still rocked by the steadily rolling waves. Gwen pushed to a sitting position and then stood, resting her hands on the rail of the ship so she could stay upright. As when they'd crossed the Irish Sea in the other direction, she felt hollowed out—her stomach, her heart, her eyes. For all that she hated being separated from Gareth while on board ship, part of her was glad that he hadn't been with her in her darkest hours, for his sake, if not for her own.

The last two days had consisted of unending hours of misery and little else. She supposed her illness had one single benefit: none of the Danes, nor Cadwaladr, had shown any interest in approaching her. And she'd slept so long that either everyone had forgotten about her, or they were too preoccupied with their own concerns. Fine with her.

Gwen scanned the beach, counting the ships on the shore and then the men moving around them. She counted again. Only six ships were drawn up on the beach. Two boats were missing. Where were they?

Another check of the symbols carved into the ships' bows and she realized that Godfrid's flagship was one of the missing. Unable to dampen her rising panic, Gwen clambered out of the ship and fell to her knees when her legs wouldn't hold her up. The grittiness of the sand was welcome in her clenched fists, along with its warmth. She checked the sky. It was late in the day, nearly sunset, which meant that she'd endured two full days of sailing, despite the easterly wind.

Cadwaladr had found a post on the top of a dune that gave him a good view of the land to the east of the beach. Gathering herself and careless of his status, which she'd never respected anyway, Gwen marched up to him, pleased to see his usual, perfectly-turned-out apparel ruined by salt and spray. She cleared her throat, forcing the words through the parchedness. "Where's G—"

"We've seen no sign of his ship since the storm," Cadwaladr said, not waiting for her to clear her throat again. "Godfrid's is the only one missing. We've another scouting a possible landing site to the south of the Menai Straits."

"Why would we want to move?"

And then Gwen didn't need an answer because she saw what had caught Cadwaladr's attention: a line of tents and cooking fires, a quarter of a mile away. The flag flying above the tents showed the unmistakable Gwynedd lions. Owain Gwynedd had come, unannounced and unlooked for. It must have been very disappointing to Cadwaladr to find himself caged. He'd raged for most of the night at the Fates for causing the storm, and now had cause to curse them again.

Owain had placed his tents in such a way that Cadwaladr's company couldn't leave the beach except by sea. His choice now was to take his Danes and flee again—whether south to his burned castle at Ceredigion where he could try to marshal support among his subjects against his brother (unlikely), or to the other side of the Straits so that he'd have free rein for a time near Caernarfon. Or he could negotiate. Cadwaladr had to know, however, that loosing his Danes on the local populace would not endear him to Owain, and might permanently sever their relationship. He'd brought the Danes to threaten his brother, not because he thought he could conquer Gwynedd with them.

"What's your plan?" Brodar had pushed his helmet back from his face and now scratched his ear with a sandy hand.

"I must speak to my brother," Cadwaladr said. "I will go alone."

"Oh, no, you don't!" Brodar caught Cadwaladr's arm in a tight grip, as if he thought Cadwaladr planned to set off towards King Owain's lines at that very moment. Maybe Cadwaladr would have if Brodar hadn't stopped him. "What's to prevent you from turning on us, now that you're here? You owe us two thousand marks!"

"Then what do you propose?" Cadwaladr gestured towards Owain Gwynedd's lines. "My brother has come too soon."

It looked to Gwen as if Cadwaladr had just realized the truth of his situation: that the Danes weren't his servants. He was their hostage, held against his will until he paid what he owed. He should have known better than to think he could get the better of his Nordic cousins.

"I will go," Brodar said. "Or King Ottar will, to speak to Owain Gwynedd on your behalf."

"King Ottar knows no Welsh." Cadwaladr sniffed and stuck his nose into the air. "And if you think—"

A shout from the shore distracted Cadwaladr from his unfinished sentence, and before he could conclude it, Brodar left him at a run. Gwen turned to see what had excited them: Godfrid's ship was sailing into the cove. His distinctive sail with a hind in its center—indicating it was the ship of the prince and heir to Dublin—grew larger with every stroke of the oars. Godfrid himself perched at the front of the boat like a conquering hero. The ship reached the beach and pulled up. Among general shouting and jubilation at his survival, nobody seemed to notice Gwen's state of near collapse.

Finally, she was able to pull Godfrid aside, tears already pouring down her cheeks at the news she'd yet to hear. "Where's Gareth, Godfrid?"

He leaned in, brushing her cheek with his lips and whispered close to her ear: "Alive." Then he straightened and cuffed Cadwaladr's shoulder. "Your countryman fell overboard; didn't know when to huddle in the boat like a sane man."

Cadwaladr's eyes narrowed. "He is your only loss?"

"Not much of one," Godfrid said, "though if you were his friend, I am sorry."

"No friend of mine." Cadwaladr turned away and strode back up the beach to resume his post on the dune.

Brodar moved in close, allowing the other men to disperse out of earshot. Gwen stayed where she was. Brodar glanced at her and then back at his brother, prompting Godfrid to put his arm around Gwen's shoulder.

"Speak so Gwen can understand," Godfrid said.

Brodar obliged. "All is well, brother?"

"We play a greater game," Godfrid said. "Two thousand marks is hardly worth our time in comparison to what I have planned; what Father has planned."

"What of Prince Cadwaladr?" Brodar looked past Godfrid's shoulder at the Welsh prince. "Owain Gwynedd has come. His men stand just there..." Brodar gestured to the east. "I told

Cadwaladr that we wouldn't give him leave to go to him; that I would speak to King Owain for him."

"Good," Godfrid said. "We shouldn't let him out of our sight. We cannot trust him."

The trio headed up the beach towards the campfires. Gwen's stomach growled. She hadn't eaten anything since they'd left Dublin, and not much even then because she knew it would end up in the sea anyway. At their approach, other men stood, including Ottar, who rubbed his hands together—*in anticipation?* Godfrid nodded his greeting and released Gwen. "The men must discuss the future. Don't wander off."

Gwen made a moue of irritation, her eyes never leaving his, but obeyed. She moved towards another fire pit, noting as she did that Cadwaladr had left his post. It was dark enough now that he couldn't see anything, other than the cooking fires of his brother's men. They were at a stalemate, if a temporary one. She gazed eastward herself, wondering what was going to happen next, and hoping *next* included Gareth.

33

Godfrid had come back from his meeting with Ottar and Cadwaladr in a foul mood. He'd worked for over an hour, making Gwen a bower of a sort, hollowed out of a dune with driftwood forming a makeshift roof. And hadn't spoken more than a grunt to Gwen the whole time.

"You'll be all right for tonight," he said, finally breaking his silence. "I'll be keeping watch not far away, and Brodar too."

"Thank you, Godfrid," she said. "It's more than I expected."

"Well, it shouldn't be," he said.

"And Gareth?" Gwen lowered her voice. "How did you get him safe?"

"Suffice that he is. Better you don't know." Godfrid grumbled something she didn't catch in Danish, and then stalked away to a campfire Brodar had lit and now sat next to with half a dozen of Godfrid's men.

Gone was the merry Dane and in his place was a very serious and worried prince. Gwen watched him go, more concerned than she wanted to admit. *How much should she be worried too?* She'd eaten and drunk just enough to feel comfortable for the first time in a week. It gave her renewed energy and strength and she thought about the various ways she might get herself free, now that she was back in Wales. King Owain's camp wasn't far. Might she find a moment when the guards were inattentive and escape?

But then she glanced to where Godfrid sat with his men and thought better of it. She couldn't quite put her finger on the virtue in staying—the honor that seemed to emanate from Godfrid in particular, but it applied to her as much as it had to Gareth when he'd come to Dublin. To escape would imply that she was Godfrid's prisoner, and that he couldn't trust her, and somehow that felt wrong. Still occupied with these thoughts, Gwen tucked herself into her blankets and closed her eyes.

She was almost asleep when footfalls in the sand had her opening her eyes again and searching beyond the rim of the dying fire for whoever had made the noise. She glanced towards Godfrid's fire. More time must have passed than she'd realized because the men had lain down to sleep, leaving only a single sentry awake who wasn't looking her way. She eased to her feet, a blanket wrapped around her shoulders, and took two steps away from the fire. Another few steps and darkness encompassed her. What had she heard?

She was about ready to give up and dismiss the footsteps as her imagination, when she spied a black shape flitting across the sand, heading away from the camp. Fearing the worst, she followed, peering into the dimness ahead and hardly able to make out the person's shape in the darkness. A moment later, however, a white face looked back towards her and she stilled. *Cadwaladr*. She hoped he couldn't see her silhouetted against the light behind her.

And then the shape disappeared into the scrub to the east of the beach. Her thoughts whirling, Gwen let out a deep breath. Should she follow him, or did honor mean that she should turn back and warn Godfrid that Cadwaladr had gone?

She headed back to the camp at a run, past the spot where she'd slept, and pulled up at Godfrid's campfire. She knelt, her hand to Godfrid's shoulder, and shook once.

Godfrid's thick hand fisted around her forearm and he sat up. "What is it?"

"It's Cadwaladr. He's gone," she said.

"Stinking Welsh traitor!" Ottar's rough hand grasped her arm and yanked her away from Godfrid.

"What—?" she said, in reflex, her voice going high.

Ottar loomed over her, shouting words she couldn't understand. Godfrid sprang to his feet and spoke rapidly. Never had Gwen wished she understood Danish more. The argument became heated very quickly—not that Ottar wasn't already fired up—and didn't resolve in Godfrid's favor. As she struggled to stay on her feet, Ottar hauled her with him through the darkness and the seething mass of angry men to his tent, one of the few the Danes had brought.

When they reached it, he forced her inside and shoved her to the ground. She landed on a fur rug that formed the floor of the tent. She twisted to look back at him. He glared at her, a knife in his hand. Nearly hysterical with fear, she crab-walked towards the back of the tent to get away from him. By the time Godfrid pushed inside, Brodar right behind him, she cowered in the far corner. Taking in the scene at a glance, Godfrid grabbed Ottar's arm but in a flash, Ottar pressed the knife to Godfrid's throat instead of Gwen's. Godfrid's hands came up and he stepped back, retreating towards the entrance he'd just come through and almost stepping on Brodar's toes.

King Ottar spit out an order to someone outside the tent whom Gwen couldn't see. Gwen's heart threatened to beat right out of her chest while she waited for whatever would happen next. She blanked her mind, trying not to think and to focus only on her breathing. *I will get through this.* Then, a man entered with a length of rope and wound it around Gwen's wrists and ankles until she was tied like a pig for the spit. At this, Ottar seemed to calm and Gwen herself gave in to relief. Tying her up was minor, compared to what he could have done to her.

Brodar had been speaking fiercely to him, and now Ottar laughed and put away his knife. He clapped Brodar on the back, sneered something into Godfrid's stony face, and left the tent without another glance at Gwen.

"Why is he doing this?" Gwen said to Godfrid before he too could leave. She was sick of these silent men who tossed her around like a sack of turnips with little regard for her wishes, thoughts, or feelings. "I could have run like Cadwaladr, but I didn't!"

Godfrid hesitated, half in and half out of the doorway. "It would have been better if you had." He didn't look at her, and she realized he was afraid—he, Godfrid, a prince of Dublin. He spoke over his shoulder. "You are now the only leverage Ottar has against Owain Gwynedd. Let's hope that King Owain has more honor than his brother."

"But—"

"Don't speak another word. It isn't safe." He shook his head at her, just once, and was gone.

The transition from asleep and free to bound prisoner had happened so fast Gwen was having a hard time keeping up with the change. She took in a deep breath, trying to slow her frantic thoughts, and assess her situation. She'd gone from being Cadwaladr's prisoner to being Ottar's; from hovering on the edge of Ottar's consciousness, to landing smack in the center of it. Like Cadwaladr, he still thought she was pregnant with Hywel's child. It seemed that was the only reason she was still alive.

34

Gareth stared across the dunes that separated him from Gwen. "It was the right choice," Hywel said, coming up beside him. As usual, he was more perceptive than Gareth felt comfortable with. Gareth had just been thinking that he wasn't sure he should have allowed Godfrid to leave without him. "For all that Godfrid is a Dane, he is my cousin. He will protect her."

"If he can," Gareth said, feeling that familiar growl forming in his throat. He'd felt it often around Gwen—that possessiveness that she would have dismissed as foolish but that had the hackles rising at the back of his neck at the thought of her anywhere near another man.

"He'll be able to protect her far more than you could as a potential prisoner," Hywel said. "Cadwaladr is mistaken, of course, that Gwen carries my child, but even if she did, my father wouldn't necessarily do what he asked in order to save her life."

"I know it," Gareth said. "And though I would do everything in my power to save her, I can't ask a king to sacrifice his kingdom for one woman."

"Hopefully, it won't come to that," Hywel said.

Together, they turned back towards the fire pits and the pavilion where Owain held court. Given that the weather remained clear for now, King Owain had opted not to retreat to Aberffraw but to remain close to the beach with his men. They'd gone only a few paces, however, when Rhun intercepted them. Gareth couldn't make out his features so far from the torch lights, but his voice was grim.

"Bad news," he said.

Gareth looked past Rhun to the encampment. Men moved about, but in no great hurry.

"What is it?" Hywel said.

"Our uncle is here."

"He's what?" Gareth said. "The Danes let him go?"

"It appears he snuck out," Rhun said. "He's meeting with Father now."

"*God have mercy!*" Hywel said. "What a sorry excuse for a prince. We'd better find out what he's got to say."

They hurried to the king's tent. Knowing his place, Gareth skirted the inside wall while Hywel and Rhun strode to where the two royal brothers spoke. Although Cadwaladr's voice didn't carry far, it was otherwise completely silent in the tent and Gareth had no trouble hearing their conversation.

"I'm sorry for Anarawd, brother," Cadwaladr was saying as Gareth came to a halt about ten feet from him, to the right of the king's position. "I never thought—"

"You never do think, *brother.*" King Owain had brought a chair specifically for himself so he wouldn't have to lounge on the ground, a fallen log, or stand like everyone else, but he wasn't using it. Instead he folded his arms across his chest and stared at Cadwaladr, using all of his considerable height to intimidate his brother. "It's been a long while since this was about Anarawd, though his murder is what so starkly revealed your cowardice to me."

"My cowardice?" Cadwaladr sputtered at the word.

King Owain turned up the fire. "Yes, your cowardice!"

"What are you talking about, Owain?" Cadwaladr said. "I did what I had to—"

"Why did you have Anarawd killed?" Owain said.

Now, that is a question.

Cadwaladr straightened his shoulders and lifted his chin. "I did what I thought was best. I believed it was more advantageous to us for Cadell to become King of Deheubarth. If I was wrong, I am sorry."

Owain Gwynedd seemed struck mute by this speech, but then reddened. He stepped closer to his brother and this time, he kept his voice low, having gone past anger to rage. "If you were sincere in your regrets, why is there a fleet of Danes at your back? Why do you seek to force my hand by threatening my people—our people—with ruin unless I give you what you want?" King Owain looked away, glaring over the heads of his men to where the Danes waited on the other side of the thin fabric, across the sand. "Whatever it is that you want."

For the first time in his life, Cadwaladr appeared momentarily cowed. "I haven't threatened you. The Danes are merely alli—"

"You dare contradict me?" King Owain returned his attention to Cadwaladr and his voice back to thundering. "You stand before me, claiming brotherhood, and yet your actions belie your words. *Give me back my lands or I loose my Danes on Anglesey?* And what of that poor girl, Gwen, who you've brought into this? Why haven't you returned her to her family?"

Cadwaladr opened and closed his mouth like a fish, not giving an answer, because of course, he didn't have one.

"You hold her hostage, don't you, *brother*," Owain said. "If I don't give you what you want, or better yet, slit your throat, your Danish friends will harm her. Isn't that it?"

Cadwaladr stared at King Owain for a count of ten, and then threw himself to the ground at the king's feet. "Please forgive me, brother," he said, groveling, his nose almost to the ground. "I didn't see until now how wrong I was."

"*Mary, Mother of God!*" King Owain blasphemed. "You sicken me." He toed Cadwaladr's ribs and gazed down at him, disgust written in every inch of his body. "Am I to assume by the fact that you came alone that your Danish friends don't know you're here?"

"I saw an opportunity to speak to you alone and took it." Cadwaladr lifted his head so his voice wasn't muffled. "Is that so wrong?"

Owain snorted under his breath. "And if I take you back, with or without promising anything, including your lands, what of the Danes?"

Cadwaladr sat back on his heels, his face radiant. "Together we can drive them from Abermenai. It will be a simple matter, as you so wisely encircled them just as we arrived."

"And what about your promises to them, Cadwaladr?" Owain said. "With what did you buy them?"

And again, what about Gwen? Gareth added, a cold fear settling into his chest at what King Ottar might do to her, even over Godfrid's objections and defense, once they realized Cadwaladr was missing.

When Cadwaladr didn't answer, King Owain said, "What did you promise them, Cadwaladr? My head after you'd killed me?"

"No!" The word burst out as if it was the truth, which perhaps it was. "I only promised them two thousand marks. That's all."

"And do you have two thousand marks?"

"Of course not," Cadwaladr said, as if there was any 'of course' about it.

More silence from King Owain, and then he held out his hand to Cadwaladr. "Give me your seal."

"My seal?" Cadwaladr said, aghast, eyes wide. A man's seal was his life, his honor, even more than his sword. "But … but… ."

King Owain sighed. "I'm not consigning you to the gallows, Cadwaladr, merely a room at Aberffraw until I've cleaned up your mess. I need your seal so that when I send for the cattle and goods to account for the gold you owe Ottar, your people will know that you agreed to the bargain."

"You're going to make me pay them to go away?" Cadwaladr said, clearly horrified at this unexpected turn of events.

"You will either give them two thousand marks—or its equivalent—or I will give them you," King Owain said. "It's your choice."

Cadwaladr still didn't seem to believe him. He stuttered through another dozen heartbeats while King Owain stood still as a stone, arms folded, observing Cadwaladr as if he was a chained animal on display at a village fair. Hywel, standing to his father's left, merely looked pained—and resigned.

And then Gareth understood that Cadwaladr had won again.

When Cadwaladr's protests had died down, Owain turned to his sons, though his gaze took in Gareth as well. "Rescue the girl." To Cadwaladr, he said, "We will give the Danes what you owe them. When that is done and they are gone from my shores, we'll talk again."

He strode out the tent opening and into the darkness. What was going on inside his head, Gareth didn't know for sure, but could guess that it was only his iron will that had stopped him from disgracing his brother further, or worse, running him through. Cadwaladr, on the other hand, once Owain had left, popped to his feet like a youth, even as four of Owain's guards grasped him around the shoulders and turned him in the direction Owain had gone.

"You heard him," Cadwaladr said to the trio as he passed them. "Go rescue Gwen."

Christ!

35

"Why don't you just send Cadwaladr back to the Danes," Hywel said. "This is his doing, isn't it? All of it?"

Owain Gwynedd and Hywel stood together twenty feet away on the perimeter of the camp, illumined by the light of a flaming torch jammed into the ground. The light wavered in the wind that blew from the west and allowed their voices to carry to Gareth who halted in mid-stride at the corner of the last tent. He glanced around, but no one else was in evidence. He shrunk back into the shadows so as not to interrupt them.

"Make him find the money to pay the Danes or face the consequences," Hywel continued. "He'll bankrupt himself, but make *him* do it. If you don't, he'll blame you for his lack of fortune and lands. He'll never take responsibility for his actions if you do this for him."

King Owain sighed. "He is a prince of Wales, son. You should know, if one day you are to aid your brother in his rule of Wales, that I can't allow the Danes to make free with him. He hasn't the wherewithal to face them. He's run from them now. When they discover how he deceived them, they'll lay waste to half of Gwynedd before they go home. I preserve him because by doing so, I preserve my people."

Silence. And then Hywel asked the question that burned Gareth up inside. "Will you give him back his lands in Ceredigion?"

"And if I did, would you still do my bidding?" Owain Gwynedd said.

"Always," Hywel said.

"That is why I will not," King Owain said. "Ceredigion is yours."

Hywel had been gazing out to sea, avoiding his father's eyes, but now looked into Owain Gwynedd's face. "Mine?"

"You've earned it," Owain said. "It's time you took your proper place as a prince of Wales."

For once, King Owain had cut through Hywel's façade of cynical unconcern. "Thank you, Father," Hywel said. "You won't be sorry for your trust in me."

"I know it," King Owain said. "Now get me that girl. I won't have Ottar use her as a bargaining chip. Besides, my bard will never forgive me if you don't."

"Yes, sir!" Hywel said.

King Owain turned towards the center of the camp just as Rhun came trotting across the sand to his brother. Gareth decided it was safe to join them.

"Dawn is coming," Rhun said.

"What are we to do?" Gareth came to a halt in front of Hywel, whose eyes were brighter than he'd ever seen them. "We don't know where Gwen is being kept, or even if she's being kept at all. Perhaps she's still free, as she was when she was in Cadwaladr's charge."

"We'll soon find out," Hywel said. "If we're to move, we have to do it soon. The moment King Ottar discovers Cadwaladr's absence, he is going to be one very angry Dane."

"The three of us need to rescue Gwen," Rhun said. "Just us. Right now."

Hywel studied his brother. "You are too valuable to lose."

"That is why it must be we three," Rhun said. "Even if he captures us, King Ottar will not harm us; he's not harmed Gwen, at least as far as we know. He knows that the only way he's getting out of here alive, at worst, or with his money, at best, is if he cooperates. Killing the son of Owain Gwynedd would ensure a massacre of his men and enduring enmity between Aber and Dublin. He won't want that."

"Prince Rhun is right, my lord," Gareth said. "Even if King Ottar is angry now, he hasn't killed Gwen. That would be wasteful and the Danes are a most practical people."

"Then we'll go as you said, brother, before the sun rises, and while they're still in disarray from Cadwaladr's defection," Hywel said. "If we wait any longer, it will be too late."

"They may be more alert than usual," Gareth said.

"We'll surprise them," Hywel said. "They'll be focused on Cadwaladr, not on Gwen."

Rhun snapped his fingers at one of the sentries as the three men passed him, heading for the narrow path that led through the brush to the Danish camp. "Tell the king we do his bidding. He'll know what to do if we don't return."

"Yes, my lord!"

With Hywel in the lead, Rhun behind him, and Gareth bringing up the rear, they dodged among the scrubby bushes that dotted the windswept dunes. Gareth understood that a recklessness had come upon the two princes. They'd fought battles together, risked their lives dozens of times—but this was a different matter. Gareth could picture the glee rising in Hywel's chest at this sudden chance at adventure and risk.

A cluster of stunted trees had found a niche on the edge of the beach, some thirty yards from the Danish fire circles and command tents. They dropped to their stomachs in the grass under the branches and took a moment to catch their breath. Then, Rhun lifted his head.

"Do you see anything?" Hywel said. Of the three of them, Rhun had the best night vision.

"Men surround the fires," Rhun said. "Outside their light, it's hard to see anything." And then... "Wait, a man comes."

Rhun and Hywel ducked their heads. In contrast, Gareth popped his up, unsure of what instinct made him less cautious. He gazed at the man, noting his bulky shape silhouetted against the fire. Again it was instinct—and only his instinct—that told him what to do. He put a hand on Hywel's shoulder. "Wait here."

Before the princes could protest, Gareth leaped up and ran at a crouching lope to where the man had paused. He fell on his stomach at the man's feet. Instead of calling to the other sentries, the big Dane turned his back on Gareth and faced the sea.

"Where is she?" Gareth said in a hoarse whisper.

"King Ottar's own tent," Godfrid said. "Third from the left,"

"Is anyone with her?"

"Two stand guard outside the entrance," Godfrid said. "You'll need a diversion to get inside."

"Right. You'll know it when you see it." Gareth scuttled back to where Hywel and Rhun waited. "That was Godfrid. We need a diversion to get to Gwen."

"I'll go," said Rhun. "Give me a slow count of one hundred and then move."

"What are you going to do?" Hywel said.

Rhun shot Hywel a mischievous grin. "I don't know. Like my brother, I make it up as I go along." And with that, he was off.

Still sprawled in the grass, Hywel groaned and put his head into his hands. "I don't even want to know."

Gareth kept his head just above the level of the grass. A dozen torches lit the Danish camp, ruining the Danes' night vision, but the darkness wouldn't hide Gareth and Hywel much longer. Sunrise was a long way off but they had very little time before the sky lightened in advance of it.

A flame shot into the sky further down the beach, near the shore of the Menai Straits, followed by roars of surprise by men in both camps. The soldiers around the Danish fire pits surged to their feet. Rhun had set the grass to the south of the camp on fire.

Godfrid had moved the instant the fire had been lit, the first to shout the warning to his companions.

"Now!" Hywel said.

He and Gareth ran to the rear of the tent, Gareth held his sword to counter anyone who challenged them and faced outward, on guard. Meanwhile, Hywel cut through the rear of the tent with two quick slashes of his belt knife. They ducked inside.

"Watch the front, Gareth," Hywel said as he ran to Gwen.

"I prayed you come. I don't know what would have happen—"

"We're here now." Gareth touched the top of Gwen's head in greeting, though he wanted to pull her into his arms, and then bounded to the entrance of the tent. He peered through the opening. Only one guard had remained on duty, though he was now twenty feet further from the tent entrance than he should have stood. He wouldn't be able to hear anything they said from that distance. Behind him, Hywel struggled to saw through the ropes that bound Gwen's hands.

"Hurry," Gareth said.

"I'm trying," Hywel said, through gritted teeth.

They were out of time. "He's coming, my lord," Gareth said. The guard appeared to be remembering his duty and was backing towards them, his shadow bouncing in the firelight. "We need to get out of here now!"

Hywel freed Gwen's hands and then pressed the knife into them. "You do your feet. I'll defend the rear." He stood, pulled his sword from its sheath, and stuck his head out of their ad hoc doorway. "Clear."

Gwen's captors hadn't done as complete a job on this second rope and Gwen severed it more easily than Hywel had freed her hands. She got to her feet, more than a little unsteady. "I'm ready."

Gareth caught her elbow and helped her out hole in the tent behind Hywel, who'd already gone through it. Once outside, they crouched low in the shadow of the tent before daring to venture across the sand to the trees. The distance to safety looked a lot further than it had on their way to rescue Gwen. The darkness had also turned to a murky dawn. Another dozen heartbeats and the shadows would no longer protect them.

"Stay low." Gareth clasped Gwen's elbow and tugged her forward, cat-like, across the sand.

"Down!" Hywel said.

Gareth dove to the ground, Gwen half-beneath him.

"Up!"

This was a new voice, and one that came from further east. They obeyed it, running flat out for the protective woods. Gwen tripped on the hem of her dress and Gareth clasped her around the waist to haul her to her feet again. A dozen heartbeats later, every one pounding so loudly in Gareth's ears he could hear nothing else, they'd crossed the scrub and reached the safety of the Welsh lines. Gareth pulled up short in amazement at who had joined their venture.

"Hello, Father," Hywel said.

Owain Gwynedd had come, along with Rhun (grinning madly) and a dozen men-at-arms, to ensure that the Danes stayed on their side of the beach. The King smiled and tousled Hywel's hair like he was a boy. "Son. Why should you have all the fun?" Then the king reached for Gwen and pulled her into his arms for a rib-crushing hug. "Quite a chase you've led us on, young lady."

"That was never my intent," Gwen said, her voice muffled by the king's thick cloak.

"Ha." King Owain allowed himself a genuine laugh and then released her.

She turned then to Gareth and it was as if her whole world stood still. All she could see was him. All she could think about was him. She hadn't realized she'd taken a step, but then she was in his arms and they were holding on to each other like they would never let go.

"*Cariad,*" Gareth said. "I was so scared for you."

"I know," Gwen said. "I was scared for me too. But—" She eased back from him just enough to reach his mother's cross and pull it out. "You were with me. You've always been with me."

Gareth gazed down at the necklace and then touched the cross with one finger. "All these years?"

"Yes," Gwen said.

"Perhaps we'll have a wedding at Aber after all," Hywel said.

Gwen had all but forgotten where they were. Her eyes widened, but Gareth laughed and pulled her to him again.

"I'll speak to my bard on your behalf." King Owain clapped a hand on Gareth's shoulder. "Come. It is time to make peace."

36

Alone on her pallet in an otherwise deserted room at Aberffraw, Gwen stared at the blade in her hand. It glittered in the light of the fire, almost transparent in places, the notch along the top edge glaringly apparent. She wished Gareth were here to help her decide what to do, but Hywel had sent him south within an hour of rescuing her from the Danish camp, with orders to gather the two thousand marks worth of goods and cattle from Cadwaladr's lands to pay the Danes. She and Gareth hadn't had a chance for more than a fleeting goodbye.

But he would return and they would talk then; they'd talk about *their* future instead of Hywel's—which faced her now. She took in a deep breath, stood, and walked down the hall to Hywel's rooms. He was still awake, as she'd felt certain he would be, maybe even waiting for her.

"Good evening, Gwen." Hywel looked up from the documents on his desk. Contracts maybe, or reviews from the law courts. Without answering, she set the knife on the edge of his desk and stepped back. Silent, they gazed at it together, and then Hywel nodded. "You see it, then."

"Too much didn't make sense in the end for it all to be Cadwaladr," she said, "but the knife gave the game away."

"It wasn't a game, Gwen," he said.

"Wasn't it?" she said. "You manipulated everyone—me, Gareth, your father—from the start."

"It was necessary," he said.

"That's what you think?" she said, her voice rising. Then she forced herself to moderate the tone so the sound would only carry to Hywel and not to neighboring rooms. "That's your excuse for killing Anarawd?"

Hywel shook his head. "You misunderstand. That's not how it was."

"You mean you didn't kill him?"

"Oh, I killed him all right." Hywel leaned back in his chair, an elbow on the arm, as if discussing manor accounts instead of the death of the King of Deheubarth. "But there's more to it than that." He gestured to the knife. "I could have thrown it away."

"You should have."

"But then you wouldn't have ever known the truth, would you?"

Gwen swallowed hard. "Why did you want me to know?"

Hywel turned his head to look out the window. "I don't know. I'd put the knife away and only wore it tonight on impulse."

"So tell me."

Hywel pointed to the chair across from him and Gwen obeyed, out of habit maybe, or because she was tired. Hywel, however, stood. He paced around his desk to stand at the window, staring out. It was open onto the green fields beyond the castle. The moonlight made a square of light on the floor behind him.

"Word reached me that a band of men from Ireland—Danes or Irishmen the messenger didn't know—had landed near Caernarfon the day before Anarawd reached Dolwyddelan. That concerned me, of course, as my western cousins aren't known for their gentle passage through a countryside."

Despite herself, Gwen smiled. Even his excuses were more droll than those heard from the average man.

"I gathered several of my men—Gareth not among them as you know—and picked up their trail. I went myself, on a whim. I had no idea what their plan was, or mine for that matter, or if I had a plan at all. But it seemed like a good idea at the time. We headed south from the standing stones at Bwlch y Ddeufaen, avoiding the roads and instead taking a trail that led into the mountains and would intersect the main road." He shrugged. "We reached one of the many falls tucked into the hills and I called a rest to water the horses. It was a mistake to stop, of course, because in those moments of rest, the mercenaries attacked Anarawd's band."

Gwen sat up, confused. "What are you saying? You weren't there?"

"I wasn't tired or hungry, and I had a tickling in the back of my neck I've learned not to ignore. So I left my men to personally scout the ridge above the falls that overlooked the road. The Danes timed the attack perfectly. Anarawd hadn't the least notion of their presence. The Danes killed them all."

"But..." Gwen stopped, trying to picture the scene in her mind's eye: Hywel lurking above the ambush site while the Danes descended on Anarawd's men. "What happened next?"

"Gareth crested a more northern ridge, in my line of sight, but his eyes were only on the battle. Then he raced back the way he'd come, I presumed to go for help."

"You saw Gareth and didn't—?" The rest of the question caught in Gwen's throat.

Hywel gave Gwen a pained look. "You think so badly of me, do you?" And then went on, not requiring an answer. "He could do nothing other than what he did. Anarawd's men weren't outnumbered, just unprepared. And when danger came, instead of fighting, Anarawd ran, leaving his men to fight the Danes alone."

Gwen leaned forward. "You're telling me King Anarawd abandoned his men to save himself?"

Hywel tsked through his teeth. "Even if he wasn't the man I knew him to be, it could have been the right choice. His life was valuable, more valuable than that of his men. At times, running is the only option."

"But not in this case?"

Hywel shook his head. "Anarawd's captain was killed in the first onslaught and his men were never able to organize themselves properly for a counterattack. By the end, it was a slaughter."

"And where was King Anarawd by this time?"

"Cowering in the woods," Hywel said. "The Danes didn't notice he'd run. They searched among the bodies—for the seal, it seems—left the dead as they lay in the road, and beat a retreat west, just as I told you. My choice was to return to my men and track them immediately, or..."

"Or to find Anarawd," Gwen said.

"As you say," Hywel said. "He was so happy to see me that he held out his arms to greet me. I put my knife into his chest instead. It was quite a job getting him back on the road without getting his blood all over me, I can tell you. That's why I dragged him face down."

"And left a trail for Gareth to find," Gwen said. "Along with dirt and scuff marks on Anarawd's toes."

"Oh yes," Hywel said. "I was worried when Gareth so quickly identified that the body had been moved. Admittedly, Gareth's skills are the reason I brought him into my company in the first place, but that he could read the signs so easily..."

Understanding grew in Gwen's mind. "So once we all were at Aber, you hid Anarawd's body yourself to prevent Gareth from making further discoveries. That was you."

"I buried him in unconsecrated ground," Hywel said. "Anarawd was a coward. I couldn't allow my sister to marry him."

"And Anarawd's seal?" Gwen said.

"Ah yes, the seal." He tapped a staccato on the window sill. "The Danes realized they were never going to get their money if they didn't bring the seal to Cadwaladr. I imagine he'd demanded it as proof they'd done the deed. When they didn't find it among the dead, they may have believed they'd ambushed the wrong party, which is why they returned to the road for the second ambush."

"Perhaps I can shed light on that, at least," Gwen said. "One of Cadwaladr's guards was at Dolwyddelan. I saw him there and at Aber. Later, he was one of my guards at Aberffraw, after Cadwaladr abducted me. If he met the Danes after the first ambush, he could have ordered them to finish the job. Bran, Gareth's milk-brother, implied as much before he died, though we didn't understand his meaning at the time."

"And thus, my men and I were unable to pick up their trail. They didn't head west, back to their boats, but took another route north to intercept you."

"So it was you who took the seal from Anarawd's body and hid it in Cadell's room to divert suspicion."

For the first time, Hywel looked slightly guilty. "How was I to know that Cristina would come snooping?"

"That's..." Gwen tried to find the word but the best one she could come up with was *diabolical* and just couldn't quite say it.

Hywel gazed at her intently. "Do not forget that it was Cadwaladr who sent the Danes to murder Anarawd, not I. That they did not succeed does not absolve him of his crimes."

Gwen studied Hywel's face. She wanted to believe him. She'd served him because she believed what he'd told her. But now ... something still didn't add up.

"Tell me the real reason you killed Anarawd," she said. "There's something more; something you haven't said. Was it personal gain? Your father has given you Ceredigion."

"Again, you think so little of me?"

"Is this really about Anarawd?" Gwen said. "Or about Cadwaladr?"

"It's always been about Anarawd."

"What grudge did you hold against him?"

A long silence followed through which Hywel held his expression, and then his eyes darkened. "Cowardice isn't enough?" He gave her a small smile. "No. For you, it's only the truth that is enough, isn't it?" He walked back to his desk and sat heavily in his chair. He picked up his pen and then dropped it.

"Six years ago, I fought beside my father in Deheubarth in the rebellion that put Anarawd on the throne. Even all these years later, the brutality of that war haunts me." He paused, seeming to search for the words. "Anarawd's father was old, but not to death, not like my grandfather who was blind and could no longer travel. The King of Deheubarth's sword arm was still strong. But in the midst of some heavy fighting along the Teifi River—the last battle we fought that turned into a victorious rout for us—Anarawd came upon his father from behind and murdered him."

Gwen blinked. "Just like that? And you a witness?"

The rueful smile was back. "The whole truth, eh? It was the last of the fighting but my first real experience in war. I was puking my guts out behind a tree—dry heaving by then—when Anarawd's father came to rest some ten paces from me. He put a hand on a tree, holding his heart and breathing hard. We were fifty yards from the fighting—not exactly safe, but out of it. Anarawd came up to his father, all solicitous, and then stabbed him through the heart."

"As you did Anarawd."

"Yes," Hywel said. "I call it justice."

"Why didn't you tell your father?" Gwen said. "He would have listened to you."

"Would he?" Hywel said. "You know my father. The alliance with Deheubarth was well-established by then; Anarawd was in his confidence and when he brought the body of his father into the hall and laid him in state upon the table, tears pouring down his cheeks at what the Normans had done, how could I stand then and gainsay him?"

"But in private..."

"It was done," Hywel said. "More of my ancestors than I can count took the throne by patricide. Some say that my own father killed his brother, the *elding*, in battle in much the same way."

"I don't believe that!"

"Don't you," Hywel said. "Why don't you? You've seen my father's temper."

"Do you believe it?" Gwen said.

Hywel shook his head, more in resignation than because he was saying no. "I don't believe it, but the rumors were rife ten years ago when my uncle died in battle; I couldn't stir them up again." He paused. "And then there was my sister. I couldn't stand by and see her hurt. It was my last chance to protect her."

Gwen met Hywel's eyes and neither looked away.

"I saw an opportunity and I took it. It was impulse, but still, I cannot regret my decision."

They sat together, silent, Hywel genuinely relaxed in Gwen's company, for perhaps the first time since he was ten. He had no false front to keep her from seeing him as he really was, no mask to wear. Instead, his face revealed resignation, and perhaps acceptance of who he was and the role he played in his father's world. For it *was* Owain Gwynedd's world, and Hywel was, and perhaps would always be, the son who did his father's bidding.

Hywel cleared his throat and when he spoke next, his voice came so softly, she almost couldn't hear him. "When Cadwaladr claimed you bore my child, I told Gareth that I had never taken you to my bed."

Gwen gazed at him, waiting. These words meant something to him. She could hear it in his voice.

"Do you know why?" he said.

"I've wondered why," she said. "I loved you when we were children, and there were times I would have come willingly since my father left your father's service. But you never asked."

Hywel looked up from fingering the documents on his desk and met her eyes. "It is not in my nature to be faithful, Gwen. I loved you too much to hurt you."

Gwen swallowed. As she'd suspected. *The truth.*

"I leave tomorrow for Ceredigion. Do I have your blessing? Are you still with me?"

Gwen met his gaze. "I'm still with you, Hywel." She stood. "I wish you the best." She was at the door a heartbeat later, for the first time ever without asking permission or looking back.

But before she'd gone two more steps, Hywel's parting words reached her. "As I do you, Gwen. As I do you."

Historical Background

The events related in *The Good Knight* are, amazingly enough, based on historical fact. The premise of the book, the murder of King Anarawd of Deheubarth, did take place at the behest of Owain Gwynedd's brother, Cadwaladr. Prince Hywel was tasked with rousting his uncle out of Ceredigion, and did burn his uncle's castle to the ground. Cadwaladr had retreated to Ireland and returned to Wales at the head of an army of Danish mercenaries to the extreme displeasure of his brother. This was only one of the first of many betrayals by Cadwaladr. Owain Gwynedd did accept his brother back into his favor, after he paid the Danes what he owed them.

Many of the other characters in *The Good Knight* are historical figures as well, including Cristina, Rhun, Gwalchmai, and Meilyr. The fiction comes from all that we don't know about the events that transpired, whether because nobody wrote them down, or because any such documents were destroyed in the intervening years. There is a story that one of the more recent owners of Castle Aber found a collection of papers stashed in a wall cavity in the old part of the castle—and burned them because they were in Latin and she couldn't read them.

Owain Gwynedd was born sometime before 1100 AD, the second son of Gruffydd ap Cynan. Owain ruled from 1137 to 1170 AD. His rule was marked by peace initially, at least with England, as Owain took advantage of the strife between King Stephen and Empress Maud for the English throne to consolidate his power in Wales. That conflict lasted for nineteen years, finally resolving in rule by Stephen but with the inheritance of the throne upon his death by Maud's son, Henry.

Owain had many wives and lovers. His first wife, Gwladys, was the daughter of Llywarch ap Trahaearn; his second was Cristina, his cousin, to whom he remained constant despite the active disapproval of the Church (which opposed what they viewed as consanguine relationships). Owain Gwynedd had many sons and daughters. The eldest two, from his first relationship with Pyfog of Ireland, were Rhun and Hywel, as related in *The Good Knight*.

For Hywel's part, he was a genuine warrior-bard. And he and Gwalchmai, who became the poet to King Owain Gwynedd's court, are revered as two of the foremost Welsh poets of the twelfth century.

Acknowledgments

I have many people to thank, not only for their assistance with *The Good Knight*, but who have helped make my books better and my life sane for the last five years.

First and foremost, thank you to my family: my husband Dan, who five years ago told me to give it five years and see if I still loved it. I still do. Thank you for your infinite patience with having a writer as a wife. To my four kids, Brynne, Carew, Gareth, and Taran, who have been nothing but encouraging, despite the fact that their mother spends half her life in medieval Wales. Thank you to my parents, for passing along their love of history, and particularly to my father, who died a month before I published *The Good Knight*. I couldn't finish it fast enough and he faded away before he had a chance to read it.

Thanks to my beautiful writing partner, Anna Elliott, who has made this journey with me from nearly the beginning. Thanks to Gemini Sasson, who read a late draft and made it better and to Jacques de Spoelberch, my agent, who has been nothing but supportive of my indie endeavors.

And to my readers, without whom, none of this would be possible.

About the Author

With two historian parents, Sarah couldn't help but develop an interest in the past. She went on to get more than enough education herself (in anthropology) and began writing fiction when the stories in her head overflowed and demanded she let them out. Her interest in Wales stems from her own ancestry and the year she lived in England when she fell in love with the country, language, and people. She even convinced her husband to give all four of their children Welsh names.

She makes her home in Oregon.

www.sarahwoodbury.com

Made in the USA
Lexington, KY
27 February 2015